The Rain Watcher

The Rain Watcher

Tatiana de Rosnay

St. Martin's Press ⚏ New York

THE RAIN WATCHER. Copyright © 2018 by Éditions Héloïse d'Ormesson. All rights reserved. Printed in the United States of America. For information, address St. Martin's Press, 175 Fifth Avenue, New York, N.Y. 10010.

www.stmartins.com

The Library of Congress Cataloging-in-Publication Data is available upon request.

ISBN 978-1-250-20001-3 (hardcover)
ISBN 978-1-250-20002-0 (ebook)

Our books may be purchased in bulk for promotional, educational, or business use. Please contact your local bookseller or the Macmillan Corporate and Premium Sales Department at 1-800-221-7945, extension 5442, or by email at MacmillanSpecialMarkets@macmillan.com.

First Edition: October 2018

10 9 8 7 6 5 4 3 2 1

❦

For my family

And the stars look very different today
　　　—*David Bowie, "Space Oddity," 1969*

ONE

~❧~

Je passais au bord de la Seine
Un livre ancien sous le bras
Le fleuve est pareil à ma peine
Il s'écoule et ne tarit pas

—GUILLAUME APOLLINAIRE, "MARIE"

I will start with the tree. Because everything begins, and ends, with the tree. The tree is the tallest one. It was planted way before the others. I'm not sure how old it is, exactly. Perhaps three or four hundred years old. It is ancient and powerful. It has weathered terrible storms, braced against unbridled winds. It is not afraid.

The tree is not like the others. It has its own rhythm. Spring starts later for it, while all the others are already blossoming. Come late April, the new oval leaves sprout slowly, on the top and middle branches only. Otherwise, it looks dead. Gnarled, gray, and withered. It likes to pretend to be dead. That's how clever it is. Then, suddenly, like a huge explosion, all the buds flourish. The tree triumphs with its pale green crown.

No one can find me when I'm up here. I don't mind the silence. It's not really silence, because so many small sounds fill it. The rustle of the leaves. The moan of the wind. The buzz of a bee. The chirp of the cicadas. The flutter of a bird's wing. When the mistral is up and rushes through the valley, the thousands of branches swishing sound like the sea. This is where I came to play. This was my kingdom.

I tell this story now, once, so that I don't have to tell it again. I am not good with words, whether they are spoken or penned. When I'm finished, I will hide this. Somewhere where it won't be found. No one knows. No one will. I've never told it. I will write it and not show it. The story will remain on these pages, like a prisoner.

I T'S BEEN LIKE THIS for the past two weeks," says the listless
taxi driver. The rain pours down, a silver curtain, hissing, obstruct-
ing all daylight. It is only ten o'clock in the morning, but to Linden,
it feels like dusk glimmering with wetness. The taxi driver says he
wants to move away for good, flee Paris, find the sun, go back to
balmy Martinique, where he is from. As the car leaves Charles
de Gaulle Airport and edges along the jammed highway and ring
road that circles the city, Linden cannot help agreeing with him.
The sodden suburbs are dismal, clustered contours of cubic volumes
bedecked with garish neon billboards flickering in the drizzle. He
asks the driver to turn on the radio, and the man comments upon
his perfect French, "for an American." Linden grins. This happens
every time he returns to Paris. He replies he's Franco-American,
born in France, French father, American mother, he speaks both
languages fluently, with no accent at all. How about that, eh? The
driver chortles, fumbles with the radio, well, monsieur certainly
looks like an American, doesn't he, tall, athletic, jeans, sneakers,
not like those Parisians with their fancy ties and suits.

The news is all about the Seine. Linden listens while squeaky
windshield wipers thrust away rivulets in a never-ending battle. The
river has been rising for five days now, since January 15, lapping
around the Zouave's ankles. The huge stone statue of a colonial soldier
situated just below the pont de l'Alma is, Linden knows, the popular

indicator of the river's level. In 1910, during the major overflows that inundated the city, the water had crept all the way up to the Zouave's shoulders. The driver exhales, there's nothing to be done to prevent a river from flooding, no use fighting nature. Men need to stop tampering with nature; all this is her way of lashing back. As the car inches along sluggish circulation, unrelenting rain pounding on the car roof, Linden is reminded of the email the hotel sent him on Tuesday.

> *Dear Mr. Malegarde,*
> *We are looking forward to your arrival and stay with us as from Friday, January 19th, at noon, until Sunday, January 21st, in the evening (with a late checkout, as requested). However, the traffic situation in Paris might be problematic due to the level of the river Seine. Fortunately, the Chatterton Hotel, situated in the fourteenth arrondissement, is not located in an area liable to inundations, and therefore will not be concerned by the inconvenience. For the moment, the prefecture informs us there is nothing to worry about, but our policy is to update our guests. Please let us know if you need any assistance. Kind regards.*

Linden read it at the airport on his way from L.A. to New York, where he was booked to photograph a British actress for *Vanity Fair.* He forwarded the message to his sister, Tilia, in London, and to his mother, Lauren, in the Drôme valley, who were to join him in Paris that Friday. Linden had not included Paul in the email because his father only appreciated letters and postcards, not emails. His sister's answer, which he received when he landed hours later at JFK, made him chuckle. *Floodings?! What?! Again? Don't you remember there was already a scary flood in Paris last November? And what about the one in June 2016? It took us years to organize this bloody weekend, and now this?!* She signed off with a series of scowling emoticons. Later, his mother replied to both of them: *Will come by boat if we have to, dragging your father away from his trees! To at last be together! No way will we cancel this family gathering! See you on Friday, my loves!* The Malegarde family was meeting in Paris to celebrate Paul's seventieth birthday, as well as Lauren and Paul's fortieth wedding anniversary.

Linden had not given the hotel's warning another thought. When he left New York for Paris on Thursday evening, he felt weary. It had been two full days, and before that, weeks of hard work around the globe. He would have preferred to fly back home to San Francisco, to Elizabeth Street, to Sacha and the cats. He had not seen much of Sacha, nor the cats, in the past month. Rachel Yellan, his dynamic agent, had landed him one job after the other, a dizzying swirl from city to city that left him depleted and longing for a break. The narrow blue house in Noe Valley and its cherished inhabitants would have to wait until this special family event was over. "Just the four of us," his mother had said, all those months ago, when she had booked hotel and restaurant. Was he looking forward to this? he wondered as the plane took off. They had not often been together, just the four of them, since his teenage years at Sévral, where he grew up, and more so, since he had left Vénozan, his father's familial domain, in 1997, at nearly sixteen. He saw his parents once or twice a year, and his sister whenever he went to London, which was frequently. Why did "just the four of us" sound both so cozy and ominous?

On the flight to Paris, Linden read *Le Figaro* and realized with a jab of apprehension that the situation described by the hotel was, in fact, disquieting. The Seine had already flooded in late November, as Tilia pointed out, after a wet summer and autumn, and previously, in June 2016. Parisians had kept a wary eye on the Zouave, and the little waves lapping up his shins. Fortunately, the flow had stopped increasing. *Le Figaro* explained that thanks to modern technology, one could predict the river's engorgement three days ahead, which left ample time for evacuating. But the actual problem was the torrential rain, which had not lessened. The river was on the rise again, and threateningly fast.

After traffic jams and more foreboding talk on the radio, the taxi crosses the Seine at Concorde. It is raining so thickly, Linden can barely make out the river below, just enough to notice the churning flow seems unnaturally foamy. The taxi crawls along waterlogged boulevard Saint-Germain and boulevard Raspail, and reaches the Hôtel Chatterton at Vavin crossroad. In the one minute it takes Linden to leap from car to entrance, the rain plasters his dark blond hair to his head, dribbles down the back of his neck, seeps into his socks. The chilly winter air enfolds him and seems to follow him into the lobby. He is greeted by a smiling receptionist, he smiles back, hair dripping, shivering, hands her his French passport (he has two), nods back at *"Bienvenue, Monsieur Malegarde."* Yes, his sister is arriving later on today by Eurostar, and his parents from Montélimar by train. No, he's not quite sure at what time. Is he aware that his parents' train will be diverted to Montparnasse and not be arriving at Gare de Lyon, because of the inundation risks? No, he knows nothing of this. But that will make it much more practical, he realizes, as Montparnasse station is barely five minutes away from the Chatterton.

The receptionist, whose badge reads AGATHE, gives him his passport and room key, and tells him, not too effusively, how much she admires his work, what an honor it is to have him at the hotel. Is he here for fashion week as well? she inquires. He thanks her, then shakes his head, explains this is a family weekend, that he will not be working, not a single shoot scheduled for the next few days, a well-deserved rest. He has only one camera with him, he tells her, his beloved vintage Leica; he left his gear in New York, with his agent, and the only people he plans to photograph are his parents and sister. As for fashion week, that's certainly not on his list; he'll leave those glitzy creatures tottering on their stilettos to their own confederacy of glamour and catwalks. The receptionist laughs. She heard on TV that if the Seine continues to rise so alarmingly, fashion week might be canceled. Now it is Linden's turn to snort, and he feels a furtive pang of guilt, and cannot help thinking of what it would mean to actually cancel fashion week, which starts tomorrow, what a colossal waste of effort, time, and money. The receptionist then refers deferentially to his father and says what a pleasure it is to have "Mr. Treeman" with them, and Linden is amused at her fervor (little does she know how much his father resents that sobriquet, how ridiculous he finds it, and with what difficulty he deals with his illustriousness); his father is such a respected figure, she goes on; his struggle to save notable trees around the world is admirable. He warns her, genially, that his father is shy, not easygoing and talkative like himself; however, she'll have a ball with his mother, who is the true star of the family, and his sister, Tilia Favell, is quite a number, as well.

The room on the fourth floor, giving onto rue Delambre, is warm, comfortable, and prettily furnished in tints of lilac and crème, although a trifle small to accommodate his long-limbed frame. A basket of goodies awaits on the table—fresh fruit, roses, chocolates, and a bottle of champagne on ice—with a handwritten welcome note from the hotel's director, Madame Myriam Fanrouk. He remembers his mother choosing the Chatterton two years ago when she decided to go ahead with the anniversary and birthday weekend. It was labeled a "charming, delightful boutique hotel on the Left Bank, bang in the heart of Montparnasse" and TripAdvisor comments were positive. Linden had left the organization up to her. He had booked his flights when he was sure of his agenda, not an easy feat for a freelance photographer. Lauren had also picked the place they were having dinner tomorrow night, Villa des Roses, a one-star Michelin restaurant on rue du Cherche-Midi, behind the Hôtel Lutetia.

Why Paris? he wonders as he unpacks his small suitcase and hangs up the dark green velvet jacket he'll be wearing tomorrow evening. Tilia is based in London with her daughter and her second husband, art expert Colin Favell; Lauren and Paul live in Vénozan, near Sévral, in the Drôme valley, and he is established in San Francisco, with Sacha. Yes, why Paris? Paris does not mean much to his parents. Or does it? Linden gives it a thought as he undresses, casts aside his damp clothes, and steps under a hot shower with relish. He knows his parents met in Grignan, during the ferocious heat wave that desiccated France in the summer of 1976, when Paul was working as head landscaper for an ambitious garden-design firm on the outskirts of the small town. Tilia and he know the story inside out. Lauren, barely nineteen, was visiting France for the first time with her sister Candice, two years older. Born and bred in Brookline, Massachusetts, they had never been to Europe. They started with Greece, then Italy, and made their way up through France via Nice, Avignon, Orange. A halt in the Drôme had not been planned, but it had been too hot to pursue their route and they decided to spend one night in a modest but welcoming bed-and-breakfast in Grignan. At the end of the sweltering day, the sisters were enjoying a glass of chilled rosé in the shade of the cool square, where a fountain tinkled, beneath the statue of regal Madame de Sevigné, whose imposing château graced the top of the hill, when Paul drove by in his pickup. He wore faded white overalls that had a Steve McQueen aura to them, a frayed straw sun hat, and a roll-up cigarette jutted from his mouth. Lauren's eyes followed him as he parked the truck and hauled various pots and shrubs from the trunk into a nearby shop. He was broad-shouldered and muscular, of medium height, and when he swept off the hat to wipe off a perspiring forehead, she noticed he had hardly any hair, just a segment of brown fuzz at the back of his head. Nearly bald, but young, not even thirty, she guessed. Candice asked why she was staring at the guy in the overalls, and Lauren whispered, "Just look at his hands." Candice replied blankly that she couldn't see anything special about his hands at all, and Lauren, in a sort of trance, murmured she had never seen anyone touch plants the way that man did. Their father, Fitzgerald Winter, was something of a gardener; so was their mother, Martha. The girls had grown up in a verdant, tree-filled neighborhood in Brookline, near Fisher Hill, where residents spent a lot of time tending to their gardens, with shears in one gloved hand and a watering can in the other, anxiously appraising a rosebush's growth. But this man was different, and Lauren could not take her eyes off his robust, tanned fingers, watching the way he tilted his head to stare at each flower, how he caressed the branches and blossoms of every plant he handled, cupping it in a strong yet gentle hold that mesmerized her. Paul must have felt the pressure of her gaze, because he at last looked up and saw the two sisters sitting a little farther away. Tilia and Linden knew this part by heart, as well. He saw only Lauren, her legs, her long hair, her slanted eyes, although Candice was just as beautiful. He walked over to her table and silently handed her a small potted olive tree. She spoke hardly any French, and his English was non-existent. Candice mastered French better than her sister, so she was able to translate, but to them she was invisible, just a voice choosing the right words. His name was Paul Malegarde, he was twenty-eight, and he lived a few kilometers away, near Sévral, on the road to Nyons. Yes, he loved plants, especially trees, and he had a beautiful arboretum on his property, Vénozan. Would she like to see it, perhaps? He could take her there, would she like that? Oh, but she was leaving tomorrow with her sister, off to Paris, and then London, and then back home at the end of the summer. Yes, she could maybe stay a bit longer; she had to see. . . . When Lauren got up to shake his proffered hand, she towered over him, but neither of them seemed to mind in the least. She liked his shrewd blue eyes, his infrequent smile, his long silences. "He's not half as good-looking as Jeff," said Candice later. Jeff was Lauren's preppy Bostonian boyfriend. Lauren shrugged. She was meeting Paul again later, by the fountain. There was a full moon that night. The heat did not abate. Candice was no longer there to serve as translator, but they did not need her. There was not much talking. David Bowie, Paul's favorite singer, sang from the cassette deck in the pickup as they gazed up at the stars, their hands barely touching. Jeffrey van der Haagen felt thousands of miles away. Lauren Winter did not make it to Paris, nor to London; nor did she go back to Boston at the end of that scorching summer of 1976. She visited Vénozan and ended up never leaving it.

Linden grabs a towel, dries himself, and slides into a bathrobe. He remembers his mother's mentioning that meeting up in Paris was more convenient for the four of them. She was no doubt right. And this was to be a "no spouses, no children weekend," she had pointed out. That meant no Colin, no Mistral (Tilia's daughter from her first marriage), no Sacha. Just the four of them. He draws the curtain back and watches the rain cascade down to the gleaming pavement. Scarce passersby dash through the drops. His mother had scheduled several walks and visits to museums for tomorrow. The rain and cold will no doubt hamper her plans. A gloomy noon in Paris, and three o'clock in the morning in San Francisco. He thinks of Sacha sleeping in the large bedroom on the top floor, the tousled dark hair on the pillow, the gentle, regular breath. His phone pings and he turns to retrieve it from his coat pocket. *Dude, have you arrived?* Tilia always calls him "dude," and he retaliates with "doll." *Doll, I'm in my room. Number 46.*

Moments later, he hears an authoritative rap at the door and opens up. His sister stands there, drenched, hair flattened and dripping, eyebrows and lashes spiked with wobbling droplets. She rolls her eyes, outstretches her arms, and staggers forward like a zombie, which makes him laugh. They hug, and, as ever, she is small compared to him, small but robust, built exactly like their father, with the same broad shoulders, square jaw, the same quizzical blue eyes.

Whenever Linden and Tilia are together, they never know which language to choose. They grew up learning both at the same time, speaking English to their mother, French to their father, but between them, it is a confusing, rapid jumble of both, a Frenglish potpourri of slang and personal nicknames that give other people headaches. While Tilia dries her hair on a towel, then with the hair dryer, Linden notices she has put on weight since the last time he saw her, just before summer, when he was passing through London. But it suits her, this new plumpness, giving her a femininity she sometimes lacked. She had always been a tomboy, the kind of girl who climbs trees, plays *pétanque* with the men in the village, whistles with her fingers between her teeth, and swears like a pirate. She disregarded style, makeup, and jewelry, although Linden notices that today she is wearing a well-cut, if sopping, pair of navy blue trousers and matching jacket, attractive black boots, and a gold necklace. He compliments her on her appearance, and she mouths "Mistral" above the blast of the hair dryer. Her poised eighteen-year-old daughter, a fashion student born of a Basque father (a renowned chef), is Tilia's fashion police, and it appears her efforts are paying off. Her hair now dry, Tilia walks across the room to turn on the TV, saying she wants to watch the news about the river, and Linden notices her limp is worse than usual.

They never talk about the car accident she had in 2004, when she was twenty-five. She refuses to ever mention it. Linden knows she nearly died, that parts of her left leg and hip were replaced, that she underwent extensive surgery and spent six months in the hospital. The accident happened near Arcangues, when she was returning to Biarritz with her best friends from a party. One of the girls was getting married the following week. They had hired a car with a chauffeur in order to be able to drink safely. At three in the morning, an inebriated driver speeding along the small winding roads smashed into their minivan. Four girls were killed on the spot, as well as their chauffeur and the other driver. Tilia was the single survivor of a car accident that made headlines. It took her years to get over it, mentally and physically. Her marriage with Eric Ezri broke up a few years later, in 2008, and she obtained custody of their only daughter. Sometimes Linden wonders if his sister has ever gotten over the tragedy, if she is aware of the toll it has taken, like a chunk out of her life.

"How's Colin?" asks Linden carefully as Tilia switches to the news channel. They both know—the entire family knows—that her elegant British spouse, an eminent art expert specializing in old master paintings at Christie's, her charming, bespectacled, smooth-skinned husband with his quick-witted small talk and toothy smile is a drunkard. Not the social type of drunkard who, clutching his tepid champagne glass, will careen through parties, delightfully tipsy, ensconced in a haze of innocuous gibberish, but the hardcore, bad-news type of drunkard who starts his day knocking back gin at ten in the morning and who ends it in a coma, curled up dead to the world on his doorstep at Clarendon Road in a pool of his own urine. Tilia takes her time to answer, perched on the corner of the bed, eyes on the TV screen, where old black-and-white photographs of the 1910 Paris flooding file past. She answers, tonelessly, that the situation is the same. Colin promised he would stop, that he'd go back to the clinic (for the third time), but it is not better. Things are becoming problematic at work. He had been able to hide it for a while, but not anymore. She is fed up. Colin is aware of it. He says he loves her, and she knows he does, but she is running out of patience. For the first time, Linden glimpses defiance in his sister's face. She looks bitter, resentful. When she married Colin Favell in 2010, she had no idea he was an alcoholic. He hid it cleverly. He was dashing and handsome. Nineteen years older than she? So what! It did not show. He was marvelous to look at, such a seductive Jaggerish smile, all those teeth. He also had been married a first time and had two grown-up sons. They met in London, at an auction, where Tilia had gone with a friend. Mistral had liked him, too. In the beginning. And then, gradually, well after the wedding, the truth was revealed. The drinking, the lies, the viciousness. He never hits her, nor Mistral, but his insults are odious daggers of venom.

Tilia is going to be forty next year, she reminds her brother with a smirk; that hideous age, that ghastly number, and her marriage is a disaster. Her husband is a disaster. The fact that she has no job and is living off him is a disaster. But she never really had a job in her life, so who's going to hire her now, at her age, with no diplomas or experience of any kind? Linden interrupts her. What about her painting? She scoffs at her brother. Her painting? Another disaster! He cannot help laughing, and so does she, in spite of herself. Yes, of course she still paints, and she loves it, and it saves her, but no one gives a shit about her paintings. No one wants to buy them, at least not her husband's snobby friends from the art world; they turn up their noses at everything that's not a Rembrandt. Everything around her is a disaster except for her daughter. Her daughter, born in December 1999 during a mighty storm, her baby named after the powerful northwesterly wind that blustered through Tilia's childhood, is the apple of her eye.

At the end of her rant, Tilia turns to Linden and says brightly, "And how's Sacha?" Sacha's fine, quite a bit of work at the start-up, a fair amount of stress, but Sacha knows how to handle stress. The only problem is that they don't see each other much right now, with Linden always on a plane, and that wedding date, which always gets postponed because of traveling, well, they are going to have to do something about it. Tilia asks if their father has ever met Sacha. Linden says no, he hasn't. Lauren and Sacha were introduced to each other in New York in 2014, and they hit it off fine. They met again, later, in Paris and it had gone just as well. Their father leaves Vénozan only to save remarkable trees, not to visit his family. Doesn't Tilia know that? Linden adds drily. Tilia plays with her necklace. Does Linden think their father perhaps doesn't want to meet Sacha? Linden is aware that question is coming; his sister has always been outspoken, so he is not surprised. But he finds he has no answer. He glances toward the TV, where a map of the Seine is now being shown, alarming red arrows darting here and there, marking possible flooding. He says cautiously that he does not know. He has never asked his father outright and he has not discussed it with Sacha. All he knows is that Sacha and he have been together for nearly five years, that they plan to get married, and that Sacha has never met Paul. Tilia observes that San Francisco is not exactly close to Vénozan. Linden agrees, but he reminds her that there was that one time, not very long ago, when their father had flown to California, somewhere near Santa Rosa, to prevent a plantation of an uncommon species of redwood trees from being axed to enlarge a railroad. Paul had spent a week battling the authorities with his cluster of followers, composed of arborists, dendrologists, scientists, botany students, activists, historians, nature lovers, and ecologists. He ended up saving the trees, but he never went to visit his son and meet Sacha, a mere hour's drive away. There had always been an excuse: He was too busy, or too tired, or there was another rare tree to save.

Linden changes the subject, focuses her attention on the news. The previous November's flooding had apparently been a narrowly averted disaster, thanks to the four giant lakes created upriver between 1949 and 1990. A drone films from above the lakes, situated near Joigny and Troyes, roughly two hundred kilometers away from Paris. They act as reservoirs when the flow is too high, and the past November's swell was reduced at least half a meter due to the lakes. However, the present problem, the journalist continues, is that the lakes are still full from the previous inundation, unable to empty themselves, and the rain has not stopped falling for the past few weeks, which means that the ground is thoroughly sodden, no longer absorbing water.

"Shit, that looks bad," mumbles Tilia. If only the bloody rain would stop. They can't even go out, it's so wet. Will the river truly flood? Surely the authorities, or whoever, will prevent a catastrophe. Surely nothing bad will happen. They go on watching; the same topic comes up on each channel: the Seine rising, the unstoppable rain, the growing anxiety. Oh, why don't they turn it off, Tilia groans, and Linden reaches for the remote control. The only noise now is the pitter-patter outside. They talk about the presents for their parents. Linden was able to get his hands on the only Bowie vinyl Paul was missing, *Station to Station,* which he somehow misplaced years ago and could not locate. Tilia had procured the latest biography in French about Bowie. As for their mother, for her wedding anniversary, they decided on a joint present, which Tilia went to get on Old Bond Street, a diamond-studded Tiffany key, snug in its turquoise box.

"I think I'll have a snooze," Linden tells his sister diplomatically. His jet lag is not overpowering—he travels too frequently to suffer from it—but he wants to be alone for a while, before his parents arrive. Tilia takes the hint and gets up to leave. On her way out, she mutters, ironically, that he does indeed look shattered, but the older he gets, the more gorgeous he becomes, while she looks like a hag; it's too unfair. He good-humoredly throws a pillow at her as she slams the door.

Layers of weariness have been building up in the past weeks, and he can feel their hold in the tightness around his neck and shoulders. He misses Sacha's warm, supple hands, kneading away his tiredness. There is a list of things about Sacha that he misses, he realizes. Let him count those things, he thinks as he lies down on the bed: the sense of humor, smile, wondrous cooking, laugh, hazel eyes, sometimes brown, sometimes green, depending on the light, the entrancing fragrance just below the jawbone, the love for opera and *La Traviata* in particular, the enthusiasm, sensitivity, creativity, and sheer magnetism. Sacha and he have never spent much time in Paris together. Their story started in New York in 2013.

Yet Paris is clandestinely special to Linden. He keeps a personal bond with the city, an intimate history of love, sadness, and pleasure, buried deep within him, like a bittersweet secret, and often thinks back to the twelve years he spent here, from 1997 to 2009. He sees himself, gawky and skinny, painfully self-aware, turning up on Candice's doorstep with his backpack and his joy of being here, away from Sévral, his parents, Vénozan. What the hell did he mean, leaving home, his mother had thundered, to go where, do what? Linden's grades weren't all that good; the English teacher even wrote to say Linden was "arrogant." As he listened to his mother's remonstrance, Linden was aware he could never explain, never describe how different he felt, in every way; he was a stranger, yes, even in the very town where he was born; he was a stranger because his mother was an American who had never lost her accent, and he was therefore half American and reminded of it every single day in class, even if his father came from an old Sévral family, even if his great-grandfather, Maurice Malegarde, had made a fortune with his lucrative carton-packing factories and bequeathed a touch of magnificence on all descendants to come by creating Vénozan, an early-twentieth-century folly built to resemble a Tuscan villa. As for the English teacher, cantankerous Madame Cazeaux, how could he explain to his parents she was infuriated by his perfect English, which only drew out her own abysmal accent? No, he could not reveal how uncomfortable he felt at school, with no one to talk to, no one to confide in; it was almost as if he came from another planet, as if the others intuitively sensed his difference and rejected him. He did not fit in, and it made him miserable. It had gotten worse with puberty, when he shot up in one go and the others felt belittled. He almost told his mother they spitefully nicknamed him *"l'Américain,"* increasing his wretchedness, which he found despicable, considering he was born in the Sévral clinic, like most of them. They used other names, other insults. He felt unwanted, unhappy, lonely. And the worst part was that when his mother sometimes came to fetch him in the old pickup, wearing her short jean dress and her cowboy hat, each one of them, boys and girls, ogled her. How could they not? She was the most beautiful woman they had ever seen, a vision of loveliness with her honey hair and curvaceous figure. The only person who was aware of his daily agony was Tilia. She had flamboyantly taken his side once his mind was made up, and had faced their parents, sputtering with wrath, why on earth couldn't Linden go and live with Candice, attend a Parisian lycée, spend a couple of years with his aunt? What was their problem, for Christ's sake? Why were they being so old-fashioned? What a bunch of fuddy-duddies. Linden was going to be sixteen in May. There was nothing complicated about changing schools in the middle of term; these things were done, had been done before! Linden needed to get out, to go see the world, to discover other places. Couldn't they see that? There had been a silence, his parents had glanced at each other, then back at him, and then Paul had shrugged. If that's what Linden wanted, deep down, then he wasn't going to stop his son. Lauren had added she was going to call Candice right away and make arrangements for a school transfer. Linden had stared at his sister with overt admiration, and she had winked back, flaunting a *V* for victory at him. It is amusing to think that most of those contemptuous, insufferable pupils of the Sévral lycée he put up with for all those years now flock to his Facebook page, liking every single one of his posts, and he has even seen some of them turn up at his exhibits, groveling, patting him on the back, saying they knew he was going to become a star.

His aunt Candice lived at 1, rue de l'Église, in the unremarkable fifteenth arrondissement. Her building was on the corner of rue Saint-Charles, a long, bustling street stretching from rue de la Fédération all the way south to place Balard. It was not considered a hip area, but he did not care. When he arrived on that nippy March day in 1997, Linden felt free for the first time in his life. He stood on the balcony of Candice's sun-filled sixth-floor flat and looked out, elated, his hands gripping the railing. How well he remembers standing there, like a captain at the helm of his boat, Paris enticingly spread out at his feet, the rising roar of the traffic sounding like music to his ears, thrusting bucolic Vénozan and his parents farther and farther away. He did not mind the uncomfortable sofa bed, the complications of Candice's love life, the new faces at the lycée on boulevard Pasteur. He did not miss spring at Vénozan, the cherry trees boastfully blossoming first, the scent of fresh air and lavender whipped up by the merciless wind. He did not miss the twitter of the birds, the exquisite perfume of bloodred roses that grew outside his bedroom window, the view over lavender fields studded with fig trees, inky green cypress, and silvery olive trees. There was nothing from Vénozan that he pined for. Not even his father's arboretum, which he had loved so as a boy. He embraced his new life as a Parisian. He blended in at school. He was popular for the first time ever. No one realized he was a country boy, born in rural territory, not afraid of insects, not even the black scorpions lurking on the stone walls; a boy who knew the power of the wind, the supremacy of a storm, the Latin names of trees, and no one could tell he had been raised in the company of eagles, deer, boar, hornets, and firebugs. The others thought he was "cool," with his flawless bilingualism, his impressive command of American swearwords, and his faint southern accent. They did not make fun of his first name; they did not care who his father was. He was invited to parties; girls had crushes on him, mooned over his blue eyes and wide smile. He was even considered good-looking. No one here thought he was different.

The phone on the bedside table beeps, startling him. It is the receptionist, announcing the arrival of his parents. Does Monsieur Malegarde wish to come down? He says he will do so immediately. He flings off the bathrobe and fishes around the closet for clothes. A moment later, dressed, he leaves the room, using the stairs to go faster. The first thing he notices when he gets to the lobby is how exhausted his father looks. It is a shock. Paul is slumped in an arm-chair, his hand propping up his face, his skin crumpled and unnaturally pale. He is wearing a dark anorak, which makes him seem even whiter. He looks thinner, too, almost gaunt.

"Oh, sweetie, there you are!" His mother's voice, husky, warm. She hugs him, then steps back to look at him. And he, in turn, looks at her, his stunning mother, still a beauty at sixty-one, standing tall and long-legged in her boots and jacket, ash-blond hair swept back. Wrinkles and sags, although they have insidiously appeared, have not been able to tamper with the symmetry of her face, her elegant beak of a nose, which he inherited, her full mouth, the slant of her almond-shaped blue eyes, framed by the dark sweep of lush eye-brows. As usual, she wears no makeup, and, as usual, she turns heads. He leans down to embrace his silent father, then swivels backs to Lauren questioningly. Yes, Paul is not feeling too good, his mother tells him, lowering her voice, he must have caught cold, he just needs a rest, a hot bath, he'll be fine. Tilia comes down; more hugs ensue. His sister notices their father's state instantly. Con-cerned, she squats down to speak to him; he opens heavy eyelids, mumbles something about a headache. Well, why doesn't he go up and have a rest? It's raining far too hard to go out, and no one wants to anyway, so why not make the most of it? Lauren motions to the receptionist, and the luggage is carried up to their room. Linden listens to his mother telling Agathe that her husband is tired, could they possibly have a cup of tea, something to eat? Her French, after all these years, is still hesitant and slow. But it adds to her charm, and he can already see how the receptionist has fallen for it. Once his parents have gone upstairs, he turns to his sister.

"Papa's face! So awful, so white . . ." he murmurs. She nods, concerned. Paul usually has a healthy glow about him, even in the middle of winter.

For the first time, their vigorous, hardy father looks like a shriveled old man. The thought sobers them and they do not speak for a while, sitting in the hotel lobby, shoulder-to-shoulder, hushed, while the rain drenches the city.

⚜

At the end of the day, Linden goes to check on his parents. He knocks softly on the door of room 37, and his mother opens it. She is wearing her reading glasses; her phone is in her hand. Over her shoulder, he sees his father in bed. Lauren whispers he is having a good rest. She canceled the dinner plans for that night. Dining at the animated Rotonde on boulevard du Montparnasse was not the best idea for Paul in his present state. She'll order room service for them later on, which means Tilia and Linden can do as they please. Linden toys about having a meal with his sister. On the one hand, he is tempted; Tilia's company is diverting, her stories amusing. On the other, this is a family weekend, and they will be together for three entire days. Maybe he should make the most of his unexpected freedom and look up an old friend. He tells his mother he'll do that. Tilia won't mind.

Linden tiptoes around the bed to have a look at his father's face. His skin still seems gray and furrowed.

"Is he all right?" he asks his mother uneasily. Shouldn't they call a doctor? Lauren is bent over her phone, fingers flying over the keyboard. Paul looks ghastly, she admits, but he'll be fine; she's not worried. He's been overdoing it lately, as usual, she adds, pushing her glasses up over her head. Paul can never say no to a new tree to save, even if it's on the other side of the country. He hasn't had a proper rest since last summer. And when he is at home, he's constantly on the go, roaming every square inch of the domain, keeping an eye on his beloved lime trees. It was difficult to get him to come to Paris, she goes on, lowering her voice; they are all aware of how much he dislikes the city.

Linden has no urban reminiscences of his father. Everything to do with Paul Malegarde steeps in nature. His earliest memory of his father was watching him tread the craggy land at Vénozan with his precise, steady gait, followed by Vandeleur, his faithful gardener, a dog or two on their heels. Paul's hands seemed perpetually grimy, but Linden soon learned it was not filth that coated his palms, but the grit of soil, and the fine, dusty powder that lined bark. His father caressed trees as if they were the most beloved creatures in the entire universe. A tree is just as much alive as they were, Paul told his little boy, lifting him up so he could also touch the rugged, coarse surface. A tree must fight for survival, his father told him, and it must do this every single second. It has to fight to find water, space, light; it has to ward off heat, drought, cold, predators; it has to learn to battle storms, and the bigger the tree, the more vulnerable it is to wind. It seems simple, Paul told him, how trees live, standing in the sun with their roots in damp soil, but there's much more to it than that; trees can anticipate; they are aware of seasons, of sunlight, of temperature changes. They transfer huge amounts of water; they channel rain as it falls; they have a power man must learn to respect. Humans would be nothing without trees, his father said. He could go on and on, and it never bored Linden. Even the botanical appellations of trees fascinated him as a child. *Quercus, Prunus, Ficus carica, Olea, Platanus* were the ones he remembered by heart—oak tree, prune tree, fig tree, olive tree, and plane tree. And his father's favorite, *Tilia,* for lime tree, or linden, after which both he and his sister had been named. The arboretum, situated just above Vénozan, was composed of fifty majestic limes, planted over two hundred years ago, well before the house was built in 1908 by Maurice Malegarde, Paul's grandfather. This was, Linden knew, where Paul had taken Lauren, during the heat wave of 1976. She, too, had fallen under the spell. How could she not? The lindens created a wide canopy with the velvety abundance of their interlacing branches and leaves. To stand beneath their magnificence in June or July was like showering in a honey-perfumed green glow, encircled by the humming of bees darting from bud to bud.

As he looks down at his father, Linden remembers he has never been to Vénozan with Sacha. Sacha has never seen the lime trees in full bloom, knows very little of that part of his life, because Linden has pushed it behind him. In the almost five years they have been together, a trip to the Drôme with Sacha has never been mentioned. Why? Is it because his father has never officially invited them? Is it because Linden has not mustered up enough courage to go? It is not the first time these thoughts have visited him. As usual, he brushes them away, troubled.

A few moments later, up in his room, Linden calls Sacha on FaceTime. It is ten o'clock in the morning in California. Sacha is at the start-up, in Palo Alto. The beloved face shows up on the screen, the hazel eyes, the desirable smile. Linden tells Sacha about his day—the rain, the river, his father's haggard expression. Sacha talks about the start-up, the cats, the weather, which is so glorious that it's hard to imagine the Parisian downpour. After saying goodbye to Sacha, Linden starts thinking about how he is going to spend the rest of his evening. He scrolls through the contacts on his phone. There is one name, of course, that jumps to his mind without even having to read it. A name that isn't even in his list anymore. Hadrien. The number he remembers is no longer in service, but he still knows it by heart. And he remembers the address, too: 20, rue Surcouf, Paris 75007. Third floor, door on the right. The sadness. The pain. Why is it some memories never fade?

The next name he picks is Oriel Ménard. He gets her voice mail after a couple of rings. She is a photographer he met when he graduated from Gobelins, École de l'Image in 2003, the prestigious Parisian school of visual communication. A few years older than he, she was already by then a fully-fledged photographer, and she gave him a few helpful hints when he started out on his own. She

now works for a French photo agency and specializes in author portraits for renowned publishers. He is in the middle of leaving her a
message when she calls him back, delighted to hear he is in town
for a family gathering. They agree to meet in half an hour at Le
Dôme, on the corner of rue Delambre and boulevard du Montparnasse. Armed with a hotel umbrella, a warm scarf around his neck,
Linden runs down the street in the icy deluge, leaping to avoid large
puddles. People hurry past, enfolded in raincoats. Cars roll by,
wheels making rubbery squelching sounds. At the Dôme, almost
empty, save for another couple, a dour waiter tells him it's never been
this bad: the rain, torrential, incessant, terrible for business. He might
as well hand in his notice, get the hell out of Paris, before the serious trouble begins, before the river wreaks havoc on them all. Linden asks him if he really believes the Seine will overflow. The man
stares at him and inquires politely but with a touch of sarcasm if
monsieur has been living on another planet.

"I live in San Francisco," admits Linden sheepishly. And over
there, he adds, it's the earthquake that everyone is afraid of, the
famous "big one," which doesn't stop people from getting on with
their lives. The waiter nods, it's the same thing here; Parisians are
getting on with their lives, but the rain has not stopped, the forecast is not good, and the Seine might well flood just like it did in
1910, and then what? The city will be paralyzed, thousands will
be homeless, economic activity will freeze, and the government, he
thinks, should be taking the matter more seriously, like they did
last November. What are they waiting for? Why are they being so
circumspect? They need to act now, fast, while the river is up to
the Zouave's ankles; after, it will be too late. To Linden's relief, the
waiter's diatribe is interrupted by Oriel's arrival. Linden has not
seen her for a while. She still has the same wiry brown hair, tiny
button mouth, gray eyes. She is pretty, waiflike, always dressed in
black. They speak in French. It feels good to let forth in his father's
tongue. At first, the French seems rusty; he senses American into-
nations popping up here and there, fights against them, readjusts,
and then after a couple of minutes, he regains his usual complete

fluidity. They order chardonnay, and all of a sudden, as they click their glasses together, Oriel lets out a peal of laughter.

"I've just remembered something!" she says. Does he recall what happened when they first met, in 2003? Linden, amused by her mirth, says he doesn't. Oh, it was excruciating, she says, sipping her wine. He was twenty-two; she was twenty-four. They were at a party held for Gobelin graduates in a loft near the Bastille, and she had made a fool of herself by trying to seduce him. It does come back to him now, her doggedness in a dark corner, pressing her lips against his. He had kissed her back, nicely, and when she wanted to take matters further, he had politely pushed her away. Still, she did not get the hint, kissed him again, running her hands against his thighs, under his shirt, murmuring he didn't have to be shy, that she'd do everything, he could just relax, close his eyes, until he had stated, as simply as he could, that he wasn't into girls. She had stared back at him, gray eyes fluttering wide open, had remained silent for a few seconds, and then had muttered, did he mean he was . . . and he had finished her sentence: gay, yes, he was gay. And she had looked so crushed, he felt sorry, stroked her face, and said it didn't matter. Then she had said, and he remembered that part well, that he certainly didn't look gay, so how could she tell? It was unfair; he was so good-looking, tall, masculine, how could she ever know? He had asked, sotto voce, with a wicked grin, if she could describe what *looking gay* meant, and she had clapped her hand to her mouth and muttered sorry. Did he realize they had been friends for over fifteen years, she now asks. Isn't that rather remarkable? What about another glass of chardonnay to celebrate? Linden gestures to the waiter. Oriel goes on to insist it is indeed notable, especially since he has become who he is, Linden Malegarde; she utters his name exaggeratedly with her beguiling French accent. Famous worldwide for his arresting portraits, and the best part is that he has not changed, not one bit; all that success could have turned him into a conceited prig, but no, he remains such a nice guy. She claps him heartily on the back. Linden feels uncomfortable with this sort of chitchat, wondering if the other person harbors any well-concealed bitterness regarding his fame, and as she continues, he stares into his wine, listening to the rain fall onto the glass roof. Oriel says she could tell the world all she knows, when he wore the same black leather jacket and black jeans, over and over again, when his hair was long and wavy, like a Pre-Raphaelite hippie (he cringes), when he lived in the fifteenth with his American aunt, who spent her evenings waiting for a phone call from her married French lover. Linden soberly tells her his aunt Candice died six years ago, that he had not been able to make it to her funeral and had felt so guilty. Candice had been crucial to him during the years he had lived in her flat. He refrains from telling Oriel how Candice died, the miserable aftermath of her death, how it had left its mark on him.

The glum waiter brings the second round, and when he is gone, Linden whispers under his breath that the guy was being most disheartening about the Seine flooding before she got here. Oriel's expression is solemn. She whispers back that the waiter is right; inundating could well occur and it would be hell. Linden jeers at her, what is she going on about? She sounds like those pessimistic journalists on the news, painting the bleakest of pictures and frightening everyone.

"This is perhaps not the ideal weekend for being in Paris, you know," Oriel says matter-of-factly. Because of the rain, she means? She stares at him again, as if he were an idiot. Yes, the rain and the flood, does he realize what might happen, in a city like Paris? He has no idea, does he? Her tone is irritating. Well, there haven't been any governmental warnings, have there? No one's being told *not* to come to Paris. Isn't she exaggerating a little? Not at all, she retorts. She has a close friend who works at city hall, and they're getting all worked up. The river is up to 3.80 meters at the pont d'Austerlitz, she says, and if this goes on for any longer, according to her friend, they'll stop all fluvial traffic, to begin with. If the rain does not cease, they're in trouble. The level is rising too fast. Puzzled, Linden says he thought centennial flooding occurred only once a century, that the city had learned its lesson well since 1910, that Paris is prepared. That's what everyone thinks, she points out wryly, everyone thinks Paris is safe. Everyone thinks the Seine has been tamed, that the flooding will not happen again. But Paris is not safe. Her friend Matthieu said the situation could well become disastrous, quickly, much more quickly then anybody could ever imagine, and they would know more by tomorrow, she says, or even during the night. Matthieu told her the Seine's flow was constantly monitored, that the tricky part was trying to anticipate whether the swelling was an ephemeral one that could abate in two or three days, like in November, or, on the contrary, one heralding a dramatic flood. Last time, even before the water rose to six meters, under the Zouave's waist, the prefecture had sent out dire warnings, displaced citizens situated in certain areas of the twelfth, seventh, and fifteenth arrondissements, dispatched the army, closed some Métro stations, shut down the Louvre and d'Orsay museums, but the river had finally subsided. The government had been criticized for getting the Parisians agitated and worried for nothing. Two months later, the authorities were watching their step and were conscious they could not go wrong.

"I'm here for my father's birthday and my parents' wedding anniversary," Linden tells Oriel. It is not an event he can easily cancel. Surely he can make sure they avoid all flooded areas, wherever those might be. Oriel looks serious again. She'll text him if she hears anything from Matthieu. The Seine will make headlines; of that, they can be sure. Good news, or bad news. Most probably bad news. Linden interrupts her, this is sinister; it's getting him down. What about a bite to eat? And what about her work? Is she still photographing authors? Aren't they a pain? He's had a few of those recently, some bestselling ones who think they are kings of the world because they've sold millions of copies. They order seafood and more wine, and Oriel is now happily chatting about her job. A couple of hours later, when they part, it is still raining.

When Linden gets back to the hotel, at midnight, there is a note under his door from his mother. *Your father seems better. Had vegetable soup and is now fast asleep. See you tomorrow.* Tilia texted to say she'd had a drink with an old friend and gone to bed early. He does not turn on the television. Instead, he takes his iPad out of its case and logs on to the hotel's Wi-Fi. Sacha has sent him some messages, which he responds to swiftly. His agent, Rachel, who is aware that he is not working for the next few days, has emailed him some propositions. He'll check them out later.

Linden looks up the word *Seine*. The name comes from *Sequana*, used by the Gauls and Romans who navigated along the river and settled by its swampy shores to later form Lutèce, the future city of Paris. An ancient Celtic goddess with healing powers, called Sequana, was worshipped at the river's source, near Dijon. She was represented in a small boat, graceful arms aloft. Linden reads on. He is amazed to discover that the river had often destroyed the city it nurtured; there have been at least sixty serious inundations since fluvial recordings were first registered in the sixth century. The most drastic one to be measured against the pont de la Tournelle was in February 1658, when the Seine gushed to 8.96 meters, its highest-ever recorded level. Dozens of people drowned as houses built on the pont Marie were whisked away by torrential waters.

When sleep takes over, Linden's last thought is not for Sacha, nor for Sequana and her ornamental headband, nor for the rain still drumming outside, but for his father, sleeping in the room below, with his mother; his father, whom he loves but whom he cannot talk to. Something always holds him back. Timidity, apprehension, whatever it is, it means they cannot have proper conversations. They never have had. To make matters worse, Paul is the reserved type, apart from his two favorite topics, trees and David Bowie. Linden wonders if Lauren hadn't carefully crafted this family weekend with hopes of interaction sprouting between father and son. The uneasy feeling perseveres. What if Paul does not want to know more about his son, who he is, whom he loves?

T W O

❧

A photograph is a secret about a secret. The more
it tells you, the less you know.

—DIANE ARBUS

I remember her name. But it was never spoken after the thing happened. I remember her face, too. Soft and round. Pink velvety cheeks. Her voice. Her hair, light brown. Her scent, lemony. She was young. Probably seventeen, maybe younger. She was a village girl from the area. Her father was a truffle harvester. She was hired to look after me, two afternoons a week, because my mother was expecting. I was four. I didn't know how to read or write yet. I was too small for school. She came, always smiling, and we would go for walks around my grandfather's property.

There was so much to see. Especially in summer. The black pond high up on the clump, near the pass, where toads croaked. We would throw pebbles at them, and laugh while they swam away. The cypress trees at the end of the vale, rising high and proud like warriors. She called them "the Mohicans." Careful, the Mohicans are coming to get you, she'd say playfully to scare me. Sometimes they did look like giant Indians with huge feathers in their headbands, striding down over the hills. We would sit in the lavender fields quietly. She made daisy chains and strung them over her head. Oh, she looked pretty. We sang "À la Claire Fontaine." We counted butterflies. We coaxed caterpillars into old matchboxes to examine them as they writhed. We picked apricots from over-laden branches in July. We fetched milk and eggs from the neighboring farm. They had sheep out in front, their white collie herding them in. I was a happy little fellow. When horseflies stung me, she knew how to make it better. She'd blow on the ugly pink bite and hum a little tune for me under her breath.

A couple of times, in February, when the mistral blew strong and it was freezing, she took me to her father's well-protected truffle field to watch him harvest the rare wild mushrooms from beneath the oak trees. His bitch was trained to sniff them out and locate them under limestone and roots. I loved watching the dog glue her nose to the ground, scratching the earth with her paws. The girl's father then carefully extracted the truffles with his special spade. The mushrooms didn't look like anything extraordinary to me, small, black, irregularly round, sometimes lumpy, but the girl's father said they were priceless. He always made me smell them. Such a musty, strong odor. I wasn't sure if I liked it. But when I took my truffle home, carefully wrapped up in a cloth, my parents were always pleased.

I need to choose the right words now. I have to explain exactly what happened and how it felt to me, as a child.

Go back to that child's mind, those childlike eyes. Not looking back as a grown man. Say it right, say it true, even if it fills me with horror.

THE GATES TO VÉNOZAN stand on the road to Nyons, when one exits Sévral from the east. The nearest village is Léon-des-Vignes, renowned for its olive oil and truffles. The house cannot be glimpsed from the road. The pale, pebbly path winds up, weaving its way like a long ribbon though stretches of apricot trees, vineyards, and lavender fields. It is a quiet area, with only the occasional rumble of a nearby tractor infringing upon the silence. Tourists do not venture up here—they fear the rocky path might damage their car wheels—but hikers sometimes appear, sticks in hand. Up and up, the path turns and twists steeply, so that cars need to shift gears, so that the walker or cyclist might become a little short of breath. The house can now be glimpsed, and those who have never laid eyes upon it are frequently awestruck. Vénozan looks like it was built in the Renaissance, when it was, in fact, erected in 1908. Maurice Malegarde, Linden's great-grandfather, wanted it to resemble the Tuscan hunting lodges of the Medici family. Maurice had never been to Italy, had never seen a Medici hunting lodge; he was a humble farm boy born in a cottage near Sévral. But the significant wealth due to his money-spinning carton-packing factories gave him, at age thirty-five, a certain *folie des grandeurs*. Nothing could be too good for him and for his becoming wife, Yvette, also of modest extraction. His thriving chain of factories produced carton boxes, the first ever to send live silkworms worldwide, thanks to ingenious holes punctured in the sides, which prevented fragile larvae from suffocating during the long journeys. The silk industry had caught on swiftly; then the perfume and cosmetic companies had ensued. Malegarde boxes were all the rage; they were prettily decorated, handy, easy to craft, and they generated jobs. At the turn of the century, the flourishing production of these cartons was a boon for Sévral and its area, not only for Maurice Malegarde, who was one of the first to set up his factories, but for all those who followed suit. Entire trains supplied with boxes left Sévral station twice a day, heading for Marseille, Paris, Lyon.

When Maurice Malegarde decided to build his house, he searched high and low for the perfect spot. It did not take long for him to find it, a large terrain at Vénozan, a farming locality not far from Léon-des-Vignes, just below the arboretum of limes planted by an inspired farmer before his time. One tall linden appeared much older than the others. Its beauty had no doubt drawn the nature-loving farmer to the place, and had given him the idea to plant fellow trees around it. Acquiring the land demanded a subtle pulling of strings, envelopes lined with wads of banknotes administered unceremoniously under tables. Maurice appointed a stylish Parisian architect who worshipped Italian art and the Quattrocento. The house, which took two years to construct, was a sturdy fortress built of creamy stone with a crenellated roof. It sat with a weathered indolence beneath the arboretum, facing the valley as if it had been there for centuries, its flanks adorned by an oak, a maple, an elm, and two plane trees, the northwesterly wind blowing powerlessly at its mighty back.

Maurice Malegarde, a gregarious, mustachioed fellow, hosted lavish parties with comely Yvette, which were the talk of the county. People came from far and wide to attend them, making Vénozan the place to be. With a swagger and a top hat, Maurice greeted his guests on the steps of his property, a rented orchestra playing a waltz, waiters offering champagne. A decade later, he added the locality name to his own and invented a false title, flaunting "Baron de Malegarde-Vénozan" on his calling cards and on the label of a white wine he had the audacity to produce for a couple of years. The ostentatious Maurice died of a heart attack at seventy-nine, in 1952. His son, François, born in 1908 with the house, did not inherit his father's panache. He was a quiet, self-conscious man who never felt at home in his father's vast domain. His wife, Mireille, from Montélimar, was struck with ennui in such bucolic surroundings. She missed the busy town she was from. Nothing went on here, she felt, no excitement; just trees, lavender, and wind. When she had her two children, Paul, born in 1948, and Marie, in 1952, she felt she had accomplished her duty. Mireille remained at Vénozan long enough to raise them, but when her son, Paul, turned twelve in 1960, she started a discreet affair with a neighboring farmer from Visan. Five years later, François placidly agreed to a divorce. Mireille remarried and moved away. François met a widowed schoolteacher called Brigitte and had a peaceful relationship with her. Never would he have dared use his father's false title, which conniving Maurice had managed to incorporate in property and family documents.

Under François Malegarde's hesitant directive, the splendor of Vénozan faltered and faded for twenty years. François did not possess his father's golden touch, did not exploit the factories with such a sure hand. The reign of carton packing had peaked and was slowly drawing to a close. François found the house difficult to run and maintain. In winter, without central heating, the large rooms were freezing, in spite of the oversized fireplaces. Vénozan was situated high above the village, and snow was not a surprise come December. The gardens Maurice had been so proud of were neglected, taken over by brambles and weeds. The house was damp, not tended for. There were leaks in some ceilings.

In 1970, François Malegarde succumbed to liver cancer at age sixty-two. His son, Paul, was by then in his early twenties, installed at nearby Buis-les-Baronnies, where he made his living working for a landscaper. Paul and his sister, Marie, inherited the house, but it was soon decided that Paul should take it on. Marie was engaged to a surly cultivator called Marcel, from Léon-des-Vignes, who had no intention of investing a centime in Vénozan. Paul moved back in the winter of 1970. An enormous task lay before him: tending to the gardens, to the arboretum, to the house, with limited means. It was an unhurried process, but he gave it all his attention. He worked day in, day out with his bare hands and the help of his friends, lads from the area who knew and loved the land as much as he did. There was no question of reproducing his grandfather's extravagance, of hosting fancy cocktail parties.

Six years later, when Paul met Lauren, he had already succeeded in shaping the domain into what it is today, a little paradise on earth.

The silver curtain of rain is still fizzing outside the window when Linden awakes. It is a few minutes past nine. He sends a text message to his mother to find out how Paul is. Lauren's answer is swift: *Fine! Having breakfast. Why don't you join us?* After a shower, he goes downstairs to the dining room near the lobby. His father still looks pale, he notices, and strangely puffy. He is eating cereal, bent over his bowl. Every movement he makes seems to be in slow motion. Lauren appears jaunty, her smile slightly too bright. So what if it's raining? They can still make it to the museums—she reserved all their tickets online—and if anyone is tired, they can rest, she says, plenty of places in the museum to do just that. Tilia? Still asleep, as usual. Linden talks to his father gently, asking him how he feels. It's his birthday, after all, and they will celebrate tonight. Paul responds with a feeble, croaky voice. His eyes are watery, red-rimmed. He looks so unlike himself that Linden cannot understand why he has not seen a doctor.

"I don't need a doctor," his father tells him in the same wispy tone. "I'm fine."

Linden wonders for how long he has been looking and sounding like this. He wants to ask his mother, but he is aware she will not answer him now, at least not in front of Paul. She is already changing the subject, artfully, reaching out to pour her husband another cup of coffee. Linden marvels that she should act so natural, as if nothing at all were wrong with Paul. Has Linden seen the news, she asks. No, he came straight down. Lauren prattles on as Paul silently munches his cereal, his spoon moving in the slowest-possible manner, all the more surprising, since his father usually wolfs down meals, finishing what's on his plate before others have even started. His mother sounds uncommonly loud this morning, he finds. God knows how all these people are going to manage, she blares on, waving a bit of croissant in the air. Surely the authorities are going too far, canceling everything at the last minute, sending everyone packing, all those models, those hairdressers, makeup artists, photographers. . . . Linden realizes she is talking about fashion week. All the designers are livid, apparently, and one can imagine that they would be. Linden picks up his phone to check Twitter. Fashion week, which was supposed to start today and last till next Thursday, has indeed been canceled by order of the pre-fecture. The Seine's level is still mounting, splattering at the Zou-ave's calves now, well over four meters, and the authorities are taking measures, just as Oriel said they would. There is no way the shows can be accommodated elsewhere, at such a key moment, just when the government is waiting to determine which steps to take. All fluvial navigation has ceased, he reads, and some museums will be closed today, like the d'Orsay, the Branly, and no doubt the Louvre (he reads this out loud to his mother, who groans). Bulwarks are being constructed around certain Métro stations in order to protect them, and the quai de la Gare, near where the Seine enters Paris, has been flooded. A problem due to the water spill has been reported in the sewers, and the situation could worsen within a couple of hours.

His perusal of the worrisome news is interrupted by Tilia's en-trance. Her hair is tied up in a straggly bun. She is wearing a loose-fitting sweater and baggy jeans. It must not be easy being Lauren's daughter, Linden thinks (not for the first time), not having inher-ited those looks, always being compared, unfavorably, to her mother. Does Tilia care? She never shows it, but Linden imagines she must have suffered, and no doubt still does. At nineteen, Tilia also left Vénozan and went to live in the Basque country with Eric Ezri, whom she married soon after their daughter's birth. Yet Linden knows how strong the bond is between Tilia and her parents, how tender and caring she is for them, and he sees it now as his sister takes Paul's hand, obviously disturbed by his swollen, fatigued face. Paul grumpily mutters the same response to his daughter: He is fine, no doctor needed, he is just fine, could they please stop worrying? Oh well, they have the river to worry about now, says Tilia, reaching for a *pain au chocolat*. Aren't they lucky to be in a hotel that won't be flooded? Clever Lauren, figuring that out two years ago, when she booked! Lauren replies she had no idea the rue Delambre was in a water-safe district, and come to think of it, so is the restaurant they are going to tonight. She checked on one of those online maps. Mother and daughter chat exactly like they used to, while father and son shut up. It was always that way in their family. Yet when Linden left home, settled down in Paris, he stopped being silent. The awkwardness he felt at Sévral when he used to walk into the school and bear the weight of critical eyes thawed away. It had a lot to do with Candice. His aunt resembled his mother, in the sense that she, too, was also a tall, shapely blonde, but she had a feature his mother lacked: She was an extraordinary listener. When Linden settled down in the apartment on rue de l'Église, she asked no questions; she was even-tempered and warmhearted. She made him feel welcomed the minute he arrived. He noticed she was more sophisticated than his mother, both in her appearance (hair cut in a stylish bob, pencil skirts, and stiletto heels) and in her everyday life. Books lined the walls of each room of the flat, and many a time he would come home and find her reading on the sofa, engrossed, her cat Muffin curled up in her lap. They spoke in English, although Candice's French was remarkably good, with only a faint trace of an American accent. She had been living in Paris for a while now, over fifteen years. There had been talk of marriage with a Frenchman with a fancy name, whom Linden had never met, but it had not happened. Candice seemed to wait, and wilt. She gave English lessons at a French university, made friends, but time slipped by, and in 1997, when Linden moved in, she was in her early forties, and had, as she wryly put it herself, "lost her bloom." She never asked questions, and he did not, either, but that suited them. In the beginning, they talked about everything but themselves. Linden soon understood she was unhappy, although she never mentioned it. She was still seeing the Frenchman, who had married another woman. She did not reveal any of this to her nephew, but he soon figured the situation out, noticing how some evenings she'd leave with a spring in her step, her cheeks flushed, elated, wearing a pretty silk frock, only to return at midnight, dress and hair rumpled, head down, trailing sadness in her wake. Linden never knew the Frenchman's name, only his initials, J.G. Somehow, Candice understood Linden more than anyone else did. Perhaps it was her empathy, her discretion. He was comfortable in her presence; he always had been, ever since she came to spend summers with them at Vénozan and raced him to the end of the garden and back. She did not like being called Aunt Candice. She was always "Candy" to Tilia and him.

"Dude, what are you thinking about? You look sad."

His sister's voice jolts him back to the present moment. Linden says, "Candy," and regrets it when his mother's eyes tear up. He murmurs he's sorry, that being here in Paris inevitably brings her back; he can't help it. He misses her. His mother says nothing, dabbing at an eyelid with a napkin, but he can hear her voice clearly, just as if she had uttered words out loud: *Sure, you miss her, Linden, but you didn't even make it to her cremation. You were on a photo shoot you supposedly couldn't cancel, and you left me and Tilia to deal with Candy's death and the horror of it.* No one speaks for a long moment, and the only sound Linden hears is the slush of the rain, Paul's spoon clicking against the porcelain, and voices coming from the lobby. He does not speak, either; he balks at the idea of evoking the painful subject of his aunt's death, in 2012, the shocking text message he received when he was on another continent, in another time zone, but that he would never forget: *Please call, urgent.*

Candy dead. The remonstrance in his mother's eyes is unfair; he did try to fly back as swiftly as possible, but the photo shoot, which was for a perfume brand and involved an enormous budget and a famous American actor, could not be postponed. By the time he landed in Paris, Candice's body had been cremated. She had left a clear letter: no Mass, no ceremony, no grave, and no flowers. Her ashes were to be disposed of by her parents and sister, as they saw fit. For a long time, the ashes remained in a small urn in Lauren's dressing room at Vénozan, until she mustered enough courage to scatter them near the wild roses that Candy loved.

❧

Huddling beneath umbrellas, they trudge along boulevard Raspail in the downpour. Lauren and Tilia march on ahead, while Linden slows his step to match his father's bizarrely dawdling one. He is accustomed to Paul's brisk pace, and this new rhythm unsettles him. Yet his father looks better, he notices, less pallid, less bloated. The Louvre, Branly, and d'Orsay museums are closed, so Lauren switched to plan B: shopping in Saint-Germain-des–Près. The monsoonlike rain appears to have put off passersby, and even the traffic seems fluid. By the time they reach the Bon Marché, Linden's feet are wet and cold. He imagines the others are suffering in the same way, but none of them complains, so he doesn't, either. The luxurious department store is heated; waves of warm perfumed air waft by them. The shop is full of bedraggled, wet customers rejoicing in the hot haven. His father's arm is still tucked into his own.

"Everything okay?" he asks Paul in French, leaning down to him. He and Tilia never speak to their father in English, just as they don't address their mother in French. Paul nods. He seems content, slightly dazed. His cheeks are flushed, two little red spots that look like they have been painted on. Linden asks his father if he wants to sit down, and Paul nods. Tilia says there is a place to have coffee on the second floor. They manage to find a table in spite of the throng. Linden looks at his father's hands nursing his mug of coffee. Fascinating hands, both powerful and graceful. Now he notices how the skin on them is puckered and spotted. They are no longer the hands of a young man. He takes out his Leica and photographs them. His family is so used to this, they hardly notice.

Linden started to photograph them when he was twelve, at Vénozan. He had a summer job with a wedding photographer in Sévral, old Monsieur Fonsauvage. It had started out as a chore, but the attraction emerged swiftly. The ambience of the darkroom delighted him. He observed the elderly photographer choose the right images on contact prints, bending down to glue his eye to the linen tester, pushing his glasses up over his wizened forehead. Monsieur Fonsauvage was always finicky about the final choice. He did not want his clients to be disappointed. After all, their wedding was the most important day of their lives, *n'est-ce-pas?* The trick for developing was managing the deed in total darkness. Monsieur Fonsauvage painstakingly showed him how, lights on, using leftover bits of film. Linden watched the old hands cautiously wrangle the top off the film canisters, holding the feeder between gnarly index and middle fingers, deftly inserting, handling, and cutting each spool. Linden learned by practicing. The old man, delighted with the progress and zeal of his young apprentice, offered him a battered but operational Praktica L2 camera, manufactured in 1979. It wasn't an easy camera to master for a beginner, but Linden soon became enthralled with his gift. His parents and sister were his favorite models. At first, it bothered them, this business of him constantly shoving the lenses at them, but he soon learned to become less obtrusive, and they got the hang of either forgetting him or learning how to pose. He shot his mother sunbathing, his father watching his trees, his sister playing clown and giving him the finger. He shot his friends, the few of them he had. He preferred black-and-white, and developed his prints himself under the tutorship of Gaspard Fonsauvage. He learned about light and shadow by experimenting, all by himself, by trial and error. He hadn't meant to become a photographer. It was just a hobby. He hadn't realized how much space photography took up in his life. When he was fifteen, the family went to Venice for a week. Paul, Lauren, and Tilia were equipped with disposable cameras. Linden stuck to his Praktica. When they got home, all the photos were assembled into one album. There were three identical sets, and one that was entirely different: Linden's. He had not gone for the obvious shots of the Bridge of Sighs, of the Rialto, of the Piazza San Marco. He had preferred to immortalize an old woman in black sitting on a bench, watching the sheeplike tourists lumber by, stray cats frolicking in a damp Dorsoduro alleyway, the typical Venetian brass doorbells, a waiter having a quick cigarette behind Harry's Bar, and running a hand through his unctuous combed-back hair.

Linden now turns his Leica toward his mother and sister and clicks away. He loves the different, richer sound an argentic camera makes, the characteristic mechanical whirr of film as it winds itself into its compartment. Most of the jobs he gets today demand digital equipment. He is used to that but will always harbor a soft spot for his old camera. He bought the secondhand Canadian-made Leica M4-P in Paris, at the flea market at Saint-Ouen, in May 1998, for his seventeenth birthday. All his family had contributed toward it, even his grandparents from Boston. It was cheaper than expected, due to a flaw pointed out by the vendor. There was something wrong with the shutter curtain, which tampered with the shots. It would cost even more to have it mended. As soon as Linden took the black camera emblazoned with the label Leitz into his hands, feeling its weight, its sturdy mass against his palms, he knew he had to have it. It was an iconic camera, the one he dreamed of owning. Alfred Eisenstaedt used a Leica to capture that legendary Times Square kiss in 1945; with one, Nick Ut caught the searing horror of napalm in 1972; and Alberto Korda immortalized Che Guevara wearing a beret in 1960 with his. Linden would figure out how to mend it later. His first photos were marred by strange wispy shadows, ghostlike shapes flitting through the image. The size of the shadows grew with the increase in shutter speed, he discovered. For a long time, he found he could not afford to get it repaired. So he learned to work around and with the shadows, which taught him his own technique. The Leica has witnessed much of his life. It was with the Leica that he took the memorable photograph of his father, the one that got him noticed at the age of eighteen, when he was still living with Candice, on rue de l'Église.

He has often told the story of that particular shot. On Sunday, December 26, 1999, the phone rang in the early hours of the morning, at Candy's. It was Lauren, overjoyed, announcing the birth of Tilia's baby during the night at the Biarritz clinic. A girl. The customary Christmas at Vénozan had not been held that year, as Tilia went into labor on the twenty-fourth and Lauren had rushed to Biarritz to be with her daughter. Linden had remained with his aunt in Paris, and Paul had come up to be with them. He was staying in a hotel on nearby avenue Félix-Faure. All night long, great winds had blown over Paris, but it wasn't until Linden opened the shutters after his mother called that he realized something was wrong. The public garden down the road looked like a bomb had hit it. The pavilion used as a summer concert hall had been crushed by a chestnut tree. Branches, flung here and there, were strewn all the way down the street. Linden switched on the television. He learned that a tremendous storm, with the force of a hurricane, had battered France during the night from west to east, leaving depredation in its wake from Brittany to Alsace, searing through Paris and its area. A hundred people died. Electricity was down in over three million homes. The damages were colossal. As Linden watched, mesmerized, his father telephoned. His voice was strangled, unrecognizable. At first, Linden thought there was a problem with Tilia's baby. His father needed Candy's car, now, right now. He had to go to Versailles. As quickly as possible. Versailles? Why Versailles? Linden couldn't understand. He went to ask Candice for the car keys, got dressed, and rushed downstairs to meet his father. His father said nothing as they drove out to Versailles. But Linden began to apprehend the situation when he saw the number of plummeted trees. The highway was closed because of the damage left by the storm. They had to use smaller roads to reach the château.

Police barricades halted them when they came to the great gates, but when his father said his name and the names of the persons who were expecting them, they nodded, and let them pass. Linden noticed that the château had dozens of broken windows. Near the gardens, people were waiting. They turned and acclaimed his father like a savior. There was one middle-aged man, small and bearded, who seemed desperate: the head gardener of Versailles. He took Paul's arm and murmured that the wreckage was hideous, unbearable. And as they turned toward the vast gardens, Linden saw with shock that he was not exaggerating.

A spectacle of chaos and desolation greeted them. Tree after tree had been uprooted by the storm, tossed down like matchsticks on choppy soil, fallen sentries with knotted roots rising like agonizing limbs. Some trees had been split into two, ravaged by fiendish gales that had landed on them like axes. Taking photos, Linden listened to the bearded man as he led them through a tragic labyrinth of ruin; the storm had lasted over two hours, and he had watched it all, aghast, helpless, from his window. There were 200,000 trees on the domain, and 10,000 had been devastated. The Orangerie had been flattened. The well-ordered gardens *à la française,* designed by Le Nôtre, groves, hedges, and flower beds were a dispirited tangle of splintered twigs. The worst thing, the gardener went on, was that the rare, ancient ones had been destroyed, like Marie-Antoinette's tulip tree at the Trianon, and the oldest tree of the domain, an oak that had been planted during the reign of Louis XIV. Linden could not see his father's face, as he was walking behind him, but instinctively he ran on ahead, picking his way through the rubble.

"We have lost three centuries of history," murmured the bearded man as they at last came to a stop at the vantage point in front of the Grand Canal, where the massacre could be glimpsed in all its hideous scope, a boundless spread of trunks strewn out like carcasses. Linden watched his father. He had never seen him so stiff, so silent. Paul strode back toward the château, his hands in his pockets. Then he stopped, crouching down to touch a fallen tree with his palm. Still, he did not speak, and Linden did not know what to say. He took the Leica and photographed his father three times. It was through the lens that he noticed his father was crying noiselessly, his face screwed up in pain. He tucked the camera away and went to sit next to Paul, his arm tight around him, feeling the great sobs rack his father's back.

A few days later, when Candice saw the black-and-white photograph, she gasped. Paul's white face was tilted up to the sky, furrowed in pain, two hands on each side of his wet cheeks. Behind him, the wraithlike shadows caused by the defective shutter curtain were scattered across the slain trees, darkening their bark to charcoal in a residue that resembled bloody ashes. She had never seen anything so potent, so stirring. Could she show it to a journalist friend of hers who was based in Paris and who was looking for different images of the storm? Linden agreed, presuming nothing would come from this. He had passed his baccalaureat the previous June and was employed in a photo laboratory near the Bastille, not quite sure of what he was going to do next. He worked at the till, dealt with order and deliveries. Going back to Sévral and Vénozan after nearly three years in Paris was not what he had planned, so he figured that keeping his job and earning money could help as he waited to make up his mind. Three years of cohabiting with Candy, however effortless, made him hanker for a stab of independence.

The photograph was published in the *International Herald Tribune* in the beginning of January 2000 and the calls started to come in for Linden Malegarde. Could he come and show his portfolio? The arresting black-and-white portrait of "Mr. Treeman" holding his head, tears streaming down his cheeks, as he gazed at the destruction of the Versailles gardens had not gone unnoticed. However, Linden had no portfolio to display. Only his personal work, which he was not ready to reveal. Although he was pleased at the attention his photograph got, he felt incapable of going to meet people and presenting his work. His parents were unhappy about this, convinced he should go forward and earn his living as a photographer. "He isn't ready!" barked Tilia on the phone from Biarritz, baby Mistral on her breast. "He's not even nineteen; give him time, for Christ's sake!" So he stayed on at the photo lab until he enrolled at Gobelins, École de l'Image a couple of months later, not expecting to get in. The day of the oral exam, when he showed his personal work, and the images he had taken of Versailles and of his father, one of the professors said she had seen that photograph last January and that she had never forgotten it. His parents and his aunt helped finance his three-year course, from 2000 to 2003. Linden kept working all through his studies, at other photo labs, and he shot parties, weddings, and seminars for various clients. It enabled him to pay for the small lodgings he rented until he was able, with his first serious contracts, to afford a more comfortable apartment on rue Broca, in 2005.

"Let me take a picture of you, for once," says his mother, snatching the camera from his fingers. "Oh, it's that complicated old one, isn't it? You need to figure out the light and speed and all that?"

Linden grins, takes the Leica back, and rapidly works out the focus for Lauren. He slings an arm around Tilia and draws her to him. She makes a face. No clowning around, cautions their mother; she wants a pretty photograph of her children. Paul looks on, a genial smile on his reddish face. Why does he still seem dazed? Linden wonders. He is used to his father's silences, but not to the new emptiness he now sees in his eyes, the lack of emotion, as if nothing counts, as if Paul were half-asleep, or inebriated. Lauren is complaining about how the weather has disrupted all her plans for them this afternoon. She had prepared a cultural visit to the Branly, d'Orsay, and Louvre museums, a short walk along the Seine, and a stop at a delightful tearoom.

"We can always go the movies," says Tilia matter-of-factly, as usual. "No rain there!"

Lauren applauds. What a good idea. They will do just that. There is bound to be a good film playing somewhere. For the next fifteen minutes, mother and daughter pore over their devices, finding the right movie. Paul sits there, taciturn. Not bored, not impatient, but absent. Linden yearns to reach out a hand, tap him on the shoulder, jolt him back to the here and now. But he has never been able to do that. Paul has always stood in another world, one that Linden cannot get into. Has he ever tried getting into that other world? Sacha has asked. No. He hasn't. Why? Because he doesn't know how. He doesn't know which words to use. He doesn't know how to start. Sacha said it could be done very easily, just by going to Vénozan, for example, inviting Paul out for a meal, then walking the land with his father, and starting there, in the middle of nature. Pronouncing the words that could build a bond between them. One evening, after dinner, in their house on Elizabeth Street, Linden had told Sacha, sadly, that it was too late. His father was going on seventy. He himself was going to be thirty-seven. It was too late to communicate. Besides, it wasn't as if he and Paul ever fought. They didn't. They never had. There had never been a conflict. Conflict might have made it easier. Yes, there was love. But it was not expressed. Love was tucked away, remote. That evening, with one of the cats sitting on his lap, Linden admitted he thought his father was perhaps disappointed in him. That he wasn't the son Paul had dreamed of. Sacha had stared at him; was he out of his mind, or what? Linden was a wonderful son, a perfect son; one only had to look at him. How could he say such a dumb thing? Even people who had barely met him were bowled over by his personality, his kindheartedness, his talent, his sense of humor. Not to mention his success as a photographer, and, last but not least, his looks. Linden had grinned, bashful. But he knew Sacha understood. He was aware Sacha knew what he meant. He took Sacha's hand and held it tightly. In Sacha's eyes, he saw the sadness, too, fleeting and tender, and it revived that awful, raw, buried feeling of not fitting in, of being left out, the memory of the insults the kids at Sévral would whisper behind his back.

Linden wonders what kind of relationship Paul had with his own father, François. He knew Paul was only twenty-two when his father died in 1970. At Vénozan, there is a series of framed photographs lining the stair walls. Linden had always found them absorbing to look at. Maurice Malegarde, the phony baron, holding up his champagne glass, twirling his mustaches, a buxom woman (Great-Granny Yvette, no doubt) on his arm. He must have been a character, that one. François, the grandfather he had never known, sitting on the terrace, wearing a straw hat, reading the paper. He had a gentle, kind face. Linden had never known his grandmother, either, the one called Mireille, from Montélimar, who had remarried. She passed away well before he was born. Did François and Paul get on? he wonders. He is aware his father is not particularly close to his own sister, Marie, who lives in Sévral. Whom does his father talk to? Lauren? Tilia? His gardener, Vandeleur, whom he's known for years? Or some other guy he runs the domain with, one of those burly chaps with southern accents he likes to hang out with? And what was Paul like as a teenager, as a young man? A David Bowie fan, that he knows, but that's pretty much it, apart from the fierce love of trees. Linden looks across the table at his father, feeling Tilia's interrogative gaze upon him. Paul Malegarde remains a mystery to his only son.

After the film, a undistinguished American comedy, and once they are back at the hotel, Linden's phone vibrates. A text message from Oriel: *Things not looking good. It's still raining and Seine moving way too fast. They've halted all river traffic. Stay safe. Maybe leave? O.*

Maybe leave? Linden scoffs. Surely she is amplifying the whole affair, fueled by her pessimistic fluviologist friend. He then gets a text message from Sacha: *Everything OK? News looks pretty worrying from here.* He turns on the TV. The waters have now apparently entered segments of the Métro, near the Orsay area. Panels of specialists vie for attention on all channels. Every one of them can explain the situation, it seems (and Linden is beginning to learn it by heart: outstandingly high precipitation the previous summer, warm winter causing premature thaw, saturated topsoil, nonstop rain), but no one knows how to prevent it.

The city of Paris underwent a major rehearsal two years ago, describing to residents what would happen if the water rose over four meters, the alert level, in order to prevent and prepare the population, but it appears no one seems ready to deal with the real event now that it seems imminent. Bewildered, Linden listens to one expert after another. One woman, in her forties, with reddish hair, glasses, and a low voice, keeps insisting that despite modern technology, engineering, prediction, the hemming in of the Seine by construction of higher banks supposedly controlling the course, the digging of the riverbed to make it deeper, no one or nothing can prevent the water level from reaching the same heights as that of 1910. "Which means pandemonium," she says with quiet relish. Her flustered opponents berate her with rancor; the situation is, according to them, under control, the army will be stepping in, some residents will be evacuated, but there is no way the situation will become as dire as in 1910. The redheaded woman stays calm. "You'll see," she retorts evenly. "It's mathematical. It's unavoidable. Paris will once again be inundated as catastrophically as in 1910. And that looks like it's going to be now. It will even be worse." She pursues this line, just as serenely (and Linden cannot help hanging on to every word), claiming that what people need to understand is that compared to 1910, the topography of Paris has changed dramatically. Urbanization has shielded the earth with concrete coatings, dug deep into subsoil to build parking spaces, created thousands of new roads, new housing estates. Rainwater dropping off roofs no longer infiltrates the soil, but slops directly into the river.

With mixed feelings, Linden turns the TV off. The woman's prophecies unnerve him. Maybe it is time to leave. Maybe they should all get the hell out of here, while the water is still under the Zouave's knees. Too bad for Paul's birthday, the restaurant, all that; perhaps he should take Oriel's advice and bolt. He texts his concern to Tilia. She answers immediately: *Dude! Leave? WTF??*

He suggests they make up their minds about what to do first thing tomorrow morning, Sunday. They'll need to act fast. Getting their parents back to the Drôme valley safely is their priority. It will be a nightmare finding available tickets, but they'll have to manage. And as for them, it will be back to London, and back to San

Francisco. No other way about it. Tilia complies. Isn't he being exceedingly negative, though? *Turn on the TV* is his curt reply. A few minutes later, she sends a wailing emoticon and a concerned *OMG!*

Linden hadn't meant to doze off, but when he awakes, startled, someone is knocking on the door and it's dark outside. He opens up to the maid, who asks if she can turn down the bed for the evening. He glances at his watch: nearly eight o'clock. How ever did he sleep for so long? He'll have barely a couple of minutes to get ready. He grabs his green velvet jacket from the closet, and a clean white shirt. His shoes are still wet, and he slides into them with a grimace. Downstairs, Tilia, Lauren, and Paul are waiting. Linden has to run upstairs again because he forgot his father's present, the Bowie vinyl.

A taxi had been ordered to take them to the restaurant, La Villa des Roses, situated on nearby rue du Cherche-Midi. If it weren't raining, they could walk. But no one can face getting drenched again. Paul seems more high-spirited, Linden notices. His cheeks are less red and his eyes lively. This is going to be a wonderful family evening. So why does Linden feel that niggling jab of unease? What is he worried about? That Tilia and he might quarrel? They haven't, not for a long time, but her fiery temper is unpredictable, and so is his retaliation. He sometimes hates the way she has to swear at everything, using the strongest insults. Does she do it to attract attention, to shock, to provoke? He can't figure it out. He struggles to put his anxiety aside. The restaurant is welcoming and hot, another sanctuary from the chilly drizzle. Champagne is ordered and they sit down. The place is full, but they can hear one another talk. Linden looks around at the tasteful décor: cream and pale pink tones, stylish lighting. A young waitress comes for their order. Paul is wearing a dark suit and a white shirt and tie. He seems uncomfortable in his smart attire, tugging at his collar as if it were too tight. Lauren, striking in a blue silk dress, her hair tied back, keeps sneezing. She caught a cold this afternoon, during their long walks in the rain, and is annoyed about it. She blows her nose crossly. Her nostrils are already rimmed with red and her voice sounds muffled. Linden can't help noticing she spends a lot of time checking her phone.

The meal is a success. The conversation is not strained, does not meander into hazardous zones, such as Colin's drinking problem. The four of them talk, easily, lightly, laughing from time to time. The dishes are succulent, the wine excellent. After the candles on the cake have been blown out, with neighboring tables cheering, and the presents opened, Paul gives a short speech. He wants to thank them all for being here to celebrate his birthday and their wedding anniversary. He hasn't been back to Paris for a long time and he's very happy to be here, and just wishes the rain would stop so they could get a bit of sun for the rest of their stay. Again, his voice seems queer, breathless and high-pitched. He has to pause from time to time, picking up his glass of water with an unsteady hand. His words are slurred. They can't make out what he is trying to say. Linden and Tilia exchange uneasy glances. Paul's face seems farcically lopsided all of a sudden, like a disconcerting mask. It's him, but it no longer looks like him, as if someone is jerking one side of his face up. He falls silent, and when Tilia asks him if he is all right, he sighs deeply.

It happens in the following minute, when they are not looking directly at him, signaling to the waitress for more water. There is a gasp, almost inaudible, and Paul slides brusquely forward into his chair, head hanging down, his chin on his chest. Lauren, alarmed, shouts his name, but Paul slumps farther down, his forehead crashing onto his plate, upsetting the bottle of wine. Then his body rolls over and falls to the floor with a thud. There is a moment of screaming and confusion. A sea of faces looms toward them. Linden is down on his knees, his hands cradling his father's bald skull. Paul's eyes are half-shut; only the whites are showing. His skin is gray. Tilia and Lauren seem horror-struck, incapable of moving. Linden struggles to open his father's collar, places shaky fingers on his jugular. He thinks he feels a beat, but he's not sure. He leans closer, asks Paul if he can hear his voice. Paul mustn't worry. They are going to look after him; he's going to be all right. Linden has no idea if this is true, but in this moment of dreadful panic, he cannot think of anything else to say. He doesn't even know if Paul can hear him, if Paul is still alive. He looks around him, powerless, sees all these unknown people staring. Then Tilia's voice booms out with its unmistakable vigor, and he wants to kiss her for it. "Will someone call a *fucking* ambulance?"

Her words shock people into action. The owner of the restaurant scurries off, says she will call one straight away, and a short man, napkin still in hand, presents himself to the stricken Malegarde family; he is a doctor. May he assess the situation? He squats down next to Linden and takes Paul's wrist while peering into his eyes. Lauren asks tearfully if her husband is dying. After a few minutes, the doctor says that no, he is not dying, but he must go to the hospital right away. There is not one minute to lose.

The ambulance seems to take forever. Tilia and Lauren sit together, weeping silently. Linden stays down on the floor with Paul. He waits, gritting his teeth. From close-up, his father looks dead. He cannot, will not believe it. His father cannot be dead. This cannot be happening. Yet the stark reality of the moment grips him. He can smell the synthetic odor of the carpet drifting up to him, feel its bristly texture under his knees. He can hear his mother blowing her nose. He can hear the low murmur of voices, the click of cutlery as people get on with their meals. When the medical team at last enters the hushed restaurant, things happen swiftly. He is the one to answer the questions, as his sister and mother appear unable to do so. Paul Malegarde, seventy years old. No medical treatment. Yes, he seemed tired for the past few days. Yes, his speech sounded suddenly slurred. Yes, one side of his face seemed to collapse. No, this has never happened before. No, he has had no major health problems.

There is room for only one next of kin in the ambulance. Linden tells his mother and sister to go back to the hotel. He will call or text them as soon as he has news. He will handle this. They must trust him. Lauren nods, Kleenex held to her runny nose and tearful eyes. She then motions to her son, indicating the pocket of Paul's jacket. He fumbles around, slides out his father's wallet, and takes his identity card, his social security card.

"Wait!" Lauren cries out. She rummages into her own bag, hands him a certificate, and he understands it's their health-insurance policy. As unconscious Paul is strapped to a stretcher, oxygen mask clamped to his nose and mouth, intravenous drip inserted into one arm, Linden wonders how it is that he is not panicking; how it is that he can remain so calm, so in control, nodding to the medical team, deftly stepping into the ambulance. The white van, siren howling, hurries down wet streets while two doctors are still tending to his father. Linden realizes how fast and hard his heart is pumping, the only sign of his distress. He wants to ask the men if his father is going to make it, but they seem so busy, he doesn't dare. He wants to know where they are taking them, and manages to question one of the doctors.

"Georges Pompidou hospital" is the reply.

Linden knows it is a recent medical complex situated in the fifteenth arrondissement and has a good reputation. Vehicles ahead of them glide to the side to let the ambulance pass. Paul is being taken into intensive care; Linden is not allowed to follow. Instead, he must go to the registry on the ground floor and deal with his father's admittance. He watches his father being wheeled away, and two other doctors greet the ambulance team, peering down at the stretcher. Then doors close and he is left alone. He makes his way to the admissions desk. The hospital is vast and modern, startlingly white, filled with plastic green plants. A smell lingers, that particular odor of stale air, overcooked food, and disinfectant. There is a line of people queuing up. He takes his place. He sends a text message to his mother and sister to tell them what's going on. It's a long wait. He feels tired all of a sudden. He glances at his phone, sees the time is nearly midnight. He wishes Sacha could be here. What if he called him now? No, he has to wait until he knows what's in store for Paul. He looks at the people around him. They all have the same weary, stupefied expression. He wonders what their stories are, why they are here.

It is at last his turn. He sits on a chair in front of the counter. A jaded woman on the other side barely looks at him. He hands over his father's identity, social security, and health-insurance cards. Her long pink nails click on the computer. Finally she lays her eyes on him. She is in her mid-forties, from North Africa. She is wearing a faded yellow blouse. Her frizzy black hair is tied back. She looks at him, and to his surprise, she smiles, and her smile is a kind one, lighting up her face.

"Is he your dad?" she asks, handing him the cards back. He nods, his throat tightening. She asks him for his details, entering his name and number into the file. Then she tells him to wait on the third floor, in intensive care. As he gets up to leave, she says gently, "Good luck, monsieur."

⚜

While he sits in the impersonal waiting area in intensive care, Linden reads the emails that have been piling up. His agent, Rachel, has asked him to call, which he hasn't. At one point, he'll have to let her know what is going on. There are a couple of important engagements coming up and she needs to go over certain aspects with him. Flying Linden from city to city is never an easy endeavor. He needs his team with him, his two assistants, Marlowe and Deb, and his indispensable digital technician, Stéphane. Not to mention his equipment, which seems to get bulkier by the year, his three Canons and his Hasselblad, lenses, tripod, laptop, necessary cables for cameras, backup material, flash units and lighting, light stands, umbrella heads, reflectors, extension cords, plug adapters, clamps of various sizes, Velcro straps, background stand, collapsible back-drop, memory cards, extra batteries for camera and flash, and battery charger. Gone were the days where he could travel lightly and fly with a single camera and argentic rolls of film. Rachel Yellan was not his first agent; there had been Béatrice Mazet before her, the first one to pick out Linden's work in 2005, two years after he graduated from Gobelins and was working as an assistant for a French photographer, Marc Clerget. Béatrice got him straightforward, uncomplicated jobs that he enjoyed but that did not thrill him. He disliked studio work, standard advertising shoots, and accepted them only because he had to earn a living. His first recognition came two years later, in 2007, when his latest photographs had been shown at a gallery in Saint Germain-des-Près. As usual, he had not gone for artificial lighting, which he disliked, but concentrated on reflections, superimposing faces and silhouettes using texture and natural light. The result was arresting, distinctive, and sensitive, a far cry from the Photoshopped, artificial images so often projected in the media. Rachel Yellan, a famous American agent, happened to see the portraits on the gallery's website. She checked out his work online, as well as the famous *Treeman Crying in Versailles*, the photograph he took in 1999, contacted Linden, and when she was next in Paris, they met. He had at first been intimidated by her drive, but then decided to trust her. When the jobs started to come in, they were mostly based in America. It became evident to Linden that he should move to New York, which he did in 2009, at twenty-eight. The fact that he had an American passport made it less difficult for him, as well. It was almost like coming home, except that he wasn't that familiar with the USA. Rachel found him a temporary place to live in SoHo, on Spring Street, in a renovated building above a grocery store, where he was to share an apartment with a painter and another photographer. He had been to Boston many times to visit his maternal grandparents, and to New York occasionally, with his mother, but it took him a while to settle down, to feel at ease in Manhattan. How unforeseen, that he should have felt so French upon arrival; he was even convinced an accent could be detected when he spoke English. Living in New York was another matter. Never in his life had he faced such noise. He found it deafening: the constant rumble of traffic, the thunder of construction work, the howling of sirens, the endless honking, and the loud parties. The store was open all night, and his room was situated just above it. Clients chatted on the sidewalk at three in the morning, as if it were broad daylight. His cotenants weren't bothered: They were born and bred New Yorkers. He became accustomed to it after a while, just as he became used to the loquaciousness of his neighbors, unlike his Parisian ones, whom he had barely exchanged three words with, and he marveled at how perfect strangers were sociable in the street or in shops, sparking up conversations, interested and curious in the fact that he was from Paris. Six months later, he moved to the Upper West Side, on Eightieth Street, between Amsterdam and Columbus, to a small town house with a very steep staircase of four flights, which did not put him off. Eightieth Street was quieter than others, because it ended at the pretty park just behind the Museum of Natural History. He loved sitting on his roof terrace, where he could see the sun rise over Central Park and set over the Hudson and New Jersey. His downstairs neighbor, Emilie, was a Parisian. She was a gourmet chef and an Edward Hopper fan. He enjoyed speaking French with her, which he wasn't doing much of these days. She took him shopping at Zabar's, where he followed her, entranced by the dizzying display of food, and introduced him to the famous Cafe Lalo, between Broadway and Amsterdam, where he liked watching New Yorkers and tourists mingle. Little by little, Linden found himself fitting in, but never entirely. He had boyfriends, discovered new groups of people, and enjoyed himself. It seemed to him that even if restaurants were jam-packed, there was always another new, exciting place to explore. New York was friendly, welcoming, but he began to understand that to appreciate the city completely meant having been born here. His new neighborhood reminded him of the Paris he'd grown up in, the fifteenth arrondissement and its particular combination of ugly constructions and attractive ones, its mixed population, its families, its simplicity. Rachel kept him so busy, he hardly had time to feel homesick. In the beginning, the jobs weren't thrilling: a load of portfolios for models, a steady flow of advertising work, which was well remunerated. He accepted each assignment with his usual enthusiasm. It paid off, to Rachel's satisfaction. In a couple of years, Linden Malegarde became the young Franco-American photographer that every magazine or brand wanted to hire. His portraits were different, fresh, immediately identifiable. It was a question of shadow and light, grain and chromatology, what he brought out of his subjects, how he made them pose. He didn't always go for a smile, which he found contrived or bland, preferring to seek out emotions, those that were hidden away. To him, taking a picture of a person, or a place, was like sketching unseen outlines, bringing forth imperceptible areas from the darkness, giving them another dimension, breathing new air into them. He wasn't a talkative photographer, but he had learned how to put his subjects at ease. He was aware that most of them needed some kind of guidance. What he liked best was shooting a famous person who felt comfortable with the camera, who knew how to pose, how to catch the light. He slowly got such people to put their guard down, to give him something personal, an aspect of themselves they had never revealed, a clandestine vulnerability, a sense of humor, a dash of originality.

Tonight, at the Pompidou hospital, Linden feels a peculiar and novel withdrawal from his job. He's never experienced this before. Yet he takes his career to heart; he is enthusiastic, punctual, and polite, even with temperamental movie stars and divas, even with media tycoons who try to manipulate him, seduce him, or con him. Nothing else matters at the moment, nothing except the thought of his father. He is alone in the long waiting room, his eyes fixed on the double doors ahead. He's given up answering his sister's incessant messages. He made it clear to her he'll call as soon as he knows anything. An additional worry is Lauren, who is running a high fever and has a headache. Her cold seems to have worsened. Tilia put their mother to bed; she is at last asleep, but it took a long time to soothe her, as they are both so worried about Paul. From time to time, Linden rises, strides up and down the cheerless corridor. Finally, he sits, dread gnawing at him. Why are they taking so long? What is wrong with his father? Why can't they come and tell him? He's going to go mad if this goes on. A silent TV flickers in the corner, showing the same images of the Seine flooding. He ignores the screen, wondering if he should go and find someone, just to obtain information.

At two o'clock in the morning, as Linden is half-dozing on an uncomfortable chair, a doctor in a white blouse enters and asks if he is here for Paul Malegarde. He gets to his feet, his head spinning. The woman is small, blond, his age. She looks uncannily like Jodie Foster. Her name badge reads DOCTEUR HÉLÈNE YVON. She takes him into a small office beyond, asks him to sit down. He is so tense, he cannot speak. He can only stare at her, bracing himself for what she is about to say. She must have sensed his tautness, because she reaches out with a small, slender hand and touches his wrist.

"Your father is still with us."

Even the shape of her mouth is exactly the shape of Jodie Foster's, down to the implantation of her teeth. Linden is annoyed with himself for noticing this while she is giving him such important and positive news. She goes on, explaining that Paul had a stroke, a severe one. The result is an injury to the brain, she explains, and this can cause communication problems if there is damage to areas that control language. Some stroke survivors find they can no longer speak because the muscles of their lips, tongue, or mouth have been affected. But they don't know that yet about Paul; it's too early. They will have to undertake several exams and scans to assess that. That will take a while. He might have to be operated on, so they can remove a blood clot. The thing Linden needs to know is this: Paul will be here for a while. They don't know how long. Linden listens, nodding. He wishes Tilia were with him; she would know exactly what to ask, what to say. He feels incapable. Words are stuck in his mouth.

Dr. Yvon's shrewd eyes take all this in. She gets up, pours out bottled water into a paper cup, hands it to him. He drinks thirstily. He then asks if he can see his father. She replies that he will be able to do so later on, during the day. He can come back to the hospital in the early afternoon. For the moment, the best thing he can do is go get some sleep. She'll see him when he returns. Is he okay with this? Linden nods. They shake hands and he leaves. It's too late to SMS his sister. He'll see her back at the hotel, if she is waiting up for him. When he gets outside, the stark, freezing air is a welcome one from that of the stuffy hospital. The rain falls lightly, noiselessly, but he can feel it dampening the back of his neck. The streets are empty. It's a residential area; many Parisians live here, but they don't party here. No one comes here for nightlife. Linden walks past place Balard, up to rue Lecourbe, just as deserted, and cuts across to busier rue de Vaugirard using broad rue de la Convention. He hasn't been back to this part of Paris for a while. He can't help being fond of it. This was the Paris of his adolescence, the unpretentious fifteenth arrondissement, a district that could never be considered appealing, because of the disfiguring upsurge of the Front de Seine, an urban planning project of the seventies, twenty skyscrapers marring the city's classical beauty. He used to say he lived in "Moche Grenelle," ugly Grenelle, laughingly, although he now knows Beaugrenelle recently underwent a massive refurbishment and metamorphosed into a successful shopping mall. Linden knows this area by heart: the quiet domestic streets, and the modern buildings sitting cheek by jowl with older Haussmannian ones. In 1997, when he first arrived in Paris, he knew little about the subtleties of neighborhoods. He soon realized nocturnal entertainment took place in Montparnasse, the Latin Quarter, the Bastille, the Marais. But he didn't mind heading back to the sleepy streets where Candice lived, leaving noisy nightlife behind. He always walked home in the small hours, enjoying a peaceful communion with the city. Tonight, as he heads toward rue Delambre, Linden sees himself at seventeen, coming back late from a party. His tall stature and broad shoulders deterred any assailants. Sometimes a tanked-up passerby would ask him for a cigarette. He never had any trouble. Candice did not demand he should be back at a given hour. She trusted him. His grades remained fair, not excellent, but above average.

How could he ever forget that December night in 1998, when he came back after four in the morning? He hadn't warned Candy, hadn't thought of ringing her, and when he *had* thought of it, it was already so late, he'd wake her if he did. He remembers the frostiness of the air, a little like tonight, the way his shoes slid on the icy pavements. When he had turned his key in the lock and slid into the apartment, he realized with a shock that the lights were still on and that she was waiting for him in the living room. She sat there in her pink dressing gown, her hands cupping her herbal tea.

"I was so worried," she said. "I thought something had happened to you."

He had looked away, ashamed. He mumbled that he should have called, that he was sorry, and took his jacket off. He went to sit across from her. Muffin blinked curious yellow eyes at him and then nestled back to sleep on the sofa. This was twenty years ago, and yet Linden recalls every moment, every second. Candy never asked questions. She didn't pry. She didn't ask whom he was with, where, if he had had a nice time. And yet he felt he had to talk. It was building up inside him like a huge bubble. He looked at her hands holding the cup. They were longer and whiter than his mother's. He said he had not been at a party. He had been with a friend. Her eyes remained steady, compassionate, never looking away from his, but not unnerving. The silence grew between them, but he didn't find it distressing. He was just searching for the right words. She gave him time. He finally said his friend's name was Philippe. He was in the same class, at the lycée. He had spent the evening with him, and he hadn't noticed the hours go by. The words stopped there. He couldn't bring himself to go any further. A sort of fear gripped him, a dread that she would judge him, that she might be repelled, or angry. Then she said (and he remembered those words with precision; they had never left him, ever), "Linden, don't be afraid. Tell me what you have to say."

He saw tenderness in her eyes, nothing else. He got up, stared out of the window, down to empty rue Saint-Charles with its glittering Christmas decorations. He guessed it might be easier if he didn't look straight at her. He felt naked, exposed, more vulnerable than he had ever been in his entire seventeen years. For a short moment, a couple of seconds, he thought maybe he should keep it in, not say anything, never tell, shut up about it, never mention it. But the bubble inside him was already rushing up, craving to be let out and away. He said slowly that Philippe was the person he thought about night and day. Philippe was handsome, special, and he felt comfortable with him, felt himself. He could talk to him, express things he had never told anyone. The bubble soared up, pushing at the threshold of his throat and mouth, and there was no way he could hold it back. He said he had always felt different. It started a long time ago, at Sévral. The kids at school sensed it. He didn't know how they had picked up on it, as he hadn't thought it showed, but they had guessed it, and they made his life hell. When they began to have girlfriends, at thirteen, fourteen, to be obsessed with girls, with girls' bodies, legs, breasts, he felt left out because that obsession never came to him. And instead of leaving him alone, they taunted him ceaselessly: And where was his girl-friend, then? Didn't the American have one, or what? Had he ever touched a girl that way, this way? Had he even ever kissed one? Was he downright gay, then, a *fiotte*, a *pédale*? They rejoiced in the string of insults they flung at him during recess, and the only thing he could do was to brace himself. A girl once whispered to him the other boys were jealous because he was good-looking. Why didn't he have a girlfriend? she asked. He could have all the girls he wanted, starting with her. He had not answered her. When he got to Paris, last year, he'd felt relieved. No one in his class ever mentioned him being different. No one cared if he had a girlfriend or not. He was popular. And then, one day, Philippe. Philippe and his curly hair, his merry eyes. Philippe was comfortable with himself, with who he was. He didn't have to pretend to be someone else. Philippe had taken Linden to his bedroom one day after their last lesson. How could it have been so simple? It had. They were alone in the apartment, and Philippe had kissed him. That's how it began. Recently, three students from their class had stopped Philippe and him on the stairs. The voices rose around them, taunting, jeering; the invectives hissed, always the same dreadful words, and

Linden had felt himself recoil in horror. He was projected back to Sévral, to the teasing and the scorn, and he had felt his eyes close with dread. He heard Philippe's voice ring out, calm, humorous (how on earth could Philippe remain so calm? he had wondered); his tone was unruffled, fearless, and Linden opened his eyes and saw Philippe standing there in his long black coat, superb, chin raised, a smile on his lips. Gay? Yes, he was gay. Was that a problem? Was he going to be arrested? Was he going to be mobbed? Tied up, lynched, and thrown to the lions? Should he go crying home to his mummy? Should he hate himself because he was gay? Is that what these guys were trying to tell him? Well, he had news for them. He was seventeen years old, and he was not afraid. No, not afraid. Not afraid to be gay. Not ashamed to be gay. Was there anything else these guys wanted to add? Something like *sale PD*, perhaps? There had been a silence. The three students had shuffled away. Philippe's hand grabbed his and held it tight. Linden had felt it shaking.

Linden paused again, for a long time. His breath drew a puffy white cloud on the cold windowpane. Candice waited. The bubble drifted out of him, up and out. He said, "You might not like to hear this." Another pause. And then he added, "I'm gay. Are you disappointed?"

He felt fear, wretchedness, loneliness, and then, strangely, relief. He turned around and confronted his aunt. She was smiling and her smile was nothing different from the ones she gave him each day. She got up and came toward him, putting her arms around him. Then she said, "I'm not disappointed. I love you just the same."

How he had cherished those words. *I'm not disappointed. I love you just the same.* They stayed with him during the lengthy span of time when he felt he was not ready to tell anyone else. They stayed with him when he thought about the Sévral years, the abuses, his lonesomeness. They stayed with him when he contemplated telling his father, his mother, his sister. He waited. Candy's precious words protected him, for the moment, from all the fears he had.

Linden turns left into boulevard du Montparnasse. The traffic is denser here, even at this hour. At the crossroad with rue de Rennes, the pavements are full of people, despite the cold. Linden is aware of how much he misses walking. His job doesn't let him do enough of it. When he's at home, in San Francisco, he walks over an hour a day, rejoicing in the steep streets.

Many bars and cafés on the boulevard are still open, with clients spilling out on the pavement to smoke. When he gets to the hotel, there's a note on his door from his sister. She wants him to come and see her no matter what time it is. Her face is pinched and white, her eyes red. He tells her everything he knows. She keeps asking him beseechingly if their father is going to be all right. At one point, slightly exasperated, he tells her to go back with him to the hospital, so she can ask the doctor herself.

"Dude, I can't go with you to the hospital."

He stares at her. What on earth does she mean? Tilia hangs her head, embarrassed. He waits. She clears her throat after a short silence. She explains, haltingly, that she hasn't been able to enter a hospital since her accident, back in 2004. Oh, and he can stop looking at her like that, please! She just can't do it. She can't. Yes, she knows it was ages ago; she was only twenty-five, but it's impossible. She has tried. She feels faint every time she puts a foot in a hospital. It brings back all the horror. Linden points out that she never talks about it. So how could anyone know much about the horror? She crosses her arms, puts on that obstinate face he knows so well. She cannot go, and that is that. She'll look after their mother, who is not doing well. Lauren's fever is still high. She cannot go and he'll have to make do with that.

There are so many things about his sister he doesn't know, Linden realizes as he heads wearily back to his room. It is odd to think that he spent nearly sixteen years living by her side, he is convinced he knows her backward and forward, but no, he doesn't. Shadowy areas remain. He doesn't know what happened the night of the accident except that she was the only one who wasn't killed. Yes, they are close, but how close? How close can you get to a sister? he wonders. What is close? Knowing each other's secrets? Each other's past, or even present? His sister probably has no idea what his life is like since he has become a famous photographer. She no doubt thinks it all glorious. She knows nothing of the tension, the rivalry, the drive it takes. He can hear her saying, oh yes, Linden Malegarde is my little brother, with that half-sneering, half-smiling expression. Is she jealous? He's never thought of it until now. But perhaps she is. Jealous of his success, jealous of the good looks she did not inherit? It is time to call Sacha in California. Sacha will know what to say, how to soothe him.

Later, Linden cannot sleep. He remains on his back, eyes open in the darkness. When he gets up to look out of the window, surprised by the sudden silence, he sees the rain has transformed into snow. Snowflakes circle around lampposts like a flock of insects seeking light. He settles back into bed after turning the heating up a little. No, he will not switch the TV on. The rising Seine is too alarming. He wants to concentrate on his father, even more alarming. He has to be strong for his father, for his mother, for his sister. Somehow, he understands he is the one who is going to be dealing with all this, that he is the one singled out to lead the battle. Is he ready? He has to be. He hasn't got much choice. Until now, he always thought Tilia, being the bossy older sister, was the one to take things in hand. Beneath the swagger and bad language lurked someone else, someone far more fragile than he'd imagined. Sacha had been amazed by the fact that Tilia was not going anywhere near the hospital. He had asked Linden if he was disappointed. In loyalty to Tilia, Linden had said no. But deep down, he was.

He thinks of his father, in intensive care. Has Paul regained consciousness? Does he know what happened to him? Is he in pain? These thoughts frighten him and keep sleep at bay. He remembers meeting a woman on a plane once, with whom he had had an interesting conversation, and who had suggested that whenever he felt scared or stressed, all he had to do was to conjure up a positive image, the depiction of a thing, a place, or a person that would appease him. He has never tried it out. He closes his eyes. The first picture that comes to him is his father, his father at Vénozan, wearing his frayed straw hat and dungarees; his father bending down to look at his shrubs and flowers. When he was a small boy, Linden used to follow Paul around the land. His father didn't talk much, but Linden became used to that. He still felt close to Paul during the silences; he learned not to be upset or bothered by them. He would kneel down next to Paul, knees in the limestone, wielding his toy rake and shovel, and observe. His father's hands darted here and there, pulling out weeds, straightening stems. One of his earliest memories was pointing out the different colors to his father. "*Bleu,*" he would say proudly in French. So many blues to choose from! And such magical plants! Awed, he fingered small wispy indigo globes that felt like woolly foliage, as if magical spiders had crafted them. "*Echinops ritro,*" his father replied gruffly. Linden pointed to another blue: intricate tubular flowers atop slender silvery wands. "Russian sage" came the answer. He circled around tight mounds of needlelike blades, not daring to touch the vibrant blue spikes. "*Festuca,*" his father replied. And what about the dense batches of star-shaped blue flowers that attracted ravenous bees? "Borage." He loved playing the color game with his father. Always in French. "*Jaune!*" Linden would shout excitedly, picking out all the yellows. The gorse glowed as bright as melted butter; so did the lemony bobbles on a plant his father called santolina, which sounded like a girl's name, he thought. Sometimes his father turned the game around and asked *him* to name the flowers. The Latin names eluded him, but Linden always managed to remember what the treasure flowers were called, oversized daisies with their striped orange-and-golden petals. "*Gazania splendens!*" he lisped triumphantly, brandishing his tiny spade. Paul stroked the top of his head with a grimy palm. Vandeleur, his father's favorite gardener, looked on and clapped. Linden liked Vandeleur, with his red hair and freckles. He got dreadful sunburns, but he didn't seem to care. Apparently, Vandeleur had English blood, but he couldn't speak a word of it, and Lauren teased him sometimes. Paul's garden was an enchantment at every season, even during the shorter winter days. He knew which plants bloomed in autumn, which ones stayed eternally green, which ones smelled delightful at Christmastime, like odorous sweetbox. When the storms broke and caused the electricity to fail, and after the black clouds had scurried away, leaving pearly mist in their wake, Linden couldn't wait to head back outside, because the fragrance of the garden was at its strongest. The rain intensified the intoxicating aromas and he'd breathe them in hungrily.

Linden feels a gentle peace enveloping him. He can smell those fresh scents now, and in his mind, he sees the arboretum. He sees his father standing next to the tallest and oldest linden. His father resembles the captain of a ship, sailing on a sea of leaves. There is sweet woodruff under Linden's feet, with its whorls of bright green leaves and pale, pointy buds. He sees bunches of houseleek, thick pink rosettes with jagged edges, which used to fascinate him as a child and which reminded him of an artichoke. He reaches down to caress succulent dark red sedum. Butterflies hover over purple aster flowers, and one lands on his outstretched palm, just like they used to when he was a child, slowly batting its delicate wings. The woman on the plane was right; it is working. He can see the butterfly perfectly, its tiny fuzzy head, its round eyes, its fine antennas; he can make out the texture of the iridescent wings. He notices his palm is not the one of a grown man. He is a little boy, in his father's garden. He feels safe, calm. If he walks back to the house, he can glimpse his mother sunbathing on the terrace, near the oleanders and hollyhocks. He can hear Madame Leclerc, the cleaning lady, washing up pots and pans in the kitchen. Tilia is cartwheeling on the lawn, over and over again, as if in slow motion. That's the last thing he sees before he falls asleep at last.

THREE

❧

On prit l'habitude de passer les soirées sous un immense tilleul à quelques pas de la maison.

—STENDHAL, *LE ROUGE ET LE NOIR*

My favorite place was up by the trees. In summer, it was my realm. The girl liked going there, too. She read a book in the shade while I built a tree house with branches and twigs. Sometimes she helped me construct it. My father never came. I soon understood he preferred to be in town. As for my mother, her pregnancy tired her. She didn't want to come up here. I seemed to be the only one who liked to have fun up by the trees. My friends preferred the pastures or the lawn, where they could throw a ball around or fight. My sister was not yet born. Not that I played much with her anyway when she was.

My tree house moved with the wind and made creaking noises like a ship. The girl would send the wicker basket up filled with whatever I needed. I'd pull on the cord and heave it up. She always encouraged me. I felt strong, manly, even if I was only a boy.

The girl would spread a checkered tablecloth for us to sit on. In the basket, she had carefully packed figs, peaches, wild strawberries, all from the garden, small squares of dark chocolate (which we had to eat quickly when it got very hot), and chunks of baguette.

I played with the trees. They were like living things to me, as alive as humans. They seemed to whisper secrets. Maybe I was the only one who heard them. Trees were at the heart of things. I was four years old, but I sensed that already.

How well I remember those slow, sunny afternoons. Everything around me seemed at peace. From up in the branches, I watched various kinds of insects climb up and down the trunk: beetles, moths, ants, caterpillars, and firebugs, my favorites. They were harmless and climbed on my finger. They clustered together in groups, making one red patch. I observed the bees garnering pollen, fascinated by their little yellow pouches growing larger and larger. I never got stung, even when the tree attracted clouds of bees in July.

She was pretty to look at. She had the whitest skin I had ever seen. It was like milk. She had to keep out of the sun, she told me. On her feet, she wore espadrilles. She'd kick them off when we were sitting on the tablecloth. Even her toes were pale and creamy. She was my first crush. On the afternoons she spent with me, I'd stand in front of the window on the first floor, waiting, just to watch her walking up to the house. Her father dropped her off in his blue van. She always wore dresses. On the days the mistral blew, the dress would float up above her thighs. She was called Suzanne. Every time I hear that name, something inside me breaks.

A TEXT MESSAGE FROM Oriel jolts Linden awake at eight o'clock on Sunday morning. *Are you all still in Paris? Seine rising much too fast. Never been so fast for a long time.* Rubbing his eyes sleepily, he turns on the TV. It's all over the news. Overnight, the Seine jumped up a meter, reaching the Zouave's thighs. Channel after channel shows the same images: brown water mounting higher. Linden learns water has started to flood more basements and parking lots, slowly but surely, rising into buildings from below. He hadn't realized the flooding was springing from underground, stemming from marinated soils, and not gushing from riverbanks. Outside, the snow is still falling, leaving a slushy layer on rue Delambre, but it will soon turn back into rain, apparently.

The Seine worries him, but not half as much as waiting to hear about his father. No news from the hospital. Dr. Yvon would have called had there been anything serious. Or so Linden imagines. He has another subject to fret about: canceling all their departures for this afternoon and finding out if the hotel can put them up awhile longer. He showers, gets dressed as fast as he can. Down at the front desk, not a sign of Agathe, but instead, a casual young man who doesn't seem to understand that Linden must speak to the hotel director, Madame Fanrouk, as soon as possible. He is told Madame Fanrouk doesn't come in on Sundays. Masking his irritation as best as he can, Linden asks if they can keep their rooms for a couple more days. No problem for his parents' room, but, unfortunately, only his sister's room is available tonight and tomorrow. Linden puts a reservation on both rooms. He'll have to sleep in Tilia's room, and he wonders how she will react to that.

He knocks on his mother's door, gently, and then a little louder, as there is no answer. Tilia opens up, her face and hair a mess. Linden can tell she has hardly slept. She asks if he has any news from the hospital. He shakes his head.

"Mom has a really high fever," she whispers, her voice low. "And her dry cough is terrible!"

When he sees his mother's face, Linden can tell this is not a simple cold. She is flushed, her eyes sunken. They need to call a doctor, right now. Tilia agrees, and gets on the phone to reception. She is told a doctor will come within the hour. Tilia makes some kind of joke about their family get-together turning into a nightmare. Linden grins halfheartedly. Then he suggests to his sister that she go take a shower and rest for a bit. She seems exhausted; she needs a break. He'll look after their mother now and he'll let Tilia know what the doctor says when he gets here. His sister leaves the room, thankful and weary.

Linden sits on a small sofa. His mother has her eyes closed, but she coughs from time to time, and winces when she does so. He asks her gently if she wants any water and she shakes her head. She smiles weakly at him. He smiles back. He looks around at the room. He would do anything, *anything,* to get his father back here. Every time he thinks of the hospital, his stomach churns. He is not going to say anything to his mother. He will keep his worries to himself. On the bedside table, he notices his father's reading glasses and a book. *The Man Who Planted Trees,* by Jean Giono. He is intrigued. To his knowledge, his father hardly ever reads books. It is a slim copy, only forty pages long, published by Gallimard, the famous French publisher. On the flyleaf, he discovers unfamiliar handwriting: *To Paul Malegarde, the modern-day Elzéard Bouffier, with my highest admiration.*

Linden can't make out the name scrawled at the bottom of the page. The book was probably a gift from one of his father's numerous devotees, those who followed his tree-saving exploits closely. As he leafs through the text, he gathers Elzéard Bouffier is the hero of the story, a quiet shepherd from Provence who single-handedly planted an entire forest over a time span of forty years, replenishing the dried-out ecosystem of a deserted valley. His father is similarly considered a hero by many, by those for whom trees mean just as much, if not more, than human beings. He had seen cliques gather at Vénozan just to listen to Paul. He used to make fun of them behind their backs with Tilia, mocking their fervor and veneration, but deep inside, he was awed by the influence his father seemed to have over them. Nature specialists and scientists came from far and wide to see Mr. Treeman, and Linden soon grew used to seeing cars parked in the drive when he got home from school, and his mother's mentioning his father was busy again. It was always odd to see his father, customarily so uncommunicative, speaking unbrokenly in front of strangers who drank in every word as if he were God. Sometimes Linden would go and sit with his snack just to listen to his father, hiding behind a bush, a chair, or a tree, unnoticed. The journalists always wanted to know how his passion for trees began; they asked that question over and over again, and Paul was never impatient with them. He explained, amiably, that his parents had not given a second thought to nature. Neither of them spent time in the garden. For him, it was another story. At a very young age, he learned to watch trees, how they grew, how different they were, what they needed, what they feared. It was here, at Vénozan, in the arboretum planted long before his day, that he slowly became accustomed to the world of nature. His father had allowed him to cultivate a little patch of garden all to himself. He was interested in watching plants grow, although he was too small to have an idea yet of the names of plants and flowers he loved. He spent hours there by himself with his spade and his rake, planting and weeding. He learned that anything to do with a garden, anything to do with trees, was slow. Nothing happened overnight, except the devastation left by a violent storm. Later, as a young man, when he had lovingly and painstakingly reshaped the garden at Vénozan, which his father had let grow into a tangled mess, he by then knew he was going to spend the rest of his life tending to trees, not as a landscape gardener, which was his first job, but as an arborist. Paul always told journalists and followers about the first tree he saved, when he was barely fifteen. Linden knew the story well, but he enjoyed hearing it. Paul was working on a shrubbery in the fortified village of Le Poët-Laval, near Dieulefit. A wealthy businessman from Paris had bought an ancient mansion with a walled garden. He was having the entire property redone, perhaps not in the best taste, and had convinced the mayor to ax a three-hundred-year-old plane tree on the fringe of his premises because it threw too much shade on his swimming pool. At least fifteen meters high, the tree was a beauty, with its thick, leathery leaves and its olive-gray bark flaking away in patches, divulging the smooth milky surface beneath. Paul was outraged when he heard of Monsieur Morel's intention. No one seemed to be shocked by what was going on. No one seemed to care. The mayor had other, more important things to do than to worry about an old tree. No one listened to the young boy, who became angrier and angrier. One spring evening, after the sun had gone down, Paul knocked on each door of the small village, introduced himself, and explained the situation. He told them that the villagers could not sit back and watch the tree be destroyed. The tree was just as much a part of the village as they were. It was certainly one of the oldest trees in the area. It had to be saved. It had to be protected. Too bad for Monsieur Morel's swimming pool. Little by little, the inhabitants listened to Paul. He was young, he was convincing, and he was one of them. He spoke their language, he had their accent, he was from neighboring Sévral. Not like the contemptuous Parisian who hardly glanced at them when he arrived in town. A petition began to go around, more and more people signed it. Paul sped to each local village on his bicycle, the petition in his pocket. It was creased, stained by rain, coffee, and rosé, but over four hundred villagers ended up signing it. Even so, the mayor turned up his nose at it. Evidently, he was on Monsieur Morel's side, fawning in an obsequiousness that Paul found repellent. There was only one thing left to do, Paul told the journalists, who were drinking up his every word. Chain himself to the tree. Two other citizens accompanied him on this defiant mission; toothless Violette Sediron, all of eighty-eight, and Roger Durand, his age, also a nature lover. It caused quite a stir. The lumbermen had arrived with their chain saws and lorries, to find three human beings tied to the tree. When the police were called to the scene, more villagers joined Paul, Violette, and Roger. Soon, a hundred people were fiercely guarding the tree. The local newspaper came and took pictures. Other villagers brought food and drink to the protesters. Everyone chanted: Save our tree! Save our tree! It was a magical, wondrous moment, Paul recalled, his face lighting up, and it was even more so when Monsieur Morel agreed to have the tree's branches trimmed, and never to cut it down.

On the bedside table, Lauren's phone makes a buzzing sound, startling Linden. She makes no motion toward it. After a while, it vibrates again. Linden reaches out to grab it. Perhaps it is concerning Paul. The name flashing on the screen is vaguely familiar: Jeff-VDH. Then he remembers. Jeffrey van der Haagen. His mother's fiancé from before Paul. Jeff came to Vénozan one summer, years ago, with his wife and daughters. Blithe smile, well groomed, neatly parted hair. Boring, but nice. While Linden is pondering whether to take the call or not, there is a knock. The doctor. He puts down the phone and gets up to open the door.

The doctor examines his mother and flatly announces Lauren has a bad case of the flu. It could last up to a week. There is nothing to do except take medicine to keep the fever down, and rest. When the doctor leaves, Linden calls Tilia to inform her. One of them will have to go out to buy the medicine for Lauren. Tilia says she will be right over; she is just out of the shower. Meanwhile, Linden uses his phone to cancel their train and plane tickets for later on today. This takes a moment. When he's done, he wonders whether he should call Marie, his aunt. His father is not close to his only sister. He decides to wait until he hears what Dr. Yvon has to say. He checks his watch, waiting to be able to return to the hospital. Part of him wants to go there right now, but he knows he won't be able to see Paul; he needs to remain patient. He leaves Lauren in Tilia's care. She'll deal with getting the prescription. Back in his room, he sends an email to Rachel Yellan, explaining the situation as briefly as possible. He remembers he has an important job lined up for this Tuesday, the portrait of a political figure, a senator, who has at last agreed to be photographed at home with her family in Massachusetts. It will have to be put on hold, or Rachel will need to appoint another photographer. Linden doesn't care, not one bit. How strange. His job used to mean everything to him; it used to take first place each time. Not anymore.

He must get out of the hotel. There is no way he can sit in front of the television, watching the Seine rise hourly on the screen while he waits to be able to go to the hospital. He grabs his coat and leaves. The cold stings his skin as soon as he steps out. The snow has turned into slush; the rain is back to falling steadily, as if it will never stop. No umbrella, no hat. His hair is soon wet. He walks up boulevard Edgar-Quinet, then along boulevard Raspail to Denfert-Rochereau, noticing that the area around the huge statue of the sitting lion seems strangely empty, and then reminds himself this is Sunday morning. He chooses the café on the corner of rue Daguerre and sits down, ordering hot chocolate. The place is not too full, and he appreciates the quiet. He asks the waiter for the Wi-Fi code and plugs his phone into the electrical socket in the wall. He Googles *stroke* and then wishes he hadn't. The more he reads, the more his anxiety increases. How will his father ever recover? Many people, he reads, suffer from the physical and psychological aftereffects of a stroke, and have permanent disabilities. He can't bear thinking about it. What state will his father be in later on today? He realizes he is afraid of walking into the hospital room. He will be alone, without his sister and mother for support. Without Sacha. He will have to face it alone. He will have to hide his fear from his father. This is what parents do, don't they? They protect their children; they never let their children realize they are afraid. Now he will have to do this for his father. Linden remembers his father hacking a viper to death with a spade on the terrace at Vénozan, just as it was about to slide into the house. Paul seemed calm and in control, but Linden could see his hands were shaking. Later, he learned his father hated snakes and feared them. But he never showed it. He must act like that today, by his father's bedside. Calm and in control.

He peruses the news on Twitter. The twelfth arrondissement seems to be the most flooded area so far. This is where the Seine enters the city from the east. Electrical power is failing in some streets near Bercy. More Métro stations near the river are being closed, with cement walls erected around them. The Jardin des Plantes, the botanical garden and museum that host the only Parisian zoo, is being evacuated. The government will no doubt launch "Plan Neptune" on Monday, set up in cases of utmost emergency. Linden discovers Paris is making headlines all around the world. Will the Seine rise higher? The question is on everyone's lips.

But there is only one subject that matters to Linden right now. His father. His father, and nothing else.

When he arrives at the Pompidou hospital in the beginning of the afternoon, he asks for Dr. Yvon at the medical staff office at the intensive care unit. A busy-looking nurse tells him Dr. Yvon will not be back until Tuesday morning. He feels let down, disoriented. Obviously, doctors need time off, but he had been certain she would be here when he returned. He asks the nurse if he can see his father, Paul Malegarde, and she shrugs. Yes, of course, he is in room 24. She seems so careless, so uninterested that he takes it as a hopeful sign, a sign that his father has recovered, that he is fine, that they will be able to walk out of this place sooner that he thought.

He treads down the linoleum-lined passageway, not wanting to look into the contiguous rooms, where patients lie in bed. More nurses and doctors brush by. Linden is not familiar with hospitals. He has never been ill, has never broken a limb. The last time he ever went to a clinic was to see his sister after her accident, in 2004. At that time, he was working as an assistant to a fashion photographer.

The crash occurred in the beginning of August, and Linden remembers the scorching heat of the hospital at Bayonne, his parents' anguish, and the shock of Tilia's bandaged body, her black-and-blue swollen face.

The door to room 24 is shut. Linden opens it gently. The first thing he sees is an unknown woman in her late thirties, and behind her shoulder, a dark and hairy stranger with a plump leg held up by a contraption. There is a sour stench in the room, that of flatulence and perspiration.

"Sorry," Linden mutters. "I guess I got the wrong room."

"No, you didn't," the woman replies, moving away so he can see a curtain drawn against the bed. She gestures toward the back of the room. Linden walks in, not understanding, then realizes there is another bed behind the curtain. His father is stretched flat out on the mattress, with tubes in his forearm and in his nose. His eyes are shut. His face is distorted by an unbearable, ludicrous expression, almost as if he were winking or smirking at a lewd joke. Behind him, machines monitor his heartbeat with mechanical beeps. Paul seems oddly puny, as if his muscles have wasted away. Where is the strong, sturdy figure Linden is used to? Linden feels out of breath, dazed. He doesn't know what to say to his father; he doesn't know what his father can understand or hear. He comes closer, warily, puts his hand on his father's shin. Paul's eyes remain closed.

"Papa, it's me," Linden says in French. "I'm here."

He sits down on the chair by the bed. Is his father in a coma? The doctor had not mentioned that. The patient on the other side of the curtain begins to moan. His whimper goes on and on. Linden wishes he would stop. The woman murmurs something under her breath, and the man quiets down at last. The foul reek fills up the place.

Linden leans closer to his father's ear. He whispers that Lauren has the flu and Tilia is looking after her. But what he really wants to know is how his father feels. Paul makes no sound. His eyelids twitch. Does this mean Paul is never going to speak again? Linden asks Paul gently if he can hear him, if he can open his eyes. Still there is no response. Meanwhile, the hairy man starts to whine again like a panicky child.

The door clicks open, a doctor and a nurse step in. They attend to the other patient first. Linden can't help overhearing. The fat, hairy man's name is Pascal Beaumont. He had a stroke a couple of days ago. The doctor tries to explain to Madame Beaumont that her husband is going to be operated on, but he can't get a word in edgewise. Madame Beaumont, bordering on hysteria, badgers him with incessant questions: When is her husband going to sound like himself again? Why hasn't he been operated on yet? Why can't her husband have a single room? She has a strident, annoying voice that pierces eardrums. If only she would shut up. When the doctor finally turns his attention to Paul, Linden can tell the man has little patience left. He also longs to bombard the doctor with queries, but he holds back. The doctor is his age, more or less, with long, thin, expressive features and sharp coffee-colored eyes. Linden cannot help, even in crisis situations like this one, considering a person or a place with a photographic appreciation. Dr. Frédéric Brunel would be a very interesting model to shoot, with his languid eyelids, ivory-like pallor, and the cluster of fine lines around his droopy mouth.

"Malegarde . . ." the doctor says. "You're the photographer?"

Linden nods. This happens from time to time. But he wasn't expecting it, here or now. It seems out of place, inappropriate. Dr. Brunel examines Paul's chart at the foot of the bed, asks the nurse to check his blood pressure and temperature. Madame Beaumont's face peeps around the curtain, taking it all in. The doctor goes on to say how much he enjoys Linden's work. Linden's discomfort increases. He doesn't want to hear about what the doctor thinks of his work; he couldn't care less. He wants to know how Paul is, if he is going to survive, if there will be outcomes concerning his future. At last, Dr. Brunel stops talking. He bends down, slides Paul's eyelid open. He shines a little light into Paul's eye. Paul blinks. The doctor seems satisfied. He scribbles a few things down on the chart. Then he turns to Linden. Paul needs to be monitored closely. He will have to stay in this ward for another week. It's too early yet to know exactly how his brain had been affected, but his situation is stable, not worse. And that's positive, apparently. They don't know if they will need to operate just yet. That will become clear within the next week or so. Linden wants to know what his father sees, what he hears, what he understands. Is he in a coma? He is aware his tone is urgent, demanding, and he prays he doesn't sound like the interventionist Madame Beaumont, but he must know. He must know, now. The doctor moves toward the window, away from the prying ears of Madame Beaumont. He looks out on the wet roofs, the sullen gray sky. He doesn't seem irritated by Linden's questions. On the contrary, it appears he wishes to take time to answer them. Again, Linden notices how remarkable the man's profile is, the nose with its prominent bridge, the fine protruding chin. His father is in a poststroke no-man's-land, a most uncomfortable place to be, Dr. Brunel explains. He can't talk, he can't move, but he can definitely see and hear. It is not a coma. He is like a dependent baby who can't do anything by himself anymore. He will have to learn all over again. The best thing Linden can do is to talk to him, slowly, and, above all, to be patient.

When the doctor and nurse leave, Linden decides to give it a go. He sits down again, murmurs to Paul in a muted voice that everything is going to be okay, that Paul mustn't worry. He must try to relax. Isn't this the strangest birthday Paul ever had? His tone seems insincere, peculiar, even to him. He falters, and pauses. It's awkward sitting there, with two strangers behind a flimsy partition listening to every word. How is he going to manage this? It's difficult enough talking to his father in normal times. He remains silent, his hand on his father's arm. Linden leans forward and kisses his father's bald pate. His father's skin feels dry and hot. When Linden leaves the room, Madame Beaumont says good-bye haltingly. He replies politely. They are in the same boat, after all, dealing with their injured loved ones, trying to tame their fear into something they can control.

When Linden is back out in the rain, on his way to the hotel, his cell phone rings. It is a French number beginning with area code 04, which, he knows, is the Drôme region. When he answers, he recognizes his aunt Marie, Paul's younger sister. Tilia no doubt gave her his number. He hasn't seen her or spoken to her for years. Marie is a stick-thin, austere-faced widow in her mid-sixties. Her husband, Marcel, died in 2009, in a boar-hunt accident near Taulignan. Their daughter, Florence, a hairdresser in her early thirties, lives in Sévral with her small children and husband. After Marcel passed away, Marie moved in with her daughter. She wants to know how her brother is. She was worried, because he never answered her calls for his birthday, and she ended up ringing Tilia, who gave her the news. Linden tells her what he knows. While he talks to her, he imagines her sitting in the cluttered living room, where the window blinds are always closed, even in the wintertime. Marie and Florence live in the center of Sévral, not far from his old school, near the broad, curving avenues lined with plane trees that encompass the small city. He realizes, as he answers her questions, that the last time he went back to Vénozan and Sévral was over four years ago. That was the last time he had seen his aunt and cousin. They had had lunch at the main bistro near the old train station, no longer in use. After lunch, Linden had walked around town alone, camera in hand. When he was a teenager, it had been a busier place, it seemed. He knew that in his great-grandfather Maurice's day, Sévral had been a bustling hive of activity, thanks to the golden age of cardboard packing boxes. In the eighties, production slowed as boxes were being crafted more cheaply in China. The heyday was over by the nineties, and 2000 sounded the death knell of the town, which never managed to pick up. Even in the height of summer, the narrow, winding streets of the old quarter were desolate.

Sévral was a ghost town. Nobody came to visit its fifteenth-century chapel anymore; there was a scribbled sign pinned to the door that read OPEN ONLY ON TUESDAY MORNINGS. No one booked rooms at the Grand Hotel, which appeared derelict. The only place where crowds were seen was at the gigantic supermarket situated on the outskirts of the town. It was always full of people ambling along the aisles with shopping carts stuffed with groceries. Because of the supermarket, all the little shops had closed. The beautiful ancient town houses were shuttered. No one seemed to live there; no one could afford to. The one and only bookstore was empty and for sale. The cinema and theater had gone bankrupt. He remembered boisterous old men playing *pétanque* in front of the town hall, and drinking pastis at the neighboring cafés. There were no children playing. The area was eerily deserted, save for stray cats frisking on dusty sidewalks and women wearing hijabs flitting across the streets. Each and every window of the residential buildings was equipped with a satellite dish. No one cared about Sévral. No one remembered. It was sinking into oblivion.

At lunch, Linden noted how faded the once grand restaurant seemed. This, too, had been a renowned establishment, hosting dignitaries and habitués in a Belle Époque décor of red velvet draperies and festoons, gilded lamps, a brick and ceramic tiled floor, and a large glass dome. Now the tiles were chipped, the dome cracked, and the festoons looked caked in dust. Waiters shuffled about as if they worked in a funeral parlor. The few customers whispered over their dishes. And this used to be such a jolly place! Linden couldn't believe it. He recalled celebrating Lauren's thirtieth birthday here, in 1987. He was only six years old, but the images stayed with him. The restaurant, filled with white roses, her favorites, and disco music, also her favorite, blaring from loudspeakers. His grown-up jacket and pants. Candice, as lovely as her younger sister, in a sophisticated black dress. Tilia, nine, red-faced and delighted, boogying with Paul. And his mother, the queen of the evening, radiant in a white pantsuit. Conversations with his aunt and cousin were always contrived. Nothing flowed; no one laughed. That last lunch in 2014 had not been any different. Marie and Florence were careful to not mention his personal life. They politely inquired about Tilia, Mistral, and Colin, but they never asked if Linden was seeing someone, if he had a partner. He sometimes wondered how they would react if he suddenly started to talk about Sacha; if he suddenly uttered the words *my boyfriend*. It was easier, safer for them to inquire about his job, not that either of them knew anything about photography, nor wished to.

Nothing has changed with Marie. She still has the same hard voice. Linden says good-bye, promises he'll call if he has more news. How different she is from her brother. Nature and trees mean nothing to her. She never wished to keep and restore Vénozan. Being a Malegarde is of little importance to her; she dropped the name when she married Marcel. But Linden knows how much she loves her brother, even if they are not close. She looks up to him; she admires him. And he can tell, behind the stiffness of her tone, how worried she is.

The rain has become part and parcel of his life, it seems. What if the skies remain perpetually wet and gray? What if the sun never appears again? Perhaps this is his new world. Rain. Learning to live with its dampness, its pitter-patter. Linden walks back to the hotel swiftly. His pace is strong and fast. Passersby move aside at his approach. The sensation of his body working, legs reaching out to lunge ahead, his arms swiveling up and down, does him good. His breath wreathes out behind him in puffy white clouds. He has ignored his agent Rachel's calls. She wants to know how his father is, but she also wants to know when he will be getting back to work. He doesn't have that answer for her. His priority is his father. And if she doesn't understand that, then she can go to hell. He'll be back at the hospital tomorrow. This time, he'll take the book by Giono with him. He'll read aloud to Paul. It may not be actually talking to him, but it might help.

Earlier on, he called Sacha and talked for a long while. Hearing his voice cheered him up. Sacha asked if Linden wants him to come, said he could do that, right now, could get on a plane, be there in less than a day. No, Sacha doesn't need to come, not just yet anyway, although he misses Sacha so much, it actually hurts. He feels as if he is caught in an unknown time warp, in foreign territory, dealing with fears and emotions that dwarf him. He can't look ahead, it frightens him so. Instead, he deals with the here and now.

Lying on his bed, staring at the ceiling. When he got back to the hotel, there had been an unpleasant scene with Tilia. Exactly the kind he had been dreading. She told him blatantly she couldn't afford paying the extra hotel nights. She wasn't earning the kind of money he was, and, in fact, she was earning shit right now. Did he have any idea about that? Piqued, he had brushed it aside, saying guardedly that of course he'd pay for the extra nights, it wasn't a problem; the problem was their father, not this money business. And at that, she had flown into a rage. Her face had turned purple. Who the fuck did he think he was? Did he think that because he photographed the high and mighty and lived in the lap of luxury, he could make that kind of statement, actually compare their father's state to what he had in his wallet? He had tried his best to calm her down, but he knew her well enough to be aware she had worked herself into one of her fits, and there was nothing more he could do except to leave her room, close the door, and flee to his. There was a note under his door from Myriam Fanrouk, the hotel director, saying how sorry she was about the state of his parents' health and if there was anything she could help with, would he please let her know.

Linden is still on his bed, mulling over the events of the day, when someone knocks on his door. This must be housekeeping, reminding him he has to move out of his room to join his sister. A young girl flings herself on him in a whirlwind of long black curls. His niece. Mistral.

There has always been a special connection between them, ever since she was born. She was the only baby he had instinctively known how to hold, to cuddle. Now she is growing taller every time he sees her, towering over her plump, fair-haired mother, a graceful daddy longlegs. The only item she inherited from her thickset Basque dad is his olive-skinned complexion. The rest is all Lauren, the height, the allure. Her sophistication often makes him think of Candy. Today she is wearing a Burberry trench coat tied snugly around her small waist, a vintage Hermès scarf, and black jeans with boots.

"Mom was so mad at you," she says flippantly, and then goes on
to inform him she soon put an end to Tilia's rancor. Mistral, all of
eighteen, mothers her own mother brilliantly, and has been doing
so, it seems, all her life. Now that she's calmed Tilia down, she
wants to know all about "Papy." She is the only grandchild, after
all. That's what she's here for, for Papy. She doesn't see him much;
she's worried. She wants to go to the hospital; she wants to be there.
She wants to help. She's embarrassed that her mother can't make it
to the hospital. She thought Tilia had gotten over the accident, but
obviously not. Perhaps her mother needs more time. As usual, Linden is impressed by her self-possession. He was never that mature at
her age. When he thinks back at himself, he only remembers torment, the agony of trying to fit in, the fear of being different. Watching Mistral discuss her mother, her stepfather, and her father so
reasonably and articulately dumbfounds him. She seems to have
everything figured out. In two years, she will have finished her fashion studies at Central Saint Martins, which her father is financing, and then she wants to work in New York for some big fashion
company, and if he has any pointers, she'll take them, but she
doesn't want to be a burden, as she knows how busy he is. Nonetheless, it must be said her uncle is Linden Malegarde; that might
come in handy for an interview, mightn't it? A winning smile lights
up her charming face. He'll do anything to help her, and tells her
so. She thanks him, and goes on, explaining how she must get out
of the house on Clarendon Road, how living with Colin has become
unbearable; his drinking is now nightmarish. She imitates him,
staggering from door to window with an elegant hobble, eyes
screwed up, mouth flaccid, an imaginary tilted glass in her hand.
The money problem, of course, doesn't help, the fact that Tilia earns
near to nothing with her paintings, that Colin can be insufferably
parsimonious. Mistral has a boyfriend, a British guy called Sam,
and her cheeks go pink as she pronounces his name, which Linden
finds endearing. She spends a lot of time at his place in Hackney,
near London Fields. It's far enough for Tilia and Colin to cut her
some slack. Mistral ceases her bubbling discourse. Now this won't

do at all, she's the one doing all the talking, what nonsense! She wants to know how he is, how Sacha is. When is Sacha next coming to London? She wants him to take her to the opera again. She wants to know which is the best version of *La Traviata,* and only Sacha can help her with that. She wants to know all about the famous people Linden has photographed recently. She'll shut up from now on, she promises! Linden reaches out to stroke her curly head affectionately.

"You've got it all sorted out, haven't you? You clever girl."

Mistral shrugs. She's pretty sure he had it all sorted, too, when he was her age, right? Oh, no, he hadn't, he tells her. Her black brows lift in surprise. He hadn't at all. She has to picture him as a very lonely teenager, living at first with Candice, who waited all day long for calls from maddening J.G. At nineteen, he had been out for two years, but only to Candice. His family discerned nothing about his personal life. He never talked about himself. He was unsure about every aspect of his existence. Unconfident about his professional future, worried about how he was going to attain independence, wary of revealing his real self to people he met. After cohabiting with Candy, and even though he enjoyed her company, he had moved out, to earn his living, to spread his wings. He hadn't been quite ready. It had taken awhile to get used to living alone, he explained. Later, he was working in a photo lab, earning a small salary, and having affairs that no one knew anything about. Candice knew his first love was Philippe. When there were other boys, he stopped telling Candice; he felt embarrassed. There was no love, then. Just affairs. Guys he'd meet in bars. Quick episodes he put aside, and which made him feel lonelier than ever. Then, there was Hadrien, the saddest, sweetest love story he ever experienced, when he was her age. Hadrien, and rue Surcouf. That was a secret. It was too complicated, too painful. It had ended so horrifyingly. Linden had felt lonelier than ever.

His mother, asking over and over again if he had a sweetheart. Mistral rolls her eyes. Did she *really* do that? She did, until he found the courage to tell her he was gay. He was twenty-four at that point, working for a photographer. He was living alone, on rue Broca, not very far from Montparnasse. Was it difficult telling Lauren? It was both easy and hard. Easy because it felt like such a relief, getting it off his chest. Hard because she had looked so disheartened. He tried to remember the words he had pronounced, exactly. They hadn't been the same as those he had used with Candice. He had vivid images of that spring day in 2005. His mother was sitting in front of him, in his small living room. She was wearing a jade-colored shirt, a jean skirt, and sandals. So, when were she and his father going to meet his girlfriend? He recalled her tight smile, her expectant eyes. She held her coffee cup with such intensity, he feared she might break it. For a split second, he had felt the dreaded nakedness, the sensation of being so vulnerable that nothing could ever protect him. He knew his mother would never forget this conversation. The thought was terrifying. He took the plunge, headfirst. No more hesitating. No more dithering. He had said something like "There is no girlfriend." And because she didn't seem to catch on, at all, he had added, "There is a boyfriend." And then, clumsily, said, "Or boyfriends." She had remained silent, and then came a little "Oh." And her face went blank. Mistral groans and covers her eyes. She can't believe her grandmother merely said "Oh." What happened next? Lauren had gotten up, paced the room. Did anyone else know? Had Linden told anyone? He told her Candy knew. She swung around. Candy? Her own sister? Since when? He'd told Candy in 1998, when he was seventeen. Lauren seemed thunderstruck. He told Candy, nearly seven years ago? She had hissed out the word *seven,* and he still remembers the way her lips drew back to reveal her teeth. Had Candice told anyone? Linden had been confounded by that question. No, he didn't think she had. Did it matter if she had? And then his mother had pronounced the sentence that still pained him today. "I don't know how your father is going to take this." He had wanted to crawl away, to hide, to disappear. Part of him wanted to weep; another part became incensed. Did Lauren mean his father was going to be disappointed? Well, of course, she had retorted, this was a complete shock; surely he could see that? What had he expected, that she might have patted him on the back and congratulated him? He felt the sting in her words and recoiled. How was it that his mother had never guessed? How was it she had never seen? If those kids at school in Sévral had seen it, when he was barely into his teens, how come his own mother had never noticed? The answer was clear, then. It was because she had never wanted to see it. Linden had stood up and he had said this to his mother, "Your sister told me she wasn't disappointed and that she loved me just the same." There had been a silence, and then Lauren's face had crumpled. She sobbed into her palms, and Linden had let her do so, without moving. He watched her until she regained her composure. She wiped away her tears, smearing her mascara. "I'm sorry." She murmured it, low down, but he heard it. And he never knew what she was sorry for. He never asked. When she left, she hugged him. She said clearly, just as he closed the door with shuddering fingers, that she wouldn't tell his father anything. She'd leave that up to him.

Mistral's hand finds its way into his. Her voice pipes up.

"And did you ever tell Papy?"

"Tell him what?"

"Well, that you're gay."

Linden hangs his head. He says nothing for a while. Then he looks into her eyes.

"No. I never did. And I don't know what he knows."

Later on, when Linden is back from dinner with Tilia and Mistral, there is a message for him from Madame Fanrouk at the reception desk. The hotel director is upset at the idea of his having to share a room with his sister, especially since she understands his young niece has just arrived and will be sleeping in her mother's room. The hotel is fully booked, as he knows, but there is an attic room he can use for as long as he likes, free of charge. It is heated but has no bathroom. Would he mind sharing his sister's? Linden is shown up to the last floor, carrying his small suitcase with him. The door bears no number. The attic room is long and narrow, with a single bed pushed into a corner. He can hardly stand up straight without knocking his head on the beams. The drumming of the rain comes down through the roof. The room is warm and clean, but it has no TV, nor Wi-Fi. It will have to do.

Before dinner, his sister had sheepishly mumbled an apology. He nodded and accepted it. Best to move forward and forget the entire episode. The three of them went to a pizzeria on rue Vavin, just the other side of the crossroad. The rain had thinned out to a fine drizzle. He noticed Tilia downed her Valpolicella hastily. At one point, Mistral inconspicuously placed her palm over her mother's glass. Tilia kept quiet, he noticed, but stuck to water after that. Linden had called the hospital, and the doctor in charge informed him Paul was still in the same state. No better, no worse. Linden replied he'd be there tomorrow during visiting hours with his niece. As for Lauren, they'd all been in to see her at the end of the day. She seemed washed-out, pale-faced, and gaunt against the pillows. No worse, either, but not that much better.

Linden had watched the news from his sister's room. What he saw alarmed him. The Bercy district was now flooded. Power plants had been swamped, electricity malfunctioned or failed, apartments and shops were no longer heated nor lit. Several Métro lines had been more than partially inundated. Pumping the water out had not helped. Train line RER C, built along the river, was full of water and had to be shut down. The Palais Omnisports at Bercy was closed. All events to be held there had been canceled. The nearby Ministry of Economy and Finance was about to be evacuated. The most worrying aspect of the flooding was the slow but sure accumulation in the underground sewer system. Most of the trouble was coming from deep down, up through Parisian cellars, basements, and parking lots, due to the high saturation of the water table and the persistent rain. The surge was inching up leisurely, taking its time, but rising with extraordinary steadiness. A website named Vigicrues, which literally meant "Flood Watch," had been accessed thousands of times by Parisians. It measured, minute by minute, the staggering upward curve of the river. Linden transferred it to his phone and discovered the Seine was already over six meters at the pont d'Austerlitz. The forecast for the next couple of days was bleak. Governmental action was now in full swing. No one was taking this lightly.

Oriel had been right. The flooding was not going to subside. Linden had turned the TV off. He had felt slightly nauseous. The Seine's upwelling upset him, but his parents' state worried him all the more. The bad timing of their visit to Paris stupefied him. How could their family weekend have turned into such an ordeal? He thought of his father, in the hospital, of his mother, prostrate in her airless room, of the river edging up, and his anxiety increased.

At dinner, however, he attempted not to reveal his concern to his sister and niece. He tried to cheer them up by telling them about the worse photo shoots he'd experienced, the ones where everything had gone wrong. He regaled them with stories, from the truculent model who balked at every suggestion to the overbearing artistic director who practically snatched the camera from his hands. The scariest episode was when a major power failure that affected half of New York City plunged the state-of-the-art basement studio he was shooting in into darkness. The entire team, his assistants, models, stylists, hair and makeup crew, caterer, and janitor had been locked in for the night. One of the hairdressers had had a panic attack. And then there was the calamitous moment where an inattentive assistant he no longer worked with had left most of the equipment in a taxi as they were about to embark for Australia. In fact, he told Tilia and Mistral that the perfect photo session was nothing short of a miracle. When they got back to the hotel, they went to Lauren's room. Her fever had subsided, but the cough was still there. The only word she could pronounce in a sort of rasp was her husband's name, with tears in her eyes. Her woe saddened them; they didn't know how to reassure her. The three of them sat around her bed helplessly. It was Mistral who at last found the right words, who managed to comfort her grandmother.

Now that Linden has retired to his attic bedroom, having left his sister and niece with Lauren, he feels worn out. His back aches again, and his head, as well. The Valpolicella, no doubt. The bed is too small. The rain splashing down on the roof seems unnaturally loud at first. After a while, he gets used to it. It takes him a prolonged time to settle into a troubled, patchy sleep. He wakes up suddenly, throat parched, and reaches down to look at his phone. It's one in the morning. His head still aches. He remembers he has no running water in the room. A bottle of mineral water has been thoughtfully placed by his bed. He gulps it down, lies back on the pillow. The rain taps above him soothingly. He closes his eyes and sinks back into the darkness.

The model's profile is exquisite, skin resembling porcelain, eyelashes thick with mascara spiking out like stars. She looks down, legs crossed, arms wrapped around her slender torso. He asks her to start posing, but she won't, so he puts the camera away and comes closer to speak to her. Still she won't look at him. Now he can see the tears trickling down her cheeks, smearing her makeup. Her quivering lips are bloodred and glistening. He asks her what is wrong, gently, and she shakes her head. The perfect makeup is marred, yet the model is still lovely, as if she had been brutalized and discarded, a flower ravaged and tossed aside. Maybe he should take photos anyway. The client will not be happy, but perhaps he can work something out. The short black dress clings to her, revealing most of her long, slim legs. He takes the camera in hand, starts shooting. She sobs in silence, with complete desperation. She turns her face fully to him and lets him click frame after frame. She knows how to move. She is far from amateurish, but she is not giving him what she usually offers. He is both surprised and stirred. She has removed all glamour from her stance, and the only thing she submits is her sorrow, in all its naked beauty. He checks the images in his viewer, and he can already tell, with a thrill of delight, that they are stunning, totally different from what he was supposed to do. He has a fright when she collapses onto the floor. He scrambles to her side, grabs her hand. He helps her up, leads her to a nearby room where there is a bed. She stares at him, takes a couple of breaths. Then she says, "It's my father. My father has died." She screams at the top of her voice, "My father is dead! He's dead!" Her tears come again, and he finds he cannot help her, just as he is incapable of shutting out her pain, her grief. He places her on the mattress, covers her with a blanket, switches off the bed-side light. He doesn't even know her name. She sobs and falls asleep after a moment. Drowsiness takes over, and he surrenders to it. His ears pick up faint sounds in the obscurity: a creak, a breath. They are not alone. The model has not moved. Her face looks deathly white. Someone is in the room with them; someone is standing at the far end, near the door. His eyes gradually get accustomed to the dimness and he perceives two figures hunched by the entrance, near his photo equipment. Who are they? What do they want? He shifts slightly, and they freeze. One of them creeps forward stealthily, holding a mobile phone out like a torch. He feels the dim light on his face. He feigns slumber. They go back to rummaging through his things, speaking in low whispers. The panic fades when he sees them handling his Leica. It's the only object he cares about. A slow rage begins to burn, heating him up. Why should he let these people walk away with one of his most prized possessions? Is he going to sit back and let this happen? They have wrapped the Leica up in one of their sweaters. Linden is able to make out a man and a woman. They are arguing about what to do next; the man wants to leave, but the woman keeps pointing at the smartphone near the bed where the model sleeps. The man pulls away, but she insists. She is the one who comes for the device, down on the floor, slith-ering like a snake. When her hand reaches out, Linden swings his legs from the chair, driving both feet into the small of her back, crushing her with all his might, ignoring her squeal of pain, and then makes a lunge for the man, clutching him by the hair before he has time to slide out of the room. Linden's fury empowers him, providing him with startling vigor. He grabs the Leica with one hand and wallops the man's face with his other fist, once, and the stranger sinks to his knees, moaning.

Linden awakens with a start. His heart is pounding; his mouth is even drier. The dream has a dreadful potency that leaves its slimy mark on him. Shaking, he drinks the last dregs of the bottle, then lies back, breathless, on the small bed. After a while, he feels calmer. He gets up to check that his Leica is still there. What a strange, odious nightmare. He slips on a pair of jeans and a sweatshirt, takes his iPad, and heads downstairs. It is nearly four o'clock in the morning. The hotel is deserted. There is no one in the lobby, but the lights are still on, blazing. Is there a night manager? He calls out for one. No one answers. He peers outside to rue Delambre through the rain. No passersby at such a late hour. He lies back on a sofa, sends a message to Sacha, asking him if he can call him now. Sacha is still at the start-up, and in a meeting. No, he can't talk. Later, maybe? Then he asks Linden, *What are you doing up at this hour??* Linden sends a long message describing his awful dream. The scene with Tilia. His poor parents. The river rising. The rain. He misses Sacha. He misses California. He feels miserable. He notices an email from Tilia he hadn't been able to read until now because of the lack of Wi-Fi in his attic room. Again, she tells him how sorry she is. She has to learn how to curb that temper of hers. She's relieved that her daughter is here, magnificent, fearless Mistral. Mistral will go to the hospital with him tomorrow; he'll feel less alone, won't he? *Sorry again for being such a hopeless sister,* she wrote. And then, at the bottom of the email, she had added:

> *PS:*
> *I went back to check on Mom after you went up, just to make sure everything was OK.*
> *She was fast asleep and her forehead was cooler, I thought. I looked at her phone, and there were dozens of missed calls and texts from "JeffVDH."*
> *Dude, wasn't that her fiancé from before Dad??*

FOUR

❧

La Seine, avec ses larges flaques vertes et jaunes, plus changeante qu'une robe de serpent.
—VICTOR HUGO, *NOTRE-DAME DE PARIS*

The day it happened, Suzanne was wearing a pale blue dress and her hair was tied up, so I could see the back of her neck. We took the picnic to the tree house, singing songs, holding hands. Her palm was always cool. There had been a storm during the night. The heat was back the next morning, but the earth retained moistness. The ground beneath the trees was still damp.

That same summer, my grandfather died. He was seventy-nine; to me, that was old. I was not shown his dead body. They thought I was too small. No one told me what happened. No one explained. They thought I wouldn't understand. But I saw the coffin being hauled out of his room and down the stairs. It seemed heavy; four men carried it, grunting and sweating. I saw my grandmother weepy in her black dress. My father looked dried-up and beat. The skin around his eyes was wrinkly. Strangers came to the house and spoke in low voices. One of them gave me nougat that stuck to my teeth. Everyone patted my head and said what a nice little boy I was.

My grandfather was a loud and cheerful person. I was told the entire village went to his funeral. After he was gone, the house was still and silent. I didn't like it. I missed his thundering step, his guffaw.

He didn't pay much attention to me, but I didn't mind. I don't think he cared for kids. He liked to sit on the terrace, in the shade, and drink Clairette de Die with his friends. He had a big potbelly and curly mustaches that pricked when he kissed my cheeks.

I couldn't understand death. I didn't know what it was. The only way I was able to measure it was by the fact I couldn't hear my grandfather's laugh anymore.

But I had no idea how close I would see death. How close it came to me.

All those years later, I'm still looking for signs. There was no one or nothing to warn me of the dreadfulness to come. It was one of those beautiful summer days. There were no signs. None at all.

"Monsieur malegarde . . . excuse me. . . . Monsieur Malegarde?"

Linden opens heavy eyelids. Agathe, the receptionist, is patting his shoulder gently. She asks him if everything is all right. Dazed, he stares back at her. Then he understands, discomfited; he fell asleep on the sofa and it is now morning. He gets up, murmurs an apology. Nearly nine o'clock. He must have passed out.

There's a message on his phone from Mistral saying he can come and use the bathroom if he likes, they're both awake. When she sees her brother, Tilia asks him what he made of the Jeffrey van der Haagen messages. He replies he has no idea, no idea at all. The guy called dozens of times, his sister goes on, sotto voce, so that Mistral, under the shower, can't hear. Did Linden know if their mother had planned to meet up with Jeff in Paris? Again, Linden shakes his head. Why is his sister bothering about this? Is it important? Has she been to check Lauren this morning? Yes, she has, and their mother is not looking good, still coughing and feverish. They should get the doctor to come back. Tilia nods; she will call him.

After breakfast, Linden reads his emails. Rachel Yellan wants to know if he has a camera with him. Could he get to work? She is aware of the situation about his father, but the Seine is making every single headline all around the world. Is he willing to take pictures? He doesn't have to, of course, she adds, but shouldn't he try? The river photos in the press look so crazy. What does he make of it? Linden understands it is happening. The flood is here. At about the same time he was having his nightmare, the Seine topped its banks, at Alfortville and Charenton, east of Paris. All the river's upstream tributaries, engorged by the rain, are now pouring toward the capital mercilessly. The riverbed can hold no more water, he reads. Thirty Métro stations have been closed and more evacuations are taking place in the seventh and fifteenth arrondissements. Residents are being asked to leave, but not everyone wants to go, he discovers. People are afraid of looters; they wish to stay at home and protect their goods, even if they have no more running water, no electricity, no heating.

On Instagram, the number of photos of the flood is flourishing. From Bercy to Javel, each image shows an unnaturally broad and dirty river, with tied-up barges bobbing high up near street level, banks engulfed by brownish water, trees and lampposts bursting out like aquatic flowers, almost comical. The most impressive pictures are retweeted by news channels, and the hashtags #parisfloods, #zouave are trending topics. Despite the chill and the rain, tourists are enjoying the phenomenon. Linden can't count the amount of selfies with the river in the background. He must go see this for himself. He has time, as the intensive care unit doesn't open till three o'clock. As he rushes out the door with Leica in hand, cramming rolls of film into his pocket, a voice cries out.

"Wait for me!"

It's Mistral, on his trail. She wants to see the river, too; she wants to see it with him. The unexpected company warms him. He is so used to the rain, he hardly feels it anymore. It's the cold that gets to him, piercing through his jacket and scarf. They hurry down boulevard du Montparnasse, turning right onto rue de Rennes. The traffic is dense; cars honk impatiently. The air feels humid and dewy. They reach the river through narrow rue Bonaparte. There are already masses of pedestrians going the same way. Barriers set up by the police prevent cars from turning onto rue Jacob and rue de l'Université. Linden wonders why, but as he peers down the road, he can see stretches of water, like eerie tarns, spreading over the pavement. The pont des Arts is closed, so the throng heads to the next ones, Carrousel and Royal. Never has Linden seen such a crowd along the quays. Umbrella spokes prod at them from every angle. The bridges are jam-packed with rows and rows of people gaping at the river level. Mistral and Linden have to stand in line in order to get to the front of the balustrade and glimpse the Seine. The acrid stench of the water wafts up to them.

The last time Linden had been in Paris with Sacha, in September 2016, they had ambled on the Right Bank wharves from the Louvre to the Île Saint-Louis. Linden was here for a photographic assignment, and Sacha had come over to join him from Berlin, where he was meeting investors for his start-up. Sacha had booked tickets for *Tosca* at the Opéra Bastille. In an ecological but controversial gesture, the mayor of Paris had closed the docks to all traffic from the Louvre to the pont de Sully. It was a beautiful fall morning. Although he considered himself a Parisian, rendered blasé by the city's marvels, the magnificence of the capital had dazzled Linden. He had always been a fervent walker. He had strolled through every neighborhood of Paris, and this area used to be one of the most congested and noisiest arteries of the city, clogged by cars and pollution. It was extraordinary to be actually treading the road along the river where lines and lines of vehicles used to mar the splendor of the place. The unfamiliar silence around them made it difficult for him to believe he was in the heart of the city. Sacha was exhilarated. He had not visited Paris often. Linden pointed out the Île de la Cité, on their right. This is where Paris was born, he explained to Sacha, entranced; the Celtic tribe called the Parisii lived right here, by the river. Of course, Sacha had to imagine what the banks must have looked like in 52 B.C. He'd have to wipe away the pointy green triangle of the Vert-Galant garden heading west, the awe-inspiring Haussmannian walls of the Palais de Justice, where the delicate black spire of the Sainte-Chapelle could be glimpsed peeking over the roofs. Right next to it, Linden had gone on, was the mediaeval and grim-looking Conciergerie, where

Marie-Antoinette was imprisoned until the day of her execution. The Seine eased by mildly. Linden had noticed how transparent the tranquil green-blue water was, lapping lazily at the quayside. He had been able to gaze right down into it and spot the round gray stones that lined its bed. How meek and submissive the watercourse had appeared that day, an idyllic postcard vision, with ducks and swans floating on its smooth surface.

There is nothing docile about it today. The river has turned into a gluttonous muddy monster. It has wolfed up each bank, swallowed all the bridge's footings. Plastic chairs, recycle bins, tree trunks cavort by, whamming into the bridge's foundations with cavernous whacks. The pont Royal appears truncated, lying low across the roaring current, with only the triangular tips of its stone arches visible above the eddies. These novel perspectives both fascinate and shock Linden. The river seethes like a hostile reptile beneath leaden skies and the uninterrupted downpour. The swarm around them jostles and shoves, cheering each time a piece of furniture or a plank hits the bridge. Linden clicks away, steadying his feet against the push. People laugh and jeer, holding up their mobile phones. No one seems afraid, he notices. To them, it's a joke, a display. Yet the ugly torrent gushing below has nothing comical about it. Neither does the ominous gurgle of its urgency as it pumps along like a robot in its furious marathon westwards to the Channel.

Mistral and he struggle to make their way back to the sidewalk, bearing toward Concorde and Alma. The pavement is dotted with TV crews filming the river, minivans with elevated satellite dishes parked alongside one another. Hordes of photographers angle their cameras to the waters. Linden has to fight to find a spot so he can work, as well. It takes them longer than usual to reach the pont de l'Alma and the famous stone Zouave, standing in the choppy water with dignity, impervious to the circus around him. Everyone wants a souvenir of the Zouave with the river up to his waist. Ineffectual policeman try to get people to step away from the quays, but the gatherings are too thick. Parisians mix with tourists, smiling, waving, shouting, gazing down with awe at the unusual show. Linden sees a very old man wearing a hat, puffing at his pipe, leaning against a tree. His calm, rheumy eyes take everything in. Linden politely asks the old man if he can photograph him, and the elderly gentleman replies he may. He makes quite a figure, quietly gazing over the excited bystanders.

"Don't know what they find so amusing," he tells Linden crustily. "They'll be less happy tonight when the Seine finds its way to their beds."

Linden asks him if he truly believes that will happen. The old man scoffs. Well, of course he believes it! The river will go up even higher than in 1910. Paris will sink into a cesspool. Mistral listens attentively, her face serious. So what should they do, then, she asks, should they leave? Another cackle. The old man has no teeth, but he certainly knows how to smile. Yes, they should leave! What are they waiting for? They should leave now. Go back to wherever they are from. Leave now, before the end of the world. Linden pulls on her sleeve gently, and they murmur good-bye. Mistral is silent for a while. When they reach the École Militaire, she asks her uncle if the old guy was nuts or whether he could be telling the truth. Linden doesn't want to frighten her, but after all, she is an adult. She's seen the news on TV, right? So she knows. Their priority now is Paul. They need to concentrate on him; they will deal with the rest in time. Mistral nods her head. She looks so youthful all of a sudden, her face wan beneath her hood.

On their way back to the hotel, Linden stops at a post office to send the rolls of film to his agent in New York, the old-fashioned way. He explained in his earlier email to Rachel that it was the best he could do, as he did not have any digital equipment with him. The noncommittal person who takes his package murmurs that she hopes it will get to America before too long, because postal services are beginning to feel the effect of the flooding. A little farther on, Linden buys the newspapers of the day: Every front page features the Zouave overrun by the flow. Before they reach the hotel, he checks Vigicrues on his phone. The river is rising one centimeter per hour and has reached 6.5 meters at the pont d'Austerlitz, going over the levels of June 2016 and last November. Still far from the 8.62 meters of the 1910 flood, he reminds himself, but worrying enough.

The expression on Tilia's face alarms them when they knock on Lauren's door. She steps out of the room, closing the door behind her.

"The doctor came," she whispers. "Get this. Mom has *pneumonia.*"

"Pneumonia?" echoes Mistral. "Isn't that only in novels by Dickens?"

It's not that bad, but it is contagious; Lauren doesn't have to be hospitalized, thank God, but she needs rest, medication, and she cannot be moved. After her treatment has started, she will soon get better, the doctor assured. Tilia has been to see the hotel director, who was most amenable and fully understood the situation. A nurse will be coming in daily to tend to their mother. Later on, when Linden and Mistral head to the Pompidou hospital to see Paul, Linden wonders what their next misfortune will be. He does not mention this to his niece, but his silence perceptibly stirs her empathy, because she reaches out to grab his hand. It is impossible to find a free taxi. Many Métro lines and bus lines are closed because of the deluge, so they decide to walk to the hospital, the bright blue hotel umbrella sheltering them, all the way down rue de Vaugirard to boulevard Victor. In Linden's pocket is the copy of Giono's book, *The Man Who Planted Trees.*

Mistral says nothing; Linden doesn't, either, but they savor their closeness. The warmth of her hand is heartening. They have always spoken to each other in French, ever since she was a toddler. It came naturally. When the large glass construction of the hospital is in sight, Mistral asks if he ever walks hand in hand like this with Sacha. He says it's possible in some streets of San Francisco, but that's pretty much it. They've gotten used to not touching when they are outside or in public places. It's something he learned very young, in Paris, with his first boyfriends. Mistral thinks that's so sad, so terribly sad, that they cannot show the world their love. She says she keeps thinking about the day he told Lauren in 2005 and how awful her response had been. It shocked her. She never imagined her grandmother would react that way. She herself had known about uncle Linden being gay ever since she could remember. Tilia had explained this to her daughter straightforwardly. Tilia was the first person in the family who had realized Linden was gay, probably even before he did himself, long before he ever talked to Candice. She had been a wonderful support; she knew about the kids bullying him at school. She had convinced his parents to let him move to Paris. Yes, his sister had been invaluable.

Mistral wants to know if things are better now, with Lauren. It took his mother a while, Linden admits. For a long time, several years, Lauren never mentioned his homosexuality, as if he had not revealed it to her. She wiped it away, superbly. He sometimes wondered what she told their friends when they asked about him. It was easy to say Tilia was married, with a kid. Tilia fitted the pattern. How did Lauren fill in the blanks? Did she invent girlfriends to make herself feel better about her son? Mistral winces at this; he feels the tremor in her hand. When he fell in love with Sacha, in 2013, it became simpler, he says. Sacha's solar personality was responsible. Lauren fell for it, like everyone did, when she met him. Mistral squeezes his hand and chuckles. Oh, yes, everyone fell for Sacha. How could so much charisma be assembled into a single human being? As she speaks glowingly of his partner, Linden feels a pang of yearning. If only Sacha were here, right by his side, right now. Linden looks ahead, squaring his shoulders for what awaits them there. He notices policemen and barricades erected around the hospital, barring the way into rue Saint-Charles and rue Balard.

There is something unnerving about the hospital today. Linden picks it up instantaneously. It seems oddly vacant. A few nurses dash by briskly. The lights are muted, glimmering feebly in the long corridors. An unpleasant smell of decay invades the place. There are numerous posters attached to walls along the entrance area. Linden and Mistral draw nearer to read them. Due to the flooding, the premises are to be evacuated first thing tomorrow morning, Tuesday. Patients are being transferred to the Necker or Cochin hospitals. Next of kin should contact the information desk for more details. They rush to the information desk, which is closed. There is no one around. Linden can't understand why he hasn't been warned. How are they transferring the patients? By ambulance? What about the ones who cannot be moved, like his father? Mistral tries to calm him down; they'll know more once they find a doctor.

The intensive care unit is unoccupied, barely lit. No nurses, no surgeons. Dr. Brunel is nowhere to be seen, either. Linden is incensed. What the hell is going on? How can the staff just rush off like this? A few patients sleep on, unreceptive and destitute. Paul is now alone in the room. No sign of the previous patient, Pascal Beaumont, and his wife. Behind the curtain, Paul lies, eyes closed. The monitors above him beep regularly. Linden leaves Mistral with her grandfather and goes in search of a person to talk to. He walks the whole length of the dim and silent hallway, infuriated, before he hears a murmur of voices at last. He comes across a staff office, all lights on. Looking through the glass partition, he sees Dr. Brunel stooped in front of a computer. Next to him is the Jodie Foster look-alike, Dr. Yvon. They both look ready to drop. He pauses before raising his hand to knock on the door. They appear to be going through lists, ticking names off. Two nurses sit nearby, taking notes. He feels a twitch of pity for them; it must be nightmarish vacating such a vast hospital. When they hear him, they raise startled faces. He can see them trying to recall who he is. They must see so many families here every day, so many tragedies, so many losses. Why should they remember him, above anyone else?

"The photographer. Son of Paul Malegarde," murmurs Dr. Brunel to his colleague, getting up, followed by Dr. Yvon, who nods and adds, "Room twenty-four." So they do remember. He can't help admiring them for that. They stand in front of him, and he can feel the tension emanating from them. His anger ebbs. Why give them a hard time? It must be tough enough for them already. Dr. Brunel apologizes for the lack of communication. It's been hard getting hold of everyone. Yes, the hospital must be emptied. The Seine has already flooded the basement level. The operating rooms are out of order, and the water is creeping up. Many patients have left today, but it's trickier dealing with the heavily monitored ones, who can hardly be moved, like his father. That will be done early tomorrow morning. Can Linden be there at seven? Linden replies of course, and then asks if the transfers will be done by ambulance. Dr. Brunel crosses his arms and glances at Dr. Yvon. They hope so. They certainly hope so. Linden stares at them. Why is their mien so shifty? He says he doesn't understand. Dr. Brunel heaves a sigh. His coffee-colored eyes at last meet Linden's. He asks Linden to come to the rain-stained window for a moment, and he points down. From here, Linden can see that rue Leblanc and place Albert-Cohen have disappeared under the water. The Seine is now splashing at the site's very foundations. The Port de Javel has vanished under a deceptively tranquil lake. Workers are busy installing cofferdams and pumps along the hospital walls. Linden remembers the river is rising a centimeter per hour. Is it safe for his father to stay here tonight? Can't he be transferred this afternoon? The doctors both reassure him. His father is safe. The transfer will take place, most probably by boat, in the morning. By boat? Linden is astonished. Why by boat? He arrived on foot from Montparnasse; he didn't need a boat to get here. Cochin Hospital is in the fourteenth arrondissement, no floods there, so why are boats needed? The doctor hesitates again. Boats will be needed by tomorrow because the water is rising so quickly. The Javel neighborhood is the one hardest hit by the floods. Many residents have already left, assisted by the army. Linden recalls the barriers raised around the hospital. Most of the streets around here are no doubt already flooded. What kind of boat is it to be? he asks. Who will be steering it? Is it safe enough for his father? What about the cold and the rain? How will this take place? And why can't his father be transferred today, before they even need boats? He can tell the doctors are doing their best to placate him, but it's not working. Dr. Brunel says the transfer cannot happen now because of insurance problems. Linden finds this unbelievable. Insurance problems! They must be joking, right? There is a silence. They seem so uncomfortable, he almost pities them. He can read the anxiety in their eyes. He wonders if they have ever dealt with anything like this in their careers. He can tell they haven't. Fighting back his frustration, he says he has one important question. Why on earth was this modern hospital ever built here nearly twenty years ago? Surely the architects who created it were aware it was situated in a zone liable to flooding? How did they ever obtain permits? How did the city council ever let them build here? They both shrug, shake their heads. They have asked themselves the same questions. It seems preposterous, they agree. Linden changes the subject, switches to his father's health. Can they tell him any more? Paul is the same way; there are no new facts to be passed on. Once his father is safely installed at Cochin Hospital, the surgeons there will decide whether to operate or not. He will be in the expert hands of a respected doctor, Professor Gilles Magerant. Paul's file is being transferred today.

Thanking them, Linden takes his leave, walking back down the dimly lit passageway to his father's room. He hasn't felt so low, so sad, so afraid in a very long time.

In room 24, Mistral is sitting by the bed, talking to her grandfather perfectly normally. His eyes are still closed. She is holding his hand, and her voice is merry and soft. She is describing the river, and the old man by the pont de l'Alma who told them the flood was going to get worse. She says not to worry. They're here to look after Paul; he'll be fine. When Linden enters the room, she whispers that Papy is not responding, but somehow she is convinced he can hear her. How brave and sweet she is. Linden slips an arm around her shoulders and kisses the top of her head. Then he takes the Giono book out of his pocket and starts to read in a clear, gentle voice, standing by the bed. Mistral listens. She is quite taken by the story of Elzéard Bouffier, the shepherd who planted thousands of trees. Paul's face does not move. His chest heaves up and down regularly. When Linden comes to the end of the tale, thirty minutes later, Mistral gets up. She'll leave him alone with his father now, just the two of them. She'll see Linden later on at the hotel. She slips out, blows them a kiss.

Again, Linden feels powerless. No ideas come. No words. He can only sit there, hands flat on his knees. The rain drums against the windowpane. He thinks of the river down below, inching its way up the abandoned hospital. The building is like a vast sinking ship. Is there any way he could get his father out of the hospital now? The bed is on wheels; he could push it to the elevators, but then what? How could he ever move his father to Cochin? He would never find a taxi. What about an ambulance? He almost laughs at himself. He is crazy: forget it. His father has a drip in his arm and an oxygen mask on his face, for Christ's sake! Linden drags his chair closer to his father. Paul smells of antiseptic lotion. A nurse washed him this morning. He reaches out to touch his father's hand. The skin is warm, dry. Those hands that know everything there is to be known about trees. He turns Paul's hand over and examines the palm. It is pale and leathery, surprisingly clean. The habitually dusty, grimy skin now shines palely against his tanned fingers.

"Papa . . . Can you hear me? It's me. It's Linden. I'm here."

No response. Linden clears his throat, still cradling his father's hand. It seems silly, talking to someone who perhaps can't hear a thing, but he keeps at it determinedly. He tells Paul he found the doctor. The hospital is in confusion because of the upcoming evacuation, but Paul needn't fret; Linden will supervise the whole thing. He wishes his father could see the river rising, a chilling yet beautiful sight; Paul would be riveted by the event. He tries to describe the strange new angles of the bridges, the roiling torrent's hue, the mob gathered along the quays. He depicts the rain, which hasn't ceased since their arrival; the sensation of rambling through a dusky, humid, aquatic city that bears little resemblance to what it usually is; how Paris has lost its luster, its sharpness, its delineations dwindling into a slippery uncertainty fascinating to behold and to photograph.

Linden pauses, letting go of his father's hand. An idea comes to him. He probes his pocket for his phone, swipes into his music file, finds David Bowie. He doesn't own that many Bowie songs; he's not half as much a fan as his father is, but there are ten songs on his device. The first one that comes up is "Sorrow." He turns up the sound, places the speaker near his father's ear. The unmistakable voice rings out, echoing against the bare green walls. Linden remembers his father listening to Bowie in his pickup. Although he was tiny then, he understood how important Bowie was to Paul. His father never sang along, but his finger beat the rhythm against the wheel, and Linden can imagine it, that sturdy index finger oscillating to the music. How he wishes he could see it twitching again now. The next tune is "Lazarus," one of the last Bowie ever wrote, featured on the haunting album *Blackstar,* released a few days before his death. With tremulous poignancy, Bowie declares he's in heaven, that his scars are invisible, that he has nothing else to lose. Linden was at home on that Sunday evening, January 10, 2016, when the news of Bowie's death broke. Sacha and he had finished dinner and were clearing up. Sacha was making a joke about one of the cats wanting to lap up the last spoonful of his delicious chocolate mousse. (Sacha was strict with the cats; he never fed them tidbits or goodies; Linden was more lenient.) It was Sacha who received an alert on his phone, and who murmured, awed, that Bowie had just died. Linden made him repeat it twice and switched on the TV. The demise had just been confirmed. It was seven o'clock in the morning in Vénozan, too early to call his father. Paul seldom listened to the news, or read the paper. Lauren did, but she slept later than her husband. His father would be so shocked learning about Bowie's passing. Bowie and he were practically twins, born a year apart—January 4, 1947, for Bowie, January 20, 1948, for Paul. Sacha had asked him why Paul loved Bowie so much, and Linden had found it difficult to explain. It was true that at first glance there seemed to be little in common between an iconic British artist who constantly reinvented himself and an unobtrusive, reclusive landscaper from the Drôme who fought to safeguard trees. It all happened with the album *Ziggy Stardust,* Linden explained, back in 1972. Paul was twenty-four, busy working on restoring Vénozan to its former glory. He was driving in his car on his way to Nyons to fetch saplings when a melody was heard on the radio that raised every single hair on his forearms. He was captivated by the brassy guitar strum and that characteristic voice, both high-pitched and profound, sometimes feathery-edged, sometimes husky—a style he had never heard before. Paul had an ear for music, was fond of Pink Floyd, the Rolling Stones, the Beatles, but this singer was different, his style so pleasingly odd and enchanting that the air struck a chord deep within him. He didn't understand a word of English, nor did he catch the performer's name, either, only the song, "Starman." After he purchased his olive trees, he drove straight to the record store in Sévral. He was handed an album with an outlandishly long title: *The Rise and Fall of Ziggy Stardust and the Spiders from Mars*. The artist was called David Bowie. Paul had no idea how to pronounce the name and didn't even try. The cover showed a young blond man in a tight blue jumpsuit posing in front of buildings under a neon sign at night. He wore a guitar strapped around his neck and platform boots, one of which jauntily rested above a dustbin. That was how it began, Linden explained to Sacha. Paul never saw Bowie in concert, nor did he want to; he just needed to listen. Paul bought each new album, each year, reveling in its difference, its audacity. He became familiar with his idol's emaciated, pallid face, his asymmetric eyes, due to a permanently dilated pupil, his ramshackle teeth, and his boyish grin. And what was Paul's favorite song? Linden said he wasn't sure. And today, at the hospital, he still isn't sure. He's now gone through two more songs, "The Jean Genie," with its catchy, chugging riff, and "Ashes to Ashes" (his personal favorite), with its synthetic string sound and hard-edged bass. His father's distorted features have not twitched once. Linden feels dispirited. Is it worth continuing? One last song, then: "Heroes." He places the phone by the pillow, taking his father's hand in his. Bowie sings so convincingly on this one; his words come across as both sensual and desperate, a heart-tugging combination that triggers Linden's melancholy. That song brings back his father more than ever, standing wordlessly by the house, arms crossed, gazing out to the valley, watching the clouds gather for a spatter of evening rain. The fingers clasped in his seem to shudder, or is it his imagination? He stares down at them, listening to the plaintive guitar throbbing its tune. Just as Bowie's voice cries out with tender rage that they can be heroes, only for one day, his father's hand grabs his like a vise, wrenching a cry of surprise from Linden. Paul's eyes are open, wide open, large and round, staring up at him, shining bright in a frozen, twisted face. Linden, stuttering with emotion, asks if Paul can hear him, if he can answer, if he can give one small sign that he understands. Linden's hand is being pressed again, and the huge eyes blink rhythmically, as if punching out some sort of Morse code. Linden scrambles to his feet, darts out to the corridor. He must find a nurse, a doctor; they must be told his father is responding. Surely this is very good news. There's a nurse two rooms along (he can't believe his luck; he was half-expecting to wander along the deserted hospital in vain) and she greets him with a pleasant smile. She'll be there right away. Linden rushes back to his father's room, relieved to see the blue eyes are still open and so full of life. He had forgotten they were so blue. The color of summer skies at Vénozan, a deep, pure azure he has found nowhere else in the world. Blue, and twinkling, as if all Paul's feelings were pouring out through his irises, reaching out to him. Everything is going to be all right, he's here to look after him. Paul had a stroke; that's what happened. Does he remember anything? Does he remember the restaurant? Well, it happened there, but luckily Paul was taken to the hospital very quickly. The nurse bustles in, pushing a trolley in front of her. Can Linden step out while she tends to his father? He leaves the room, still exhilarated by his father's responses. Bowie triggered all this off; he is sure of that. It was Bowie. It was thanks to Bowie. He remembered talking to Paul the day of Bowie's death. Paul was devastated; he could hardly speak on the telephone. Later, Lauren told Linden that Paul had stayed in all morning listening to his vinyl collection. No one dared interrupt him. He never spoke about it, and went back to work after lunch, his face fraught, his eyes moist. Linden sends text messages to his sister and niece, describing the scene at the hospital. He can't help feeling lifted by what he has just witnessed. When he returns to the room, he is crushed. Paul's eyes are closed again. The nurse touches Linden's arm, comfortingly, murmurs a few encouraging words. Then she slips out. For a while, Linden sits quietly, watching his father's face. The magic moment is broken. Sadness flows through him, expunging the previous buoyancy.

Linden turns on the television, positioned on the wall opposite the bed. The Seine is on every channel, even the foreign ones. Another panel of specialists resumes their dire forecasts: This could last up to a month, with a seven-day peak that had not yet been reached. The river is now up to seven meters at Austerlitz, higher than its level of June 2016. Water is slowly creeping up, oozing out from ventilation systems, grids, and manholes, spreading everywhere, using every crack, every fan plate, every pothole. There is no stopping it. The prefecture has been evacuating residents with the help of the army and the Red Cross. Patients are being transferred to other hospitals, as well as from retirement homes. Parisians are being sheltered in gymnasiums and schools in the higher-up districts, which have never been flooded, such as Montparnasse and Montmartre. The skyscrapers at Beaugrenelle are being vacated and bolted—a protracted and taxing struggle, as some people refuse to leave their homes. The government promises to secure the towers in order to prevent looting, but occupants are not reassured. Electricity has failed in all inundated areas, where Internet connections are now increasingly sluggish. Paris is not alone to suffer; most suburban towns clustered along the river have also been flooded. Mayors are voicing their discontent, as it appears governmental efforts are turned predominantly to the capital, disregarding cries for help coming from poorer communes. Getting to and from Paris is problematic, as roads accessing the capital are swamped. Half of the Métro system is down. Trains are no longer able to reach stations such as Lyon and Austerlitz. Linden can hardly believe his ears. Can this get any worse? It seems it will. For the moment, the river has seeped into the Javel, Bercy, and Invalides neighborhoods. But this is only the beginning, hammers the red-haired, bespectacled woman he had already seen on TV. This time, nobody disagrees with her. This is only the beginning and it will get much worse. The president's pale face now appears on the screen. He is filmed from the presidential palace, and Linden has never seen him look so weary. Dark circles rim his blue eyes. He seems even younger, almost lost. For a moment, he doesn't speak. Then his voice rings out with its usual vigor. Yes, dear compatriots, the hour is a bleak one. Paris and its suburbs must come together and help each other in the difficult time ahead. Yes, the river is still on the rise, and predictions say the level may be higher than in 1910. The president is giving this his full attention. At the president's command, the Ministry of Defense has launched Plan Neptune, created specifically for dealing with the floods, signifying the deployment of 100,000 soldiers. This special force, working in close alliance with the police department, with firefighters, and with the gendarmerie, will participate in rescue operations, the dispersal of food supplies, and evacuations. The people of France must obey any orders they receive from the authorities. These directives will be shared on the radio and in the press. Tourists are being requested to leave, and those planning to come are told to postpone their trip. The prefect of Paris is now addressing the nation. Passersby must observe extreme caution when approaching the river, as the current is powerful. Electricity, gas, and water shortages are probable in half of Paris tomorrow. A special emergency number has been set up. People are encouraged to use it. Linden switches the TV off, heavy-hearted. He leans forward to kiss his father's forehead. When he washes his hands in the small adjacent bathroom, he notices the water is a nasty carrot color and has a sour smell. Outside, the rain and a sharp sound of hammering greet him. Metal walkways, like the ones he once saw in Venice used for *aqua alta,* are being assembled around the hospital in rickety successions. Behind the building, the river level has risen even higher, while workers surrounded by machinery pump the water away from the building's foundation.

Linden turns his back to the Seine and walks toward Montparnasse. All he can think of, all he can see, are his father's eyes.

Tilia bombards him with questions. Can he tell the whole story over again? When and how did Paul react, exactly? What do the doctors say? What's going to happen now? Patiently, Linden reminds her the hospital is being emptied; the staff is feverishly busy. He's to go there tomorrow at seven for the transfer. He doesn't know what the doctors think. Tilia strides around her room, limping, irritated. Shouldn't Linden be trying to find out? What the hell is he doing? Mistral tries to soothe her, but she brushes her daughter off. Linden knows by the expression on Tilia's face that they're heading for a conflict. Well, then, why doesn't Tilia go to the hospital herself to talk to the medical team? He knows perfectly well this sentence will infuriate her, and he gets ready for the retaliation. Strangely, it doesn't come. Instead, Tilia drops down on the side of her bed. What about Paul's treatment? What are the doctors giving him? Does Linden at least know that? He ignores the caustic tone in her voice. Medication has been the subject to avoid with his sister ever since her accident. She harbors profound skepticism about doctor's prescriptions. It had been complicated enough getting her to approve of the treatment Lauren was receiving for her pneumonia. Tilia staunchly believes in natural solutions for all health problems. She views any kind of pill and capsule as noxious, and works her way around them. Linden launches forth firmly. Can she not see their parents are in a situation where they cannot be healed by fringe medicine and stuff with plants? There is no more time for this. Paul has had a stroke and Lauren is fighting pneumonia. Does Tilia really believe a couple of herbal pick-me-ups and honey drops will do the trick? She can't be serious! If she is unable to set foot in the hospital for her own personal reasons, then she must leave this up to him. He will deal with it. His voice rings out, fiercer than he expected. Tilia's face convulses; he braces himself for the onslaught. To his surprise, Tilia does not hit back with a spiteful string of words. Instead, she seems to shrivel up, hangs her head, and sobs, face squashed between her palms. His sister, his impetuous, vociferous, opinionated, frank (and sometimes utterly tactless) sister is crying her heart out. Linden, thunderstruck, can only look on. When is the last time he saw her weep? He can't remember. He was the crybaby when they were children. She was the one who soothed him when he fell from his bicycle, when he had a nightmare. Tilia never cried. She was the tough one. He watches Mistral wrap her slender arms around her mother. He does not know what to say, so he shuts up, torn between remorse and anger. Tilia gazes up at him, her face flushed and swollen, blotched with tears.

"You'll never understand. No one can. No one can ever understand."

Linden exchanges a cautious glance with Mistral. He wonders what his sister means. What is it they can't understand? Why is she crying? Is it to do with their parents? Is it something else? She's such a mystery, this sister of his. She camouflages everything behind her loudness, her uncouth language, her vulgar puns. She makes people roar with laughter, she's the life and soul of parties, and yet she can occasionally be heartless, as long as everyone laughs at her jokes. Does Mistral have a clue about what's going on? He questions his niece silently, raising his eyebrows. She shakes her head back at him. Linden sits on the floor, directly below his sister, who's perched on the bed. He puts a hand on Tilia's knee.

"Why don't you explain, then? Why don't you tell us?"

Tilia moans that she can't. It's too difficult to describe; besides, she wouldn't know where to begin. Mistral makes her lean back on the bed, cradling her mother's head in her lap. Her voice is appeasing, so adultlike, Linden can't help being impressed. Tilia's breathing is less ragged as Mistral gently wipes the last tears away. Silence fills the room. Linden waits, cross-legged. His mind flies to room 24, to the relief he felt when Paul opened his eyes. The hope has taken over his fear. Should he let it? Would it not be better to protect himself from bad news, from hearing his father might never recover? He desperately needs hope to cling to, to keep him going. If he can't do this, then he will not be able to face tomorrow, his father's crooked features, the tubes in his nose and arm. He needs to keep up his strength, his courage. How long can he do this for? How long can he pretend to be strong? And then, there's his mother. For the moment, she's weakened by her illness, but what will happen when she's back on her feet? How will she deal with her husband's condition? Will she collapse? Will she be brave? He can't tell. Tilia jolts him back to the present moment. Her voice is toneless, subdued. She stares up at the ceiling, her fingers laced together on her chest, Mistral's hand stroking her hair. He pays attention, leans forward. She's never told anyone what she is going to say now. She's not even sure she can choose the right words; they'll just have to be patient. She pauses, takes a deep breath, and then continues. They were five best friends. Five young girls at the start of their lives. Twenty-five years old. Such promise in each of them: Laurence, Valentine, Sylvie, Sonia, and herself. Valentine was the one getting married that summer. She was dainty and blond, with curly hair and blue eyes. It was to celebrate her upcoming wedding that they'd organized a hen party for her. Her fiancé was Pierre, a handsome guy from Saint-Jean-de-Luz. Pierre worked in a real estate agency and Valentine was a medical assistant. Sylvie was the wild one of the lot, the most unpredictable. She worked in a department store in Biarritz. She wasn't pretty, exactly, but men liked her—a lot. Her love affairs were fascinating to listen to. Sonia was dark, quiet, with pale skin. The intellectual. She never went to the beach, never sat in the sun. She read a book a day. She was about to move to Paris; she'd just landed a new job with a well-known magazine. She had a boyfriend, too, Diego, who was from San Sebastián.

And then there was Laurence, who lived in Bordeaux and who came from a family of prestigious vintners. Laurence was tall and beautiful, and compassionate. She knew how to listen. She knew how to hold your hand if you were down. Tilia met the four of them during her first summer in Biarritz, when she moved there in 1998 to be with Eric. She was the only one of them who had a four-and-a-half-year-old daughter, and a husband, but it didn't make her feel any different from the rest of them. They were her friends, and they knew everything about her. They knew her love for painting, for creating. They knew she had made up her mind to live a new life in the Basque country at nineteen, away from where she'd grown up; they knew she'd gotten pregnant, had her daughter at twenty; they knew about her marriage to Eric, how in the beginning it seemed easy. In the beginning, everything always seems easy, doesn't it? Eric gave all his attention to his restaurant, and it worked out, as the place gained fame year after year. But the marriage was not working out, and her friends knew it. They comforted her; they helped her. It wasn't entirely Eric's fault. It was also her fault. She was so young then. There were so many things she didn't understand. Tilia pauses for a long time. When she speaks again, her voice has more power to it. She isn't going to talk to her brother and daughter about her first marriage. They mustn't get her wrong. She wants to talk about the girls. About that night. About that hideous night. This is the first time in fifteen years that she will talk about it. And if she is able to do so, to manage to get all the words out and not collapse, then perhaps they'll be able to understand. She can't remember who chose the restaurant in Arcangues. The first plan had been a tapas bar in Hondarribia, a place they'd already been to, the five of them, and that they enjoyed. But this was a special event, a festive one, and it had to be different. It had to be memorable. Tilia's voice falters. They had dressed up in crinolines and rhinestone diadems for the occasion. She can't look at those photographs, the ones that were printed in the press after the accident. The girls looked stunning, her dearest friends, in their finery, with their hair done, their shimmering makeup. They were princesses. They were queens. There had been much wine, excellent wine; Laurence had taken care of that. They drank freely because they knew there was a driver, a professional guy they had hired to drive them back into town in a minivan. No one was worried about liquor, not even Sylvie, who constantly got tipsy. They were safe. They felt safe. They were having the time of their lives. The restaurant let them stay late, played their favorite music: Usher, Black Eyed Peas, Alicia Keys. It was a hot, balmy evening; Tilia remembers that clearly. August 1, 2004. It was so ridiculous, dancing in a crinoline! Mischievous Sylvie ended up taking hers off, gyrating to Beyoncé in her lace undies and stilettos, to the staff's and other patrons' delight. How they'd laughed! They'd howled with laughter, hugging one another, swearing with yet another raised glass that they'd never lose touch, never forget their friendship, that they'd still meet up when they were old, gray grannies. But that was so far away, in another galaxy! They had their entire lives to live.

Tilia halts. Her trembling hands cover her face like a mask. Linden and Mistral do not move. The only sound is the gush of the rain against the pane and voices outside in the corridor. Suddenly, the telephone rings by the side of the bed, making them all jump. Mistral answers it. She nods, murmurs a few words, then hangs up. Linden asks her who it was. She whispers that it's not important. When Tilia speaks again, she sounds breathless. It happened just before the minivan turned left into the last stretch of the road that led to Biarritz. The radio was on full blast; they were singing. Singing at the top of their lungs to a song she could never listen to ever again without wanting to break down. "Dancing Queen," by ABBA. The kind of crappy stuff their mothers listened to, but that night, at that moment, it was perfect, and it was *them;* they were the dancing queens, brimming over with lust for life. She can see them now, in the back of the car, crinolines bunched over their knees, windows open, the sweet night air pouring in. It was late, and who cared? They would sleep tomorrow. It was still with her; it was still there. The sound of it. The unbearable, ghastly noise of it: the violent crunch of steel, the earsplitting shattering of glass.

Her heart in her mouth, her stomach lurching like on a roller coaster as the car was flung up into the air, carved apart as easily as a blade slicing into a mellow fruit. Just a couple of seconds, that's all it took, and then silence. Even Abba was quashed. Tilia did not lose consciousness right away. Was she upside down? Was that the sky she was staring up at? The Big Dipper? She couldn't work out the bewildering topography around her. Her ears were humming with a muffled, yammering clamor. Her skin felt gluey, grimy. All she could see was hair, endless swirls of black hair, blond hair, curly hair, strands of hair fuzzing up her line of vision. Why was there so much of it? What had the girls done to their hair? She became aware of the stench: her own vomit, trailing down her chin and décolletage, leaving an acrimonious wake in her mouth, and then another smell, much more fearful, a tinny, meaty odor that seemed to delve into her. At first, she could not understand what it was, yet it seemed oddly familiar. And then she knew. It was the smell of fresh blood. She turned her head, moaning with pain, and there was Valentine's face, right up next to hers, against her shoulder, resting there, as if she were asleep. How gray her friend's skin seemed, how sunken her cheeks looked. Tilia had moved her arm, gritting her teeth in agony, slowly bringing a quaking hand up to stroke Valentine's skin in a comforting gesture. They were going to be all right, weren't they? They were going to be fine. Just fine. All of them.

Tilia's voice is almost a shriek now, a strangled wail. Linden finds it increasingly hard to listen. Part of him wants to get out of the room now, but he cannot do that. He cannot let his sister down. Tilia says she pressed her hand on Valentine's cheek, and all of a sudden, Valentine seemed to tumble forward into Tilia's knees, in a rush of matted curls. The sickening truth hit Tilia like a fist. What lay in her lap was Valentine's head. Just her head. Severed clean from her body. How long did Tilia lie there, screaming for help, in the mass of hair and blood? It seemed forever. Something black was creeping up on her, a dark and monstrous force, working its way up her legs, her waist, her chest. Glacial and stealthy, it snaked around her throat, clamping her mouth shut so she could scarcely breathe.

She tried to fight it, but it was weighing down on her eyelids, forcing her into an obscure lake, pulling her underwater. She gave in to it; she let the water close over her head. She thought it was death. When Tilia regained consciousness, she was in the hospital, in Bayonne, where she was to spend the next six months. The doctors didn't tell her at first. They didn't say the girls were all dead, that so was their chauffeur, as well as the inebriated man who'd plowed into them. They didn't tell her the girls had all been buried days after the accident. She had no idea of the time slipping by, that she'd been here for months. She didn't recognize her husband, her little girl, her parents, her brother. She didn't know the doctors had had to reconstruct most of her left leg and her hip; she wasn't aware yet that she'd never walk properly again. They gave her powerful painkillers, stuff that knocked her out. She slept day in, day out. She was kept in a woozy penumbra that imprisoned her. When her mind started working properly again, months later, she was told. She took in what had happened, and the shock drove her crazy. Why her? Why them, and not her? Why had all her friends died? Why had she been the one left behind? The only one? Wrath overcame her. Never had she been so angry. She screamed and yelled so much, they had to pin her down and give her more drugs. She spat the pills out, spat in their faces until they tied her up and fed her the medication through her veins. When she left the hospital for a medical center in Bidart for her physiotherapy, she was still furious. Stuck in a wheelchair, she couldn't drive anywhere. Her only joy was little Mistral, who, at nearly five, seemed to understand more than anyone else what she was going through. Tilia tenderly reaches out to caress her daughter's face. "Magic Mistral," that was her nickname then, remember? It was thanks to Mistral that she was slowly able to mend her body but also her mind. A year later, when she managed to hobble around on crutches, and drive again, she went to visit the girls' families, their boyfriends. They were all kind to her, but it made her feel even worse. How could they possibly lay eyes on her? She was the one who'd survived, the one who was still there, while their lovely daughters were no more. She went to the four graves, one after the other, alone, laden with flowers. She went to the spot where the accident happened. There was a large black splotch on the road that made her shiver. Then she did a very stupid thing. She looked up the accident online. It was another shock. Valentine's decapitation was mentioned in each article, as if no one could get enough of it. She saw grisly images of the minivan, a tangled mesh of crushed steel, with the large chunk of a red station wagon still rammed obscenely into it. She learned the drunk driver's name, learned he'd been on his way back from a nightclub. Thirty-six years old, divorced, two kids. Their chauffeur was fifty-two, married, and had three children and five grandchildren. What hurt the most were the photographs of each girl, her childhood, her teenage years: gleeful Sylvie on Côte des Basques beach with her surfboard; Sonia's class photo, a lovable bookworm with glasses; Laurence busy in the vineyard; Valentine and Pierre, about to get married, clasped in each other's arms at Miramar beach; as well as the final shots of that evening. Where had the press gotten those? The families, she supposed. The families had given the photos to the press. She recognized more from Facebook. She would stare at those photographs with all her might until her eyes ached, until her head hurt. Each of them bore a dreadful finality, an ineluctable countdown that none of them had ever guessed at, that none of them had ever felt. She despised the lurid headlines: TRAGIC BEAUTIES; DEATH OF YOUNG DANCING QUEENS; CARNAGE ON THE ROAD TO ARCANGUES; FOUR YOUNG GIRLS KILLED BY DRUNK DRIVER. And then the ones concerning her: TILIA, THE SURVIVOR; YOUNG MOTHER SURVIVES HORRIFIC CRASH. Two years after the accident, she realized how much of a survivor she indeed was, but how scarred she remained, both physically and mentally. She never told anyone; she preferred to keep it secret, buried inside. She got on with her life. In 2008 she divorced Eric and moved to London with eight-year-old Mistral to start again. She gave art lessons in a Franco-British school. Everyone thought she was over the ordeal, but no, she wasn't. She had nightmares, horrible ones, of Valentine's head falling in her lap. She refused to take the medicine she had been given by the doctors. When she married Colin, in 2010, she thought she could put it all behind her, at last. She thought she could depend on someone strong, on an older man who would protect her. How wrong she was. They all know what being married to Colin entails. So here she is, nearly forty, an emotional wreck, a failed artist, the miserable wife of a drunkard, incapable of going to see her ailing father in the hospital because of her hang-ups.

Tilia begins to laugh, a harsh, sardonic snicker that rises up in the room, startling them. She rocks back and forth on the bed, head thrown back, and after a while, Linden can't make out if she's laughing or crying. The pressure of Tilia's revelations bears down on him. He can't hear anymore. The laughter digs into his ears. He gets to his feet. He gives his sister and his niece warm hugs, murmurs that yes, he does understand, that he feels for Tilia, that it is a dreadful story, and he leaves. The idea of going up to his cramped attic room, with the patter of the rain for company, dissuades him. For a while, he leans against the passageway wall, his mind racing. The images conjured by his sister distress him. He can't seem to get them out of his mind. When he visits his mother, a little later, he finds her being tended to by a kind nurse, who informs him Madame Malegarde is doing better but needs to rest some more. Down in the reception area, Linden is surprised to see how late it is, nearly five, and how fast the daylight is fading, settling into a grayish gloom.

In the lobby, an elegant figure wearing a fedora hat, its brim damp with rain, rises and greets him with an outstretched hand.

"My dear fellow. I've been waiting here for ages! I asked them to ring Tilia's room, but they couldn't get through."

The unmistakable crisp British accent. Colin Favell, his brother-in-law.

◦❦◦

Colin suggests the Rosebud bar, a few doors down from the hotel on rue Delambre. It looks like a décor from a 1930s movie, with white-jacketed bartenders, vintage jazz music, and dim lighting.

Clients cluster over daiquiris and murmur to each other. Colin sits at the zinc-surfaced bar and places his hat cautiously on the empty stool next to him. He is clean-shaven, wearing a perfectly cut navy blue suit, white shirt, maroon tie, and polished shoes. He complains, peevishly, that Tilia hasn't been answering his calls. Most annoying. The last time they did speak, yesterday, ever so briefly, she had said snappily not to come to Paris. Downright rude, wasn't she? After all, Paul is his father-in-law, for Christ's sake. Why shouldn't he come to Paris? Why shouldn't he be here with the rest of the family? Linden remembers with uneasiness Colin's ancient grudge against his parents, who had not hailed Tilia's marriage to him with much enthusiasm eight years ago—especially Lauren, who seemed to have intuitively predicted the difficulties ahead. Their relationship had been strained ever since the start, and Colin's drinking problem had increased the tension. In the beginning, Linden hadn't been unduly alarmed about Colin's penchant for alcohol. His brother-in-law appeared to be the quiet sort, downing his drinks discreetly but furiously fast at family gatherings, and his inebriety was only detected when he turned into the limp, drooling buffoon who had to be heaved home yet again by a seething Tilia. At that time, Linden and his parents had chosen to look away, not to mention it to Tilia. The subject was taboo, and even more so when, at Lauren's recent sixtieth birthday dinner, in a West End London restaurant, Colin had turned up exquisitely dressed and utterly drunk. Once seated at the table, Colin had become uncomfortably garrulous, talking only of himself, of his marital intimacy, the number of times a month they had intercourse, in which position, what Tilia enjoyed, what she didn't. After twenty minutes of Tilia's sitting there stony-faced, with Paul, Lauren, and Mistral gaping at one another in mute agony, Linden had gotten up, a broad counterfeit smile on his face, and he had said to Colin genially: Wouldn't it be a good idea if Colin and he just left the table for a minute or two and popped outside? It was so hot in here, wasn't it? Colin's face was brick-colored, almost orange. Surprisingly, he let himself be led away by Linden, sprawled over his shoulder as if they were best friends. Once they were on the sidewalk, Linden had hailed a taxi to Clarendon Road, heaved Colin in with him, found his key in his pocket, asked the taxi to wait, dragged him upstairs, placed him on his bed, where he began to snore, and went back to the restaurant. The whole thing took thirty minutes. Does Colin remember this episode? Linden wonders.

"Well, old fellow, what'll it be?"

Colin makes a gesture toward the bartenders. Linden shrugs good-naturedly and says it'll be a Coke. Colin shrugs back and orders a French 75. They do these properly here; they always get the gin and champagne mix just right. Sure Linden doesn't want one? Linden shakes his head and points out loudly and clearly that he thought Colin wasn't drinking. He had never talked to his brother-in-law directly about his alcoholism, not even after Lauren's birthday. He had always held back, out of courtesy, embarrassment, or perhaps lack of courage. Colin rolls pale blue eyes at him, taking him in slowly. A grin bares his wolflike teeth. Aha, so has darling wifey been getting to him? So, that means she's angry with him, that's why she hasn't been answering his calls, she's got herself properly worked up, then, has she? Foolish girl. Linden doesn't answer, gazing back at him levelly. Colin swallows the cocktail in one gulp, smacking his lips, and orders another with a brisk signal. He sends a smug glance Linden's way, thumps him on the shoulder. Linden should stop acting so edgy. Colin can quit when he wants, does Linden know that? He can stop just like that; he clicks his fingers at Linden's face. Tilia gives him such a hard time; she's a real pain in the you know what. He's not a boozer, just a normal chap who likes to get sloshed from time to time. Takes his mind off things, helps him relax, so he can put up with the asinine pack he works with, all those wankers he can't bear. People like Linden's parents, for example, who hate him deep down. When he drinks, he doesn't care if he has to bow and scrape, he doesn't feel anything anymore; he just gets the job done. Does Linden have any idea of what working in the art world means? The embezzlements, the colluding, the coercions? It may sound electrifying, evaluating a decrepit old lord's dusty heirloom and discovering it's worth thousands of pounds, but that doesn't happen much. Most of his job is considering junk that's worth crap and telling people courteously— people who then switch from affable to antagonistic in the bat of an eyelid and kick him out of the door. No wonder he ends up plastered at the nearest pub. Not every evening, however. Everyone drinks. Everyone has a little nip once in a while. What's wrong with that? He's not doing anyone any harm, is he? He doesn't beat his wife up. He doesn't get drunk that often. He pulls it off—just look at him. He's always groomed, elegant. He's careful about his breath. Nothing a little mint spray can't deal with. Tilia paints the whole thing black. So do Paul and Lauren, who obviously see him as a villain. His first wife was certainly less of a crashing bore. But anyway, he's not here to spill the beans about his floundering marriage, is he? He's here for Paul. No matter what Paul really thinks of him. As soon as Colin got the text message from Tilia on Sunday, explaining the situation, he wanted to come. He had to call his wife five times before she even picked up the bloody phone. Got on the Eurostar first thing. He didn't even warn Tilia. She had said not to come, after all. The cheek of actually saying that to him! So he arrived at the Gare du Nord, waited for hours for a taxi in the bloody rain, came straight to the hotel. Then he sat there for ages, going out of his mind with boredom, waiting for his wife to come down. She never did, right? Apparently, she told the receptionist she was resting. Resting, my foot! Sulking is more like it. It was a bit of a bother getting tickets; he had to prove he wasn't a tourist, not staying in a hotel, but coming to see his family. Good friends are putting him up for the night, and thankfully they live in the dry neighborhood of Ternes. So, how is Paul? What's up? Can Linden tell him?

The jazz tune, slightly too loud, tinkles around them. Linden gives Colin the information he has concerning his father. He doesn't mention the hospital transfer in the morning. Probably because the last thing he wants is his brother-in-law tagging along. Colin listens, nods, makes a face when he hears about Lauren's pneumonia, and orders a bottle of Chablis, guzzling glass after glass as if it were mineral water. His hands are less steady and his diction, although still poised, is at times slurred. The more he drinks, the more he talks. There's no stopping him. Linden, powerless, endures the monologue. As usual, Colin rambles on about his conjugal situation. Linden has the impression he is trapped in their bedroom at Clarendon Road. He can almost behold the gold-and-green Albemarle wallpaper, the snowy white carpet, the floral bedspread. Nothing is spared him. According to Colin, Tilia has the libido of a hibernating dormouse, rolled up in a ball as soon as dusk falls, snoring to high heaven. She won't make an effort; she simply will not understand that her husband has needs. And he certainly has needs, like any bloke. He may be coming to the end of his fifties, but there is no question of using Viagra. He gets it up every time. Doesn't need bloody Viagra. Colin raises his upper arm, fist clenched, to conjure marmoreal manhood. Two young women enter, raincoats shiny with rain. Colin, slouched over the bar, observes them with a lewd grin. Ah, just his type of Parisienne. The dark-haired one, just the thing, isn't she? Steamy little number, that one. He claps his hand down on Linden's shoulder, startling him, whooping with hilarity. Good Lord, he almost forgot! Linden couldn't care less, could he? He's not into girls. Girls leave him cold, don't they? Linden watches while his brother-in-law writhes with laughter. Colin wipes away mock tears, his cheeks glowing a vivid red. He must get this straight, right away, he has nothing against Linden, or against any poof, for that matter, but he simply can't understand how a man cannot be attracted to a woman. It puzzles him, it really does. How is it that a pair of tits does nothing for Linden? It's mystifying. Because desiring women is precisely what makes a man feel virile, right? Colin's voice is loud enough for each person in the bar to hear. How long can Linden sit there and pretend this is not annoying him? How long can he keep that stiff grin pasted on his lips? Colin continues, undeterred. Must be so strange being a pansy. He would have hated to be one. Thank God neither of his sons is! Would have preferred a son in a wheelchair to a gay son. Oh, come on, he's just being funny! It was meant to be a *joke*! Honestly, Linden should take that expression off his face and get a sense of humor, for Christ's sake.

"Shut the fuck up, will you?"

Colin gapes at him with red-rimmed eyes and hoots outright, nearly falling off his stool. Oh, so there is something to him, then. What a relief! Linden Malegarde at last loses his temper, pretty Mr. Cool, who never seems out of breath, with never a hair out of place, who jet-sets around the world, photographing movie stars and politicians. Well, obviously there is more to him than meets the eye! How spiffing it is that Linden is no mealymouthed wuss. What about a toast to that? Linden, fed up, is already on his way out, tossing a couple of bills on the bar. He is relieved to be out of the place, away from Colin and the conversation. He doesn't mind the rain, offering his hot cheeks to its icy pricking.

Turning right, Linden walks down rue Delambre to the boulevard. He crosses over to the other side, in front of La Rotonde. A little farther on, he stops at Le Select. He hasn't been to this brasserie for years. He finds a seat, orders a glass of Bordeaux and a club sandwich. Then he sends a text message to his sister, telling her her husband is in Paris, at the Rosebud bar, next door. He hasn't the heart to inform her about Colin's deplorable state. Tilia writes back. Yes, she knows. The receptionist informed her that her husband had asked for her. She doesn't want to see him just yet. She'll do that in the morning. She and Mistral will be having dinner with Lauren in her room. Would he like to join them? No, he'll hang around Montparnasse for a while, eat something, answer some emails, and relax. He has to get up early for the hospital transfer, remember? He won't be back late.

Linden looks around at the busy main room, its yellowish moldings and stucco, its square tables with their wooden surfaces scratched by the patina of years. Regular customers sit at the bar, facing the glittering array of bottles set against mirrored shelves. He used to meet Candice here, when he lived on rue Broca. He remembers how she used to rush in, blond and sleek in her black gabardine, face lighting up when she saw him. It was a kir for her, a glass of Saint Emilion for him. He has very few photographs of Candy. She hated being photographed. After her death, he went through his archives frenetically, pulling up every image that had to do with her. He hoarded them, even if it was torture to lay eyes on her graceful features. His favorite was the one of her in the kitchen, with morning sunlight streaming in from the window, igniting her hair and outlining the steam from her cup of tea. She was wearing a red kimono, her splayed hand delicately holding a book open. He had crept up on her as she was reading and had taken the picture just as she glanced up in surprise when the floorboards creaked. Her death weighs on him still, a burden of pain and guilt that, he knows, will not lift. Coming here tonight brings her back, resurrects the happy epoch of their cohabitation. She was perhaps, along with Sacha, the one who knew him the best. It always saddens him to think Sacha and Candice never met.

His phone vibrates with a new incoming message. It's Oriel, asking how he is. He realizes he never answered the text message she sent him yesterday morning. He calls her, and she answers him immediately. Yes, he's still around. His father had a stroke on Saturday evening, in the middle of the anniversary dinner, and is at the Pompidou hospital, which will be emptied tomorrow morning because of the inundations. They're not sure yet about his state. Oriel sounds stunned. With empathy and sensitivity, she says she hopes his father will pull through, and what bad luck about the evacuation. The reason she texted him was because she has an interesting proposal for him. Tomorrow afternoon, she will be accompanying her friend Matthieu, from the city hall, on a boat around the flooded Javel district, in the fifteenth arrondissement. She has managed to secure a pass and a badge for Linden, so that he has a place on the boat, and can take photos. The meeting point is at place Cambronne, at two o'clock. Can he make it? Yes, he wants to see this. Depending on his father's condition, he will gladly join them. He thanks her. Is he aware of how some streets are already totally submersed? He's seen them on TV, but he imagines it's probably awfully different in real life. That's right, she says. It is. And she adds it is a shock.

They talk for a little longer while he savors the wine. Out of the corner of his eye, he observes a young man sitting in the banquette opposite him, on the other side of the room. He is in his late twenties, with a pale complexion, short black hair, and huge horn-rimmed glasses. The young man's dark eyes have not lifted once from Linden's face. He can feel the pressure of his gaze like warmth settling on his skin. When he hangs up with Oriel, the black eyes are still fixed upon him, and now there is a slight smile hovering over the well-drawn mouth. Linden looks away, down at his phone. It's a rousing game. He's played it before, but never since Sacha came into his life. Linden is not into one-night stands, painful vestiges of his adolescence. However tempting, he won't glance back at the far corner. After a while, the young man gets up, slips into a coat, not looking his way once. As he passes Linden with studied insouciance, he drops a piece of paper on the table and darts out of the revolving doors without a backward glance. On it, Linden discovers a mobile number and a name. Smiling, he crumples the scrap of paper up. He sends a text message to Sacha: *Just got picked up at a Montparnasse bar by a cutie.*

Sacha's response is instantaneous: *AND??*

And nothing. I miss you. I love you. I want to be in your arms. I can't stand going through all this without you. I can't stand flooded, rainy Paris, this family situation, and your not being here.

Sacha calls him, right there and then, and just hearing his voice fills Linden with relief and joy.

FIVE

❧

Sous le pont Mirabeau coule la Seine
Et nos amours
Faut-il qu'il m'en souvienne
La joie venait toujours après la peine
—GUILLAUME APOLLINAIRE, "LE PONT MIRABEAU"

There are many things about that day I've forgotten. But other things I see clearly, so clearly. We ate the picnic and she wiped crumbs from my lips with a napkin. She said I had lovely eyes. She said women would fall in love with me when I was grown up because my eyes were so blue. It made me blush, but it also made me happy. I felt for her all the love a four-year-old could muster, and the last thing I wanted was to grow up.

Those golden afternoons were the highlight of my summer. I put aside my grandfather's death. I wasn't worried about my mother having another baby. The only thing that counted was Suzanne. My afternoons with Suzanne.

We used to play hide-and-seek. We would go no farther than the last trees, our boundary. But the trees were planted close together and were so thickly leaved that the space beneath them was a green labyrinth you could easily get lost in. Behind which tree was Suzanne hiding? I could never tell. It was my favorite game. I was good at slipping out and flitting from trunk to trunk while she called for me. I was thrilled when she couldn't find me and got anxious.

I held my breath and waited, shivers of delight running up and down my spine while she shouted my name.

I waited until the last minute, until her voice became desperate, until I could tell she was really beginning to worry, and then I'd spring out like a jack-in-the-box, yelling at the top of my lungs. She would cry out with relief and come running to me.

The best part was when she hugged me with all her might, half-scolding me, and I felt her skin against mine and the caress of her hair.

The day it happened, I was the one hiding.

I chose the biggest tree, the ancient one in the middle, with the very thick trunk. I remember closing my eyes and hearing her count to twenty.

And then there was silence.

O N TUESDAY MORNING, LINDEN has an early breakfast at
one of the cafés on place Edgar-Quinet before he goes to the
hospital. It is still dark outside, and the rain teems down, unremit-
ting. He watches the news on a large screen above the counter. Half
of Paris is submerged. Thousands of Parisians have no electricity,
no heating, no landlines. Families with small children, as well as
the elderly, are now being sheltered in churches, theaters, concert
halls, as there is no more room in gymnasiums and schools. The
Red Cross is asking for help and donations; the army is sending in
more troops. The government is under fire, and no party seems to
have a better solution, despite constant backbiting and criticism.
The bitter-cold temperature does not help. Petrol is being rationed;
the gathering of refuse in the deluged streets is an increasing
problem. Garbage-processing plants have been inundated, as well.
Parked cars threatened by the overflow are removed hourly by the
prefecture and sent to police impounds in dry areas out of the city.
Traffic is halted in almost every arrondissement; colleges and schools
are closed. Jussieu University, near the river, has been flooded.
The heliport situated at Issy-les-Moulineaux, just outside Paris, sits
under a meter of water. On quai François-Mauriac, the Bibliothèque
nationale, repository of all that is published in France, is fighting a
losing battle with the Seine. The river is still rising, greedily. If
this goes on, Parisians must expect the worst. Over a million of

them will be directly concerned. Thousands of cellars, basements, businesses, and homes will be damaged. Linden and most of the bleary-eyed customers listen in glum stillness. On the screen, a historian in his late forties explains that in 1910, people lived otherwise. They didn't depend so much on communications and transport. Horses and carriages were able to face the floods, unlike cars, with easily swamped engines. Back then, many Parisians still used petrol or alcohol lamps, and lit fires in their chimneys to keep warm. That helped during the great flood. Today, in a world governed by electricity, the situation is quite different. A century ago, people were kinder to one another, the historian explains. They watched out for their neighbors; they made sure everyone was dry and safe. Solidarity ruled, and this, sadly, is no longer true in our modern selfish world, he points out.

When Linden gets to place Balard, he is startled by the amount of water in the streets compared to the day before. A wide black lagoon circles the building. Streetlamps are no longer functioning. Searchlights fixed on nearby army vans light up the area with harsh, glaring strands. Pockets of light pick out the undulation of the mounting water. The glass façade of the hospital seems ghostly, illuminated from within by the feeble bluish glow of emergency lights. Dozens of military personnel encompass the sector, adding tension to the scene. Clearly, Plan Neptune is in full deployment. The only way in is by crossing the elevated metal sidewalks. Linden takes his turn in the queue, under the rain. It is a long, drawn-out process. Some people are rejected by the patrol and have to turn back along the unsteady passage. There is barely enough room for two to stand abreast on the iron strips at the same time. One woman nearly slips into the water and is caught at the last moment by a soldier wearing a rubber-coated dry suit. Linden is asked to produce the sheet of paper proving his father's transfer. He says he never received one. The officer replies he won't be able to enter the hospital. No paper, no entry. Usually, in this kind of situation, Linden remains calm. His tone is always polite; his voice never rises. He is not the one with the bad temper in the Malegarde family. But this morning, confronted with the man's unpleasant, churlish demeanor, something inside him snaps. His emotions are no longer kept in check; they leap up like avid flames. Linden yells at the man at the top of his lungs. Who the hell does this guy think he is? His father had a stroke, he might die, he needs to be transferred to another hospital, and because no one sent him the paper, he's not allowed in? Is he hearing properly? Is this really what's going on? Linden rarely uses his height as a weapon; he's often embarrassed of being so tall, towering above others. This morning, his powerful stature and furious voice do the trick: The guard recoils and lets him pass. The outburst leaves a new, tearing sensation in Linden's chest, as if something had forced its way through him.

The sight that greets him when he enters the vast entry hall of the hospital takes him by surprise. The floor is entirely covered by rolling brown water; bits of garbage—plastic bottles, newspapers, carrier bags—bob up and down on its greasy surface. Wooden trestles and planks are lined up on one corner, creating an extended makeshift platform, on which Linden finds a cramped spot. Soldiers with lights strapped to their heads wade through waist-high muck, maneuvering pneumatic dinghies. The din of small waves slapping against the walls is broken by voices shouting out names. The rotten, decaying smell is stronger then yesterday; added to it is the overpowering stench of brimming sewers. As more and more people take their places on the wobbly podium, Linden can feel anxiety mounting. The wait is uncomfortable and endless. Dawn begins to break with a timid gray radiance. Two men curse, elbowing each other, while a woman begs them to remain calm. She is told to shut up. Another one is in tears and no one consoles her. A soldier warns the guard at the entrance, asks him to stop sending more folks through, or the whole structure will give in. Farther on, from a flight of stairs away from the wetness, medical teams transfer invalids from stretchers into dinghies, a long and complex procedure. Some are in wheelchairs, and it seems easier for those. A young woman by Linden's side gasps at every movement, hiding her face behind her hands. He wishes she would stop; her attitude is nerve-racking. He, too, feels anxious seeing how perilous the operations are; one false move and the patient could be tipped into the dirty water.

Above the commotion, Linden somehow catches the name Paul Malegarde and raises his arm. A doctor signals back to him, and he recognizes Brunel. How are they going to get Paul down those stairs and into the boat? And what about the rain outside? Linden sees the stretcher being heaved painstakingly down the stairs by four men. Then he notices that his father, eyes closed, with drip and oxygen in place, is ensconced within an ingenious man-size Pyrex container that looks like a glass sarcophagus. It must weigh a ton. Uneasily, he watches the casket being carefully inclined, an inch at time, and positioned into the dinghy with the help of three soldiers struggling in the water. The entire performance takes twenty minutes. The deed is at last done and Linden heaves a sigh of relief. He is told to step into a large rowboat, which is to follow his father. Behind him, on the platform, others complain. And what about them? Why is no one taking care of their sick ones? Why him, and not them? They've been waiting here for a long time, and then this guy gets all the attention. It's not fair! Linden grasps the gloved hand stretched out to him and steps into the boat.

"Ignore them," mutters Dr. Brunel, who is in the boat, as well. "Your father's transfer is our priority this morning. Everyone will be taken care of. They're worrying for nothing. Are you ready for the rain now? And the press?" he adds sarcastically.

A soldier rows the boat out of the building as the rain slams down onto them. Abundant cameras click and film the event from elevated metal sidewalks while police keep journalists at bay. Some of them, spotting a doctor in a white jacket seated in the boat, shout out, trying to attract his attention. Dr. Brunel explains that many people believe the hospital has been vacated too late. The rain flattens his fine hair. He goes on to say that no one had any idea the Seine would rise so fast. Does Linden know that presently it is going up two centimeters per hour? The Assistance publique, which runs all national public hospitals, is being severely criticized. Linden glimpses his father's dinghy ahead, towed by soldiers guiding it up to the dry land beyond boulevard Victor. He sees people peering down at the bizarre procession from balconies and windows. Part of him is itching to take photos. He left his camera behind.

Just before they reach place de la Porte-de-Versailles, the water has thinned out; they are able to step onto the sidewalk. Ambulances wait, lined up, with groups of doctors and nurses under umbrellas. Linden follows Dr. Brunel, nimbly darting through the crowd. Six firefighters lift Paul's glass sarcophagus straight to an open medical van. Paul's eyes are still closed; his skin seems pale in the morning light. Dr. Brunel greets the nurses and doctors in attendance, says a few sentences, and the others nod their heads. Yes, they are all from Professor Magerant's team. They are ready for the transfer to Cochin Hospital. Dr. Brunel turns to Linden, introducing him. Linden will be riding with his father to the hospital. Then he extends his hand with a smile; he says it has been an honor tending to Paul Malegarde, and he wishes Linden all the best for his father. Paul will be in good hands; of that, Linden must be certain. As the van moves away with father and son on board, Dr. Brunel fades away, arm lifted in a gesture of farewell. The van drives up rue Raymond-Losserand, then crosses over to avenue Denfert-Rochereau by rue Froidevaux. The fourteenth arrondissement is one of the lucky ones; it is too high up to be inundated. Queues of people line up outside cafés; Linden realizes they are there to recharge mobile phones. He hasn't yet seen with his own eyes how hard hit half of Paris is, apart from images on TV of those unfortunate families displaying apartments reduced to muddy chaos. For the moment, he is sheltered.

The entry to the hospital is situated on rue Saint-Jacques, a familiar neighborhood to Linden. He lived on nearby rue Broca for four years before moving to New York City in 2009. Cochin is an older, shabbier location, but the fact that it will never be flooded makes it feel safe. The hospital is divided into several different buildings. They are taken up to a fifth-floor wing, where Linden is told to stay. Another wait. He's been doing a lot of that these days.

Nonetheless, his job consists of waiting for the right moment. Photography is all about that—the serendipity of an instant, how the magic of it ends up in his frame. He is used to the anticipation; he has learned to become patient, but this sort of waiting is something else. The tension chews into him; he has no idea how to stop it. He walks up and down the gallery, his shoes making a squeaky noise on the linoleum. It's another hospital, but the same distasteful smell lingers. He hopes his father will have a room of his own. Around him, other people wait, as well; some are slumbering in their chairs. They all seem coated with the same doleful anguish. He probably looks like that also; how could he not, with what he's been going through? His anxiety makes him jittery; he finds it impossible to stay in his seat. Others stare resentfully at him as he paces the room, looking down at his phone. He sends the same text message to sister, mother, and niece: *In new hospital. All ok. Waiting to see new doctor.*

More emails have accumulated since yesterday; more contracts, more trips. He hasn't answered any yet. He wonders how Marlowe, Deb, and Stéphane, are coping with this. Today, Tuesday, was to be a busy day for him and his team. They were scheduled to shoot a promising young senator at her home near Boston for *Time* magazine. She had never accepted being photographed with her family, in her own house, but when she heard the photographer was Linden Malegarde, she had said yes. He had prepared the event in advance with his team; Marlowe had gone to the senator's home to check the house out. They were planning to shoot in the large, cheerful kitchen, with the senator's young children and husband. Had the session been canceled? He hadn't thought of asking his agent. Rachel probably booked another photographer at the last moment. Linden wonders how the senator felt about that. He should have written to her, and explained the situation about his father. Ever since Saturday evening and the stroke, he has shut out areas of his life that appear less important, letting them dissolve away into elements he will manage later. The only inner voices he listens to are his fear, his pain, his love for his father.

The Internet connection is lethargic, coming and going, like a flickering sunbeam. It is due to the flood. Linden heard about this eventuality on the news this morning. Little by little, Paris is becoming paralyzed. It is not happening in one go, like those sudden and spectacular devastations in the south of France, or Hurricane Sandy, in New York City back in October 2012, when the superstorm wreaked havoc with New York's waterline, an event that Linden remembers well, although he was not directly affected by it, as he was living on the Upper West Side. What is happening now is an insidious occurrence, nondramatic in its unfolding, with no human lives immediately at stake. The enemy is the stagnating water, destroying everything it invades, unhurriedly. Stone may resist, but metal corrodes, plaster disintegrates, while paper and wood rot away. Linden now knows, as most Parisians do, that the water is here to stay. When it does recede, after a crowning level that has not yet been reached, it will do so with no rush at all. The aftermath will be lingering and painful. It will take weeks, months, to return to normal. He remembers one specialist stating that Paris will be brought down to her knees.

Linden stands by a window, gazing out to a bleak, wet interior courtyard. He gets a message from Mistral, saying she is on her way. He gives her the name of the building and the floor. For some reason, the Internet connection is stronger near the glass pane. Why did he Google his father's name? Now, he's looking at all the images and links that very name pulls up. There is material he has already seen—conferences, forums, and conventions his father has attended in the past—but also new elements he is not familiar with. To his amusement, he reads that in Berkeley, California, a couple of years ago, protestors stripped naked to save eucalyptus trees about to be decimated for fire-hazard abatement. Paul was not part of that crusade, but the group claimed they did it for him, under his influence. The trees were saved. The pictures of nude, paunchy campaigners hugging trunks make Linden smile. He clicks on a recent video, duration ten minutes, titled *Paul Malegarde at Vénozan*, and plugs his earphones in. Someone following Paul around the domain

shot this with a smartphone. The result is unsteady and amateurish, and the bad connection at times freezes the scene, but it is
extraordinary to hear his father again. Cradled in his palm are the
evocative images of his family home. It's all there: the autumnal
luminance, the chirrup of the birds, the large bulk of the house, and
his father's voice, low, unmistakable. "What do the trees tell me?
Everything. They always have. Ever since I was a boy. I heard them
whispering even before I heard my parents' voices. I didn't search
for it; it just happened." Paul smiles, the rare, powerful smile Linden loves. "They found me. They spoke to me. They still do. They
tell me what lies under their roots, in the thickness of their leaves.
That's why we need trees to understand the world. Trees are living
encyclopedias. They give us all the keys." Paul is then filmed in
the arboretum. His face is tanned, glowing, a contrast to what it is
now. "My principal worry nowadays is insecticides. They are already
a disaster for bees, as everyone knows, but also for trees, which is a
lesser-known fact. Forestry management, chemicals, pesticides,
heavy machinery have degraded trees terribly. If something is not
done now, there will be no turning back. The tragedy is that people
have lost interest in trees. They take them for granted. People don't
respect trees like they used to. They treat them like objects that
automatically deliver oxygen and wood. They forget that scientists
have made incredible discoveries. Trees have a memory. They know
how to plan ahead. They know how to absorb information. They
know how to send warning signals to other trees. We've known for
a while that a forest is an intricate network that shares its data, a
place where trees care for one another, where they watch out for
one another. We now know trees connect to each other. They do
that through their roots, and through their leaves. Scientists made
all these significant discoveries quite a while ago. The problem is
that people don't attach importance to the secret lives of trees, of
how trees can help us, how they can amend our climate, our eco-
systems, but also how they can show us how to face the future. We
need to learn from them. We need to protect them because they
protect us. In this new, fast world where everything happens

instantaneously, we aren't used to waiting anymore. We have forgotten how to be patient. Everything about a tree is slow, how it
thrives, how it develops. No one really understands how slowly
trees grow and how old they become. Some trees are thousands of
years old. In fact, a tree is the exact opposite of the crazy, fast
times we live in."

Linden goes back to the beginning of the video. He can't get
enough of his father's voice; he wants to hear it all over again. Suddenly, there's a tap on his shoulder, and he turns around. A man in
his early sixties is standing there; he has astute blue eyes, a prominent nose, and an abundant patch of brown hair. He introduces
himself as Professor Gilles Magerant. Linden is shown into a large,
brightly lit office that gives on to the same shadowy courtyard.
Professor Magerant goes straight to the point. The transfer went
smoothly, but his father's condition is still under supervision. It will
be a prolonged procedure, and the professor is well aware of what
an ordeal this is for the family. As Linden no doubt knows, his
father's ischemic stroke was a thrombotic one, caused by a blood
clot in an artery of the brain. The clot blocked the blood flow, and
the urgency of the treatment was to restore the flow as quickly as
possible. That is called revascularization. However, the clot has not
totally dissolved, and it may have to be removed by an operation.
Linden nods; he read about all this online. He says he knows the
chief danger for a person who has had a stroke is to have another,
an even bigger and more fateful one, within a week of the initial
attack. Professor Magerant explains that for that exact reason, his
father has been receiving medical treatment to prevent a second
stroke from happening; this includes anticoagulants and antiplate-
let medicine. Linden asks if there is damage to his father's brain,
and, if so, will it be permanent? What can his family expect? What
can the professor tell him? His father's case was well handled at
the Pompidou hospital is the reply. Early treatment and preventive
measures are crucial, and his father got both. It is too early now to
determine his father's long-term outcome—if he will be able to
speak properly, to move both sides of his body, to see normally. The

professor's voice is calming, pleasant, but as he listens, Linden wonders how many times the man has pronounced these very words to worried families. He looks at the doctor's hands—square and capable, hands that unblock arteries, that save lives. As the professor goes on talking, Linden thinks about the patients in this hospital, those in the same situation as his father. How many of them are going to make it? And what about his father? Can he dare hope for the best? Utter sadness shrouds him as he leaves the professor's office, thanking him and then heading for room 17, where he is told his father now is.

As soon as he opens the door, Linden is greeted by the blaze of his father's eyes, set full upon his face. Half-laughing, half-sobbing, Linden cries out, clutching his father's wrist. "Papa! Papa!" is all he can utter, sounding like an unreasonable two-year-old, wiping his tears away. He knows his father can hear him. He feels it in the hand gripping his; he reads it in the irises gazing back at him. Mercifully, they are alone; there is no other bed, no other patient. Linden leans forward to stroke his father's forehead, realizing he has never made these gestures before. They are new to him, but they don't feel uncomfortable, nor do they embarrass him, and when he starts to talk to his father, he finds the effort is no longer there; the words come naturally. Paul is in a new hospital, with a new team. The relocation went well, and it was quite something leaving the swamped modern hospital that stank of sewers. He describes the glass casket, the boats, the people watching them from above. Does Paul remember anything? Paul's head moves just a tiny bit. Was it a nod? His father clutches his fingers again. So his father did see some of it? They are going to have to learn to communicate, Paul and he. Perhaps they can start with this: One pressure means yes, two means no. How about that? Paul squeezes once. Wonderful! They can correspond now. They have found a way. Linden describes the flood to his father, the astonishing images he saw on TV, like the ministers being rowed on crafts atop the creek enclosing the Assemblée nationale in order to be able to enter the building. This afternoon, he's also going on a boat, with a friend from his old school, into the most immersed part of Paris, at Javel, where Candy used to live. He's both eager and scared, not sure of what he will see, of how he will feel. Paris has become unfamiliar territory, and will be even more so, he points out, at sunset, when street lighting remains dark in practically half of the capital. There are stories of Parisians hiding in their apartments, refusing to leave, wishing to stay put until the water recedes, not realizing they are prisoners of the flood, enduring extreme and deteriorating conditions. Firefighters are on maximum alert, dealing with fire risks linked to ruptured gas pipes and the increasing amount of candles being lit. Linden tells Paul about the general alarm concerning prices soaring for fresh goods and groceries, how complicated it is for parts of the city to go on functioning ordinarily. The financial cost of this catastrophe will be colossal. On TV, a specialist said damages could go over twenty billion euros. Another thing Linden learned was how the flood of 1910 affected fewer people, because Paris was so much smaller in those days, only two million residents. Back then, suburbs were far less developed. Nowadays, ten million inhabitants live in the Parisian agglomeration. There is not only Paris floundering, he points out; the suburbs are also traumatized, like Issy-les-Moulineaux and Vanves, southwest of Paris, invaded by wave after wave of frothy mud. Linden hasn't heard of any fatalities yet, thankfully, but thousands of citizens are suffering, with more to come as the river upsurges. Real estate investors are now being condemned for building housing lots along the river since 1970, knowing all along these were areas liable to flood. Brochures boasting of "tranquility along the quiet shores of the Seine" were shown on TV, creating an uproar among the thousands of people whose abodes had been swamped. Linden tells Paul about a furious man interviewed on the news, forced to abandon his new property, which was constructed a couple of years ago and now is entirely waterlogged. If he had known this area was dangerous, if someone had informed him, never would he have spent all his savings on this house. The man was appalled at the treachery and greed of mayors and others in power who have no respect for residents and who just care for finances reinforcing their personal and political agendas. All this is because of the rain, Linden explains, pointing to the window, where droplets bead along the grimy surface with steady regularity. The rain has not stopped since they got here, last Friday, and from what he hears, it's not going to. He remembers how Paul used to wait for the rain at Vénozan. Paul could tell exactly when it was coming, how the wind shifted, how the temperature changed. Linden recalls his father telling him how essential it was, not only to the trees but also to all other plants, to nature itself. He wonders what his father would make of the indomitable Seine. As he begins to ask him, there is a knock on the door, and Mistral appears, her wet raincoat on her arm. Her face lights up when she sees that her grandfather has his eyes wide open. What a wonderful surprise! And she has another great one: Lauren is recovering; the doctor is satisfied with her improvement. She should be much better by the end of the week. Mistral hands Linden a small envelope. It's from Madame Fanrouk, the hotel director. As tourists are now leaving the city, she has empty rooms to provide. A new and more comfortable one is ready for him.

Linden pockets the envelope and watches his father and Mistral interact. It's a poignant sight. He has become somewhat accustomed to his father's distorted mouth, but what he misses the most is the sound of his voice. A touch of irony, as his father's voice was not the one that was perceived the most. It was always his mother's that reigned supreme as she shouted down the stairs or across the garden. It was Lauren he heard when he came back from school, on the telephone to her sister, her parents, or a friend. It was always his mother and Tilia who chortled the most, who jested, who sang clichéd love songs.

Linden has been missing his father's voice all his life.

⟨⟩

Place Cambronne marks the frontier between the dry land of the fifteenth arrondissement and the floods. The overhead Métro line, number 6, is no longer running. Helicopters circle above. When he arrives on foot from Montparnasse, Linden sees police blockades preventing pedestrians and cars from turning into rue Cambronne, rue Frémicourt, and rue de la Croix-Nivert. The only people allowed through the barriers are those who can prove with ID cards that they live in the inundated areas. It is only two o'clock, but the dark gray sky dampened by rain feels like nightfall. Linden looks around for Oriel. She is standing near the police with a man in his early thirties. They are both wearing red bands around their right arms. Linden is introduced to Matthieu, who works at city hall. He is part of the team dealing with the Seine crisis.

"We usually don't let anyone in here," he tells Linden, handing him a red armband and a badge; "however, Oriel explained who you were. I know nothing about photography, but you'll want to see this. It's unbelievable."

They walk down rue Frémicourt, still dry, and virtually deserted. Matthieu explains the boat will be waiting for them on avenue Émile-Zola, just ten minutes away. The city hall crew patrols the marooned areas hourly, with the help of the army, making sure no elderly or sick people are in need. Matthieu talks breathlessly, gesturing with his hands. It's been a grueling experience, and it's far from over. He's never been so tired in his life, but what he feels is nothing compared to what these poor residents are going through. He has a pointed, elflike face, with pale green eyes, ruffled sandy hair. Oriel asks Linden how the hospital transfer went, and he tells her. Matthieu raises his eyebrows, stating it must have been quite a sight. He knows there was a lot of disquiet about the relocation, and he's glad to hear it went well for Linden's father. Then he whispers, although there is no one around them to hear, how everything has been pandemonium since the river topped its banks in the early hours of Sunday. They can't imagine the screaming matches between the mayor, the prefect, and the president. He shouldn't be saying this, but it feels good to get it off his chest. It's like no one gauged how calamitous the situation could get, like no one really wanted to see. Even in his workplace, at city hall, many of his colleagues were convinced the Seine was under control, that there was no danger, that due to modern technology, they could act in time. Until the last minute, they refused to accept the dreadful reality. And now, he says, still whispering, many of them feel culpable, just as others are convinced the administration is not making the right decisions, like the fiasco with the Pompidou hospital, for instance, evacuated much too late. And to make it worse, their own offices, situated in the bottom level of the Hôtel de Ville, will also be vacated today because of the rising water level. No one was expecting that, and to avoid the hassle, he prefers being here, in action, in the rain, trying to help.

They reach the intersection of rue de Lourmel and avenue Émile-Zola, where long tongues of water lap up the paving and boats wait under the drizzle. Wooden walkways and planks rise above the water, spreading down rue de Lourmel on either side. In the rowboat, Linden greets two other people from the city hall crisis cell, Monique and Franck. He takes his Leica out of the inconspicuous canvas messenger-style bag in which he incorporated a smaller padded camera case. For a fleeting moment, he misses his Canon and its lenses; he feels unprotected without them, vulnerable, but then he reminds himself that his situation is unexpected, and that the Leica has never let him down. This is not a job like the usual assignments he gets; this is something else. He'll almost have to go back to being the young, anonymous photographer, the one who wanted to let the emotion through, who wasn't worried about lack of lighting or decisive angles. What he discovers as the boat moves along is different from the vintage shots of the 1910 flood, where Parisians donned elegant long clothing, riding coats, top hats, and bonnets. Those black-and-white photographs suggested an aesthetic sense of drama, but there is nothing beautiful in what he sees today. The turbid water is sprinkled with garbage, and the files of people shuffling along gangplanks, carrying suitcases, bags, and bits of furniture look desperate and anything but stylish. The Seine reaches the middle of each entranceway, coming up to the waists of immersed soldiers wearing wet suits. It is an even greater jolt to

Linden because this was his teenage Paris, and he knew it like the back of his hand. All businesses are closed, with iron shutters pulled down into the flood, while ladders creep up façades, and he sees bottled water being transferred through windows as morose faces peek out from higher levels. How many of them are there, trapped in their flats? Red Cross volunteers stride along the makeshift platforms with temerity, holding up baskets of groceries, calling up to the people stranded in their homes. Refuse collectors in green uniforms heap stacks of rubbish into long canoes. Another element the genteel black-and-white photographs do not express is the putrefying stench. Glazed with mounds of garbage and debris from exploded drains, the slimy yellowish liquid stinks. Linden struggles against the reek by tying his scarf around his mouth and nose. He takes each photo unhurriedly: a young girl clambering up a ladder, rucksack laden with food as her parents stare down, hands outstretched; an old woman standing on one of the gangplanks, sheltered by a flimsy umbrella, a tiny, terrified dog tucked under her stout arm. The cheerful café on the corner of rue de Lourmel and rue de Javel, which he remembers well, has not surrendered; the owners have created a large pontoon with planks and barrels and have even installed a welcoming array of tables, chairs, and sunshades. He shoots a couple of well-wrapped-up clients enjoying wine, waving as the boat drifts by.

What strikes Linden is the quiet: no more car motors, roar of buses, screeching of horns; only the mild slush of rain and water mingling with the murmur of voices. From time to time, the boat halts so that the rescue crew can confer with other colleagues, or residents in need of help or information. A dinghy jammed full of journalists and photographers swishes past them. He locks eyes with a young woman on board, camera around her neck, whose jaw drops when she recognizes him. Quickly, she snaps his picture, gives him a grin and a thumbs-up. Monique tries to console a middle-aged woman talking to them from the second floor of her building. The woman says she can't sleep, hasn't been able to since Sunday, since the water arrived. Her ailing husband has acute rheumatism, but he won't leave the apartment, and things have gotten even worse since the rats. Yes, rats have invaded the entire building, scurrying up from the flooded cellars. It is hell, she mutters, absolute hell. Monique and Franck try to convince her to go with them to a temporary accommodation with her husband, where it will be warm and dry, with no rats, but the woman won't hear of it. She won't have her stuff pinched; they'd both rather stay and put up with the discomfort than leave. As they draw away, after having provided the woman with water, bread, batteries, and other goods, Franck says that this is precisely what they are faced with: people refusing to budge, people who simply don't understand the flood is not over, far from it. These people have no more TV, no more Internet, only the radio, but even the frequent warnings emitted there are not paid attention to. The only thing the municipal team can do is to bring these people supplies every day.

When the boat turns right into rue Saint-Charles from rue de Javel, Linden is confronted with the tall redbrick building where he lived for three years, on the corner of rue de l'Église. He has not been back here since Candice's death, nearly six years ago. How disturbing it is to see all the shops shut, barricaded against the elements: the supermarket, the dry cleaner's, the optician's, the Japanese restaurant, and some, like the flower shop and the Greek takeout, plainly devastated by the flood, or pillaged. He remembers how teeming this street was on market days, how challenging it was to tread the sidewalks because of the mass of customers. Today, there are no pavements, no crowds: only desolation, silence, and ripples of water. It is as if the images of past and present of the same place have become irreconcilable to him. His old neighborhood is hardly identifiable, yet painfully familiar. Linden stares up to the balcony on the sixth floor, heart hammering. His eyes want to look away, but he forces himself, flinching as he does so. This is where his aunt fell to her death, at noon, on Wednesday, June 6, 2012. He had been told by Tilia that a salesperson in the women's clothing boutique on the opposite side of the street had seen Candice standing there for a long time, until she clambered over the balustrade and dived, headfirst, arms outstretched, like an angel, the lady had said: a beautiful and tragic angel. The lady had also admitted that she would never forget the noise Candy's body made when it plummeted down into rue de l'Église, in front of the bakery, where Linden used to buy *pains au chocolat* and croissants for their breakfast. It was not a market day, and the street was less full. The ambulance came swiftly, but it was too late. Candy's death had been instantaneous. The boat lingers over the exact spot where she probably fell. Monique and Franck talk to the proprietor of the bakery, whom Linden does not remember, or maybe it is a new owner. The man wants to know when his insurance money is going to come through. They've all been patient, but if it goes on raining, and if the river keeps on rising, what's going to happen to them all in this miserable district?

"Linden, are you all right?" asks Oriel suddenly, placing a hand on his shoulder.

The rain thrumming down on Linden's face mingles with his tears. At another moment, in another time, he would have shrugged off her hand; he would have told her he was fine, just fine; he would have gone on with his photographing. Today, he finds his nerves are raw; he can't hold anything back, not anymore. When he looks up at the balcony, it is almost as if he can see Candice standing there. He struggles to find the right words. *This is where my aunt committed suicide.* They sound so horrible, he can't bring himself to pronounce them; he can only cry silently, hugging the Leica to his chest. Never had he imagined it would be so tough coming back here; but then he realizes he has never talked about Candy's death to anyone, not even to Sacha. The shock of it has not left him, after all these years. He manages to mutter a couple of words to Oriel; this is where he lived, with his American aunt. When Oriel's small, cold hand clasps his, he knows she understands, and that she has probably guessed the reason for his grief. The boat glides toward place Charles-Michels and Beaugrenelle, now entirely submerged.

The huge shopping mall seems unlit and forlorn, guarded by a floating police patrol. The abandoned skyscrapers of Front de Seine soar into heavy gray clouds.

Lowering her voice, Oriel says her boyfriend died in the November 2015 attacks, rue Alibert, in the tenth arrondissement. He was having dinner with friends in one of the cafés that were targeted by the terrorists, where fourteen people were killed. She had been dating him for only six months, but they were in love, and happy. On the night of the attack, which had plunged France into unspeakable horror, Oriel had been with her mother, who had a slipped disk and could not move. She had planned to dine with her mother and then meet her boyfriend later. Just as she was about to join him at ten-thirty, her mother's TV program had been interrupted by the news of terrible incidents throughout the city. In the confusion and panic that ensued, Oriel discovered she could not make her way to the other side of the capital. Paris was on lockdown; incessant sirens shattered the night and citizens were ordered to stay home. Her boyfriend's cell phone did not pick up. She rang the number till dawn. A long, anxious wait began. Two days later, her boyfriend's parents, whom she had met only twice, called her to say they had identified their son's body. Listening to her, and taking in the dejection of his old neighborhood, somehow takes the edge off Linden's pain. He is able to step back from it and tell Oriel how sorry he is to hear this, how dreadful it must have been. She says she has never been to rue Alibert, and she never will. She did not bring flowers and candles there like thousands of other Parisians. On the first anniversary of the tragedy, she took roses to the Bataclan concert hall, on boulevard Voltaire, where over eighty people were killed, the same bloody night of November 13. It was her way of paying homage to all the victims, and to her boyfriend.

Later, after walking back in the rain to place Cambronne, Linden and Oriel stop at a café on avenue de la Motte-Picquet. It is a relief to be in a dry, warm place, tucked away from the wretchedness of Javel. They order hot chocolate and tea, and then Oriel says, simply, "Tell me about her. Your aunt Candice."

Candice instinctively understood him, ever since he was a child. He felt closer to her than to his mother; it had always been that way. As a result, from early on, he had sensed a smoulder of umbrage from Lauren toward her sister concerning him. It was never expressed, but it lurked there, and he felt it worsen when he came out to Candy, not to his mother. The day Candy killed herself, he was in Tokyo. It had been a frantic, mad rush to get back in time for her cremation, and he hadn't made it. He still bore the brunt of that. In the letter she left on the kitchen table, Candy explained nothing; there were only details about the fact she wished to be incinerated, and no Mass. There was nothing about why she committed suicide. But he knew. He knew why she had done it. It was that man, that J.G., who had kept her waiting for years, who promised, but who never gave, and who ultimately wed a young woman. Candy had continued seeing him after his marriage. She had admitted to Linden she couldn't help it, that she loved J.G., that she needed him. She met him in hotels at lunchtime, and it was sordid. Linden had felt hatred toward this unknown man, whose face he didn't even know. He remembered J.G. calling late at night, talking for hours. Candy had been at his beck and call. What was so special about this guy? he wondered. What did she see in him? She had a fine personality; she deserved better than shitty J.G. He explains to Oriel the odd rivalry between Candice and Lauren. He was well aware they were close, that they cherished each other, but the competition existed, and it prevailed. He somehow felt it was more his mother's fault, but he couldn't quite pinpoint why; perhaps it stemmed from their childhood, from a tradition their parents instilled back when they were little girls growing up in Brookline. Lauren didn't possess Candy's calm attitude, her tact; his mother was blunter than her sister, less pensive. Candy was labeled the intellectual, which Lauren begrudged. Physically, they were both lovely, but Candy's appeal was considered quieter, more elegant, whereas it was said Lauren's exuded sensuality. He misses his aunt. He has not stopped missing her, since that June day. And earlier on, as they passed rue de l'Église, the pain sparked up, rekindled.

When he saw the balcony from which she'd thrown herself, he had felt nauseous. How and why had she decided to take her own life? All sorts of details came back to haunt him. Imagining her getting dressed that morning, choosing her clothes. He had been told she was wearing a pale pink dress. Why that one, in particular? Did it have a story? Did she wear it for J.G.? Had she known, as she slipped into it, that she was going to die in it? Wednesday, June 6, 2012. What had that date signified? Did it have an implication for J.G., for her? He had puzzled over that date so often. It was the anniversary of D-day, he had noticed, as had his mother, his grandparents, but surely that had nothing to do with it. Fitzgerald and Martha Winter, her parents, had no ties to World War II. Lauren had said the date was probably random, and for all they knew, Candy had gotten up and gone to the window, and that was it. In summer, they'd sit there, he and Candy, on two Ikea folding chairs and sip Chardonnay, watching the sky flush pink in the evening. She'd put their clothes out to dry whenever the sun peeked out, even if the landlord disapproved. And what about Mademoiselle, her new cat? Linden shared his aunt's passion for cats; he had adored Muffin, who had lived up to the ripe age of fifteen. Candy had never known his own two felines, Moka and Leporello; she died before he adopted them with Sacha. In June 2012, Mademoiselle was only six months old; she was a mischief-maker, a green-eyed black-and-white minx. When he Skyped his aunt, it was a delight to see Mademoiselle prance around the room, and Candy laughing out loud at her capers. Candice must have gone out on the balcony without Mademoiselle. Did she lock her up in another room? Candy was so careful, so protective of her cats; she spoke to them as if they were human beings. What had she told Mademoiselle on that final day? He never found out who had adopted the kitten. When Linden had left Candy's apartment in 2000, at eighteen for a tiny room under the eaves on rue Saint-Antoine, he had missed her. That minuscule place—a *chambre de bonne*, as it was called, a maid's room—was the first witness to his new routine of living alone. It had been tough spending his first winter there: The room was freezing, badly heated, and then, he discovered, stifling in summer. He worked at a photo lab just on the other side of place de la Bastille, where he earned a meager salary, enough to pay his rent. Later, he started at Gobelins, École de l'Image, and his parents and Candy helped by financing his studies. Every two weeks, he'd go back to rue Saint-Charles for dinner. She used to invite an interesting mix of people whenever he came. She was an excellent cook, another thing he missed in his new home. She had many friends, she was popular, but deep down, she was lonely, he knew. She dreamed of a family, a husband, children, a home—everything her sister had, and that she didn't. It was her solitude that killed her; of that, Linden was certain. It was those nights, alone, when she could have shared them with someone she loved, and who loved her in return. His grandparents had never gotten over her death; they had aged overnight, and had not regained their sprightliness. Fitzgerald had passed away in 2013, and Martha followed suit a year later. When Linden had arrived in Paris in June 2012, his devastated mother and sister had greeted him, drained by the past few days. They had gone through all Candy's belongings, and there were photographs, books, and letters concerning him, which they handed over to him. They had sorted out her furniture to be sold, or to be sent down to Vénozan; they had spoken to the staff and the pupils at the university and school where Candy taught English; they had done it all. Back in New York, it had taken Linden a while, perhaps a month or two, to muster up the courage to open the large envelope. Candice's handwriting resembled his mother's—irregular, slanted to the left—but he could tell them apart. In one letter, dated September 2005, she mentioned going for a weekend in the Loire valley with J.G., and she had written his name instead of his initials, Jean-Grégoire. Linden had all of a sudden remembered the man's surname, de Fleursac-Ratigny (he had poked fun at its length and complication), and then it was easy to look him up online. He had found what he needed in a couple of clicks: J.G. lived on the outskirts of Paris; he had four children, between the ages of ten and sixteen. J.G. must have been quite good-looking twenty years ago, when Candice met him: slim, dapper, and dark-haired. How and where had they met? Linden couldn't remember; some party, he believed. J.G. was currently retired from a family printing business. It was equally easy to find his telephone number and address. Almost too easy, he remembers.

The café where Oriel and he sit is now jam-packed, full of people charging their phones and coming in to shelter from the cold and the rain. It is a cheery place, decorated in tints of red and brown; the waiters scuttle by, balancing heavily laden trays expertly on their shoulders. Darkness has settled in. Oriel orders Sauvignon for both of them. Can she have the rest of the story, please? She really wants to know what happened next. Did he end up calling that dreadful man? Linden smiles, and chuckles.

"You need to stop smiling like that," complains Oriel. "You're just too sexy."

Linden is tempted to tell how her pleasurable it is to be with her, how he has enjoyed sharing this moment with her. He's been talking for the past twenty minutes, and a weight has lifted off his shoulders, despite the toll of the day and the sorrow of evoking Candy's suicide. He takes the Leica out of his bag and aims it at her. He often does this when he feels words are needed and he cannot find them; the camera in front of his face acts like a shield. Oriel holds up her palms, half exasperated, half flattered, then finally unwinds and gazes back at him. He takes a couple of images, capturing the fiery glow in her gray eyes. When he puts the camera away, she grasps his hand, caressing the inside of his palm with her forefinger and staring right at him. There is no ambiguity in her expression or her gesture. He lets her play with his hand, not pulling away. After a while, she asks him if he is in love with someone. He answers that, yes, he is; he is in love with Sacha. She raises her eyebrows, repeats the name, softly. Is Sacha a man? He replies Sacha is indeed a man, that he met him five years ago, and that he lives with him in San Francisco. He waits, expecting more questions, and ready to answer them if they come. But they don't come. Oriel sips her wine, and her hand has left his. She says nothing for a while; the silence between them is not awkward. Then she says, "Tell me about the Jean-Grégoire thingy."

Linden called J.G. at home two months after Candice's suicide, and the man had picked up the phone himself. It was noon in New York City, and the end of the day in France. Linden had said right away that he was Candice Winter's nephew. J.G. had been taken aback, but he had not been unfriendly; he had just asked circumspectly, what Linden wanted. What Linden wanted? Well, he wished to know if Monsieur de Fleursac-Ratigny (what a mouthful of a name, and Oriel snickers) was aware that Candice Winter had died. Silence on the other end of the line, then a cough and a mumble, and the clearing of a throat. Yes, he was aware. Very sad indeed. Linden hadn't liked J.G.'s voice, high-pitched and discordant. He had wondered if Madame de Fleursac-Ratigny was around, if she was eavesdropping, if she had any inkling her husband had been having an affair with a lovely, charming American woman called Candice for the past twenty years. With the same restrained tone, J.G. had asked if he could call Linden back. Linden had given him his mobile number, never expecting to hear from the man again, but to his surprise, he did ring back, three hours later. J.G. sounded disheartened. He admitted he had been deeply shocked by the news of Candice's death. How had he found out? Another clearing of the throat. Well, Candice had written to him, announcing she was going to kill herself. He got the letter the day after she died. It had been a dreadful shock and he couldn't display his grief because of . . . Because of his wife. His wife never knew. He felt terrible. He felt guilty. He knew he would carry that pain and that guilt for the rest of his life. That would be his cross to bear. There was just one more thing. J.G. didn't care what Linden thought of him. Linden could think what he wanted. It didn't matter; but what Linden had to know was this: He had loved Candice. He had loved her deeply; he had loved her more than he had ever loved any other woman. J.G. had hung up without another word.

Linden stops talking. He lets the noisy café take over his silence. Oriel's eyes are full of sadness.

෴

Linden stands under the shower for a long time, savoring its warmth. He can't help thinking of the people he saw this afternoon, confined in their freezing and dank apartments. This Parisian trip appears to have ripped him open, rubbing salt into old wounds, creating new ones. Overtiredness and melancholy invade him. He tries to pull himself together as he gets dressed, but images flit back to trouble him: his father in the hospital, Tilia's unbearable tale, the sixth floor from which Candice flung herself. Is it because he is a photographer that he sees these pictures so clearly in his mind? How can he erase them? He concentrates on his home; he thinks of its pale blue walls, the scent of amber, fragrant souvenirs from a visit to the Marrakech souks; Leporello basking in the sun, Moka bouncing up to greet Linden, like a dog would. Invoking the cats does him good, imagining their fleecy fur, the rumble of their purrs, how they race each other up and down the steep staircase. He visualizes Sacha in the kitchen, wearing shorts and a T-shirt, loins clad in a tattered apron purchased in Naples (which he refuses to throw away), engrossed in a mouthwatering recipe, hair tied back in a ponytail, while some opera (*Lucia di Lammemoor* or *Turandot*) resounds vigorously through the room. This was originally Sacha's house. He had been living there for some time before they met; Linden went to join him four years ago. Linden knew San Francisco before moving there, but now he realizes he could not live anywhere else. He loved it from the start. After Paris and New York, the country boy he was at heart felt he had found his base at last. It had to do with the ocean views, the rosy sunsets, the nearby wilderness, the botanical gardens. Here, unexpectedly, nature rules, just like back home. The cold, blustery wind makes him think of the mistral raging down the valley at Vénozan. He doesn't mind the fog, the sudden rain, the humid chill. The clang of cable cars appeals to him. The sight of the Golden Gate Bridge never wearies him, nor does the giddiness of the steep lanes on Russian Hill. Even those things people criticized about San Francisco—the lack of parking spaces, the stink of urine down in the Bay Area, the constant gentrification that was nibbling the city's soul away—all that never got to him. What Linden enjoys most about San Francisco is living with Sacha. He likes imagining the man he loves as a dark-haired boy roaming these very hills. Sacha grew up in the neighborhood, on nearby Liberty Street, where his parents, Svetlana and Dennis, still live. Linden got to know Sacha's neighbors: elderly, coquettish Mrs. Lester, who insisted on being called by her first name, Zelda, and the Leine family, who came from Uppsala, and who invited them every June to their *midsommar* party, a Swedish tradition that celebrated the summer solstice with dancing and merrymaking. Torn between hilarity and lust, Linden watched Sacha frisk expertly around the maypole, a tall wooden post adorned with flowers. Linden had never shared a place with a lover before, had never wanted to; his independence had been precious. It had all changed when Sacha asked Linden to come live with him. The narrow blue house in Noe Valley became their haven. It was a crooked three-story Edwardian built in 1903, with a mission-shaped dormer, a cathedral ceiling in the top bedroom, stucco walls, and period fireplaces. It faced south and west, so that its bow windows always caught the sun.

At last, Parisian grayness is shoved away; Linden can now see Dolores Park on a Sunday, Sacha playing Frisbee with a bunch of kids. Whenever the sun came out, Dolores Park was the place to be; he could hold Sacha's hand there, even kiss him, and no one cared. There was much to see: people sunbathing or napping on towels stretched out over the hilly grass, others playing soccer or tennis, dancers rehearsing their moves, Hula-hoops gyrating. Linden never tired of the continuous picnics, the diverse and deafening types of music, the dogs gamboling, and the mixed smell of weed and hot dogs weaving its way through the palm trees. He has never missed home, missed Sacha, this much. If only a magic button existed, the kind he dreamed of when he was a kid, the kind that sent you somewhere else, just where you wanted to be, in a flash. Yet, he knows he can't escape; he can't run away from where he is, from his role here. He is the one in charge. He is the one holding the family together, along with his niece, but no one or nothing can stop him from imagining he's somewhere else, back on Elizabeth Street.

A chime from his phone halts his reverie. It is a text message from Sacha: *Can't imagine what you must be going through. That photo of you on Twitter is unreal! How is your dad? Love you.*

Bewildered, Linden checks his Twitter feed, which he hadn't done for a while. Sure enough, there he is on the city hall boat, surrounded by water, scarf pulled up against the stink, hair drenched, Leica in his hands. It looks like a war photograph, conveying despair and tragedy. That young woman took it from the press boat. It has been retweeted hundreds of times: *Franco-American photographer #lindenmalegarde captures disaster #flood #Paris #Javel.*

Before he has time to answer Sacha, there is a knock on his door. When he opens it, he discovers his mother, pale but upright, in the hallway. Her face is thinner, more lined than usual, but she is smiling at him, a shawl wrapped around her shoulders. She wants to hear everything about Paul now that her brain has started to function normally again. Linden must divulge all he knows, not keep anything from her. They go into his bedroom; she sits on a chair, he on the bed, and he speaks gently. He doesn't tell her how harrowing his father's face is; he mentions only the triumphant incandescence of Paul's eyes, their communication by hand squeezing. He describes the hospital transfer, realizing as he speaks that his mother knows nothing about the river, or barely, as she has been bedridden since Sunday, and she listens to him, petrified, as he describes the flooded streets. He does his best to reassure her, depicting Professor Magerant's trustworthiness, insisting on the fact that Paul's situation is unchanging, but that they must wait in order to know more, and it's the delay that makes it difficult. Lauren asks questions; her voice is almost back to normal, but more subdued. She no longer smiles. She gazes back at him, arms crossed. This trip was her idea, and look what's happened. She shakes her head mournfully; she feels it is her fault. All Linden can do is tell her firmly that it certainly isn't, and he pats her arm. His mother seems like the ghost of her former self. He wishes Mistral and Tilia were here to cheer her up. How has she been feeling? he asks. Has the nurse been to see her? How much longer does she need to take her medicine? Lauren sees through his diversion tactic, ironically nodding her head at him. Yes, she feels much better. She appears to be on the brink of telling him something else, but then she hesitates, as if changing her mind. She places both her palms on the sides of her face and sighs. When she does that, she reminds him of Candy. He doesn't want to tell her about today, about the visit to Candy's building, the painful memories resurfacing. One day, he would like to be able to mention Candy, to talk about her freely, without his mother's expression clouding over. Lauren gets up, runs a hand through his hair, like she used to when he was a boy. Oh, and by the way, there is a situation. Colin is downstairs. With a swift gesture, she mimes inebriation. Tilia won't go down to talk to him.

When Linden arrives in the lobby, Colin lolls alone on a sofa, his face brick red. His jaw protrudes, Neanderthal-like; his suit is rumpled and stained, his hair uncombed. He sees Linden and raises a shaky hand. Linden can smell the liquor even though he's standing a few feet away. Colin's voice booms across the room. Does Linden know his silly sister isn't even coming down? She won't have dinner with her husband; isn't that preposterous? She's moping in her room with her daughter, two silly cows. He couldn't give a crap. He's had it with them. Colin's voice rises even higher. He's fed up with the Malegarde lot anyway. Fed up with their attitude, their contempt, their intolerable superiority. They think he's not good enough for them, right? It's been like that since the beginning, ever since he married Tilia, for God's sake. They've always given him the cold shoulder, always made him feel crummy. Embarrassed, the receptionist, Agathe, glances over at them. There are a few other guests, a little farther away, taking in the scene. Linden has little patience left. An ominous burn simmers in his gut. He says tersely that Colin should leave. Just leave, now. Tilia doesn't want to see him in this state, and neither does Lauren. He should go back to his friends' house and sober up. There are taxis outside; he'll find one. Just go. Colin glares back at him, his lower lip bulging out. Go? Linden can shut up and stop looking at him like that. Why should he take orders from Linden? Why should he leave? He'll do what he likes; he'll wait here for as long as he wishes, until that foolish, fat wife of his comes down at last, and then he'll give her a piece of his mind. He'll tell her exactly what he thinks of the insufferable Malegarde family. For Christ's sake, he's come all the way here, from London, for her, for her dad, for them, and what does he get in return? This? Sod off, the lot of them. He's not afraid of Linden. Ha! Why should he be frightened of a fag? No one's frightened of fags.

Wordlessly, Linden strides over to Colin, grabs him by the collar of his coat; he jerks him up pitilessly, forcing him to stand. Colin snorts with glee. Oh, so Linden is playing at being the man, is that it? Is this how he gets going with his boyfriend? Do they get rough? He cackles. Must be quite something. Not his style, however. Will Linden get his filthy paws off him? Linden drags him to the door, not an easy exploit, as Colin is nearly as tall as he is, and probably heavier, but his rage spurs him on.

"What the hell are you doing?" Tilia's voice booms into his ear.

Isn't it obvious what he's doing? Chucking her husband out of the door, that's what he's doing, shoving him back into the gutter, where he belongs, out in the rain. That should clear his head; that should do the trick. He feels Tilia's ineffectual fingers on his arm as he hauls Colin outside into the wet darkness, the spatter of raindrops bursting around them. Colin groans and mutters something unintelligible, while Linden yells, telling him to shut up. Tilia looks on, amazed; never has she seen her brother so angry. Linden's face is transformed, sharpened, his eyes black with fury. He rams Colin

against the wall, bumping his head back so that Colin can see him
through the rain. He clamps him by the chin. Linden talks slowly
and clearly, as if Colin were an obtuse five-year-old. It's simple, and
it's going to go like this: Colin is going to go back to his friends at
Ternes, right now, and he's going to stay there, and he's not coming
back. If he does come back, and if he is drunk again, then he'll be
very sorry. A free taxi is slowly coming up rue Delambre, a miraculous and unexpected sight. Linden whistles and halts it. As he
opens the door, tries to thrust his brother-in-law into the car, Colin slips on the wet sidewalk and falls flat on his bottom, feet flip-
ping up in an uncoordinated and comical collapse, like a stunt
from a Charlie Chaplin movie. It takes a full five minutes to hoist
him up to his feet and to shove him into the backseat with Tilia's
help, both of them ignoring the honking of cars behind them. The
taxi driver tersely says he won't take this guy anywhere in that
state. Exasperated, Tilia reaches for money in her back pocket,
hands him fifty euros, far over the normal fare. The man takes the
banknote and shuts up. Colin can't remember his friends' address,
so Tilia asks the driver to take him to the Ternes Métro station,
hoping her husband will work it out once he's arrived. They watch
the car draw away under the drizzle, then look at each other, soaked,
Linden still heaving with ire. Clearly, Colin had been at it all day,
Tilia explains. She hadn't wanted to see Colin, not at all. He took
it badly. Yes, she had been hard on him, but what else could she
do? Was she really expected to turn a blind eye every time he got
pissed? How dare he turn up in such a state? Thank God their
mother had not seen him. And that fall! It was miraculous he hadn't
hurt himself. She imitates him, staggering backward. Linden
catches her by the sleeve.

And then it starts. It takes over, like when they were kids: the
laughter; helpless, delightful, uncontrollable laughter. They hang
on to each other, mouths gaping open, bent double, bellies aching,
heedless of the rain, of the cold. Poor Colin, how could he ever
know? That tumble! It was spectacular! It should have been filmed.
They whoop so loudly that passersby join in, chuckling. Hilarity

chases belligerence away. An easy sense of well-being flows through Linden. He hasn't felt this serene for days. Brother and sister end up locked in each other's arms, hugging each other close.

"I love you, dude," whispers Tilia, leaning against his chest.

"I love you, too, doll."

It is the first time, ever, that they have said those words to each other.

SIX

꧁❦꧂

Quand je suis parmi vous, arbres de ces grands bois,
Dans tout ce qui m'entoure et me cache à la fois,
Dans votre solitude où j'entre en moi-même,
Je sens quelqu'un de grand qui m'écoute et qui m'aime!

—VICTOR HUGO, "AUX ARBRES"

There I was, hiding behind the biggest tree. I thought Suzanne would find me right away. But she didn't. She seemed to be taking her time.

I became impatient. I couldn't hear her voice any longer. She wasn't calling my name like she usually did. Slowly, I peeped around the trunk, carefully, in case she caught a glimpse of me. I couldn't understand what I saw. It didn't make sense to me. Suzanne was lying down. All I could see was her hair, spread out against the grass, and her bare white legs.

There was something on top of her. It looked like a gigantic bag. Dark, grainy, and dirty, covering her top half. But the bag was moving, and as I watched, I understood that it was hurting her. I could hear her stifled breath, and it sounded as if she was being burned or beaten. The bag had enormous reddish hands and they were wrapped around her neck.

Never had I felt so afraid. This, I was sure, was a monster, the kind that comes in nightmares. The kind all children are frightened of. This was no nightmare; this was real life. This was broad daylight, not nighttime. She was fighting it; I could see that. She fought it with all her might. She twisted and she bucked, but it was so much stronger and bigger than she was.

I wanted to run, but I couldn't move. I was paralyzed with fear. The monster shoved on top of her, faster and faster, with a sickening frenzy. She was making choking noises, while the monster grunted, horribly.

I felt I was going to dissolve with fear. I wet my pants. I began to cry. I wanted to scream and yell. I had no idea how to get help, where and whom to run to. The house was too far away. And if I moved, the monster would see me. It would come for me.

W HY DID YOU BECOME a photographer?" was a question
Linden often got asked. He never tired of answering the
question, just as his father never tired of telling the story of the first
tree he had saved. Linden enjoyed mentioning working with old
Monsieur Fonsauvage, who had offered him his first camera, the
Praktica, and how the Leica came into his life. There were some aspects of his job, however, that he couldn't put words to. How could he
possibly describe accurately that to him, photographing was like
acquiring experience? He had no wish to sound pedantic. He had
no lessons to give. He never wanted to preach through his work,
just as he didn't like his subjects to pose stiffly. It was too intimate
and knotty a conviction for him to share out loud. Once, he had
tried to explain to a French journalist writing a portrait of him for
a magazine that the act of photographing was using a language understood all over the world, and it seemed deceptively easy, describing it as such. The woman had smiled at his choice of words.
How could he tell her there was nothing simple about it; that each
photographer possessed his or her own version of that language? It
was easier to say that even when he did not have a camera in his
hands, he was still mentally photographing everything he saw; that
every time he had seen beauty or tragedy, he had wanted to immortalize it, in his own way, with his own vision.

This Wednesday morning, at the hospital, it is his father he is photographing, both with his phone and the Leica. There is not much light in the small room. Paul is awake and gazes back at him with his wide eyes. The nasal cannula for oxygen is still in his nose. Because of his twisted mouth, Linden cannot tell if he is smiling, but he likes to think his father is content. As usual, whenever he holds the camera, he doesn't need to speak. He concentrates on photographing his father's hands, knobby and strangely pale against the yellow blanket. There haven't been any doctors yet. Perhaps they came earlier? Nurses tend to his father with practiced gestures. Some of them are more outgoing then others. High above the bed is a complicated array of screens, with red, green, and yellow stripes and numbers flashing across them rhythmically. Linden observes his father's body, shrunken and emaciated beneath the blue hospital johnny. This will be a shock for his mother, and for Tilia, he knows. In a mere four days, Paul has aged, seeming far older than his seventy years.

A woman enters the room quietly. She is middle-aged, plump, dressed in a tweed skirt and a brown cardigan, with short gray hair. She greets Linden. He has no idea who she is. He acknowledges her, puzzled. She introduces herself as Dominique. Her voice is soft and pleasant. He wonders if she is in the right room, but then she asks how his father is this morning. Is she an unknown friend of Paul's? One of those tree lovers? As if she had foreseen his questions, she explains she is a hospital volunteer. She has been working in Professor Magerant's ward for a long time. She usually comes in only on Tuesdays, but with the flooding, and new patients being transferred here, she is on tap all week. The hospital can do with all the help it can get. At first, Linden doesn't feel comfortable with her being there. Dominique is now sitting down, opposite him, placing her bag on the floor, and it looks like she is settling down to spend quite some time here. He feels a twinge of annoyance. How can he ask her to leave? It wouldn't be very polite; she seems a nice lady. She takes her knitting out of her bag and gets to work, needles clicking steadily. He watches the long trail of blue wool. A scarf? A sleeve? He can't tell. Has Linden seen the news this morning?

It's quite something, isn't it? Luckily, she lives in the fourteenth, not far from the hospital. Apparently, the Seine has reached eight meters, and it will go even higher. Only a bit to go before it gets to the historical level of 1910! Has Linden seen the extraordinary images of the Eiffel Tower? The river has encroached upon the entire Champ de Mars. The tower looks like it's been planted bang in the middle of a giant lake. Isn't it rather unbelievable, what's going on in the city right now? She heard that the best way to get around Paris, apart from a boat, of course, is on horseback. She saw it on the news: the incredible coverage of police horses with water up to their chests trudging down avenue Bosquet. And of course one mustn't forget the suburbs, where people are suffering just as much, but not getting half of the attention Paris is getting. The suburbs have always been a sensitive area, and the flood isn't making it any better; there is mounting unrest there. Dominique heard nocturnal lootings began in some of the swamped neighborhoods—apparently, gangs of youths from the northern suburbs—and the police and the military were having a hard time protecting the deserted buildings. The president was going to visit Javel later on today by boat. Did Linden know that? The president had been criticized by many for not doing this beforehand. She hopes he will make it to the suburbs, as well; the people there feel neglected. She has a cousin in Alfortville, whose home is inundated. Her tone is soothing, pleasant to listen to. After a while, Linden finds he quite likes listening to her. She goes on with her conversation, placidly, her hands moving swiftly. He is tempted to photograph her; there is an interesting halo of light around her silver hair. Dominique read in the paper (Was it *Le Parisien,* or *Le Figaro*? She can't remember) that the recent nonstop rain was the direct result of global warming. The weather was bad in all of France, as well as in other European countries. Wasn't that worrying? Didn't that mean more rain to come in the future, and more floods? Linden nods, agreeing with her. The article she read also mentioned that deforestation upstream from Paris, which had never ceased in the past decades, could also have contributed to the swift water heave. Getting rid of trees is never a good idea, is it? Linden notices his father is taking in every word. Paul's bright eyes dart from Dominique to him, like those of a spectator watching a tennis match.

"Your father hears and understands everything we say," says Dominique, seeing Linden glancing at his father. She had quite a conversation with Mr. Malegarde last evening. When Linden frowns, puzzled, she resumes: Of course, Mr. Malegarde can't talk properly yet, but he can certainly communicate. This is what she does, every week; she connects with patients who've had strokes, and she helps and teaches their entourage to do so as well. Linden wonders what she knows and learns about every family to whom she offers solace. It must be a difficult job, and not even getting paid for it is all the more remarkable. How did she end up doing this? What triggered her? What was Dominique's life like? Did she have someone to go home to, or was the hospital the only focus of her day? His father's eyes are settled on Dominique's round face, flickering down to the knitting. Perhaps Paul is comforted as well by her presence. What was Paul able to express to her yesterday? Linden feels curious. Dominique gets up inconspicuously, folding her wool away. It's been a pleasure talking to them. She will be back tomorrow. When she goes out and shuts the door behind her, there is a void. Linden struggles to find his own path in the sudden silence. Should he resort to simply chatting, like Dominique did? Just talk, let the words flow out? In his father's eyes, he reads expectancy. He pulls closer to the bed, takes Paul's hand in his. *Your father hears and understands everything we say.* He feels his father's slow pulse at his wrist, beating against his thumb. He marvels at the convolutedness of the human body, of all the unseen maneuvers going on beneath the skin. He thinks of the clot blocking his father's artery, of how his father's constitution is fighting it. He wants to be able to hope, to believe his father will pull through. Holding his father's hand like this, in this peaceful moment, makes Paul's possible death a heresy. And yet, at the back of his mind, there is a powerful image, one that he cannot erase. It seems his father's life is slowly ebbing away, with the same stealthy pace as the rise of the Seine, as if the two events are intertwined and preordained. The complex intricacies of nerves, cells, and organs composing his father's body resemble the Parisian network of streets being gradually invaded by water, shutting down power, blocking computerized data transmission. Linden looks through the spattered windowpane, and it seems to him he has become a sentinel, on the lookout for the inevitable aquatic invasion, watching over his father, over the rain, over the entire city.

Linden starts by saying Lauren is better. Hopefully, she will soon be able to come and see her husband. She looks beat, but she's over the hump. She'll be okay. His father's face twitches a little; he blinks, makes a strange groaning noise. Linden can't understand what Paul wants. He leans closer. A whisper. He makes out "You." The word *you*. Linden points at himself. Paul lowers his chin, grunts again. What does his father mean? Oh! He gets it! Paul means him. *Him*, Linden. How is Linden feeling? Paul rumbles and nods again. Linden smiles, exulted that he can decipher this new language. He's fine. He's fine, a little tired, but fine. He moves on to the Seine, convinced this will absorb his father, like earlier on, when Dominique was bringing up the latest news. He describes how the flooding is slowly spreading to the eighth arrondissement, exactly like it had in 1910, despite obstructions and pumping devices installed by the city. Another lagoon is forming in front of the Saint-Lazare train station, creeping down rue de l'Arcade, where blockades have been raised. The authorities have locked off the area, not only because the enormous station was built on unstable ground, which had been thoroughly quarried for sewers, undercrossings, parking lots, and the Métro, but also because an ancient and stagnant branch of the Seine used to flow there, centuries ago, on a northern path from Ménilmontant to Chaillot, and the flood has resuscitated it, sucking water into the vicinity. The Musée d'Orsay's ground floor is entirely swamped; artwork has been stowed away safely, but impairments to the museum are colossal. The Maison de la Radio, the circular modern building situated on avenue du Président-Kennedy, very near the river, which usually broadcasts several national channels, had to be shut down and evacuated. Gigantic inflatable rings had been fitted all around the edifice, but the flow had still filtered through. Transmissions were now being made from temporary dry offices, near Montmartre. La Défense, the major corporate area, west of Paris, where thousands of businesses have offices, has been cut off from the capital and overrun by the swollen, furious river at the pont de Neuilly level. Specialists are now saying the city will be paralyzed for over fifteen days. The peak of the surge should be reached tomorrow, or the day after, Linden heard. He realizes he might be worrying his father, so he refrains from mentioning the numbers he heard on the news, that over five million people would find themselves without running water, without electricity. The impact of this flood would be ten times worse than in 1910; he doesn't mention that, either. He tells him instead that his agent emailed him to inform him that several of the black-and-white photographs he took at Javel with the old Leica have been published in the international press. As he talks, Linden is convinced his father is aware, perhaps more than anyone else, of the supremacy of nature. Paul is listening carefully; Linden can see it in the intensity of his eyes. Part of him is crying out to talk about something else, to evoke more personal subjects. They have never done this, his father and he. How can he start? Perhaps he should ask Dominique; she might know how to help. His thoughts are interrupted by Mistral's arrival. He feels both relieved to see her and thwarted because he hasn't been able to share more intimate concerns with his father. Mistral is glowing with exhilaration; she has a surprise for them. Can they guess? She hops up and down, her face pink. They both stare at her, baffled. Slowly, she opens the door, and Tilia is standing there, pale and still. She catches sight of her father and promptly bursts into tears. Mistral pulls her into the room gently, leads her to the bed. Tilia, still sobbing, catches her father's hand and kisses it. She can't talk; she can only press her lips against Paul's skin again and again. It was quite something getting her here, murmurs Mistral to Linden. It was Tilia's idea in the first place; she wanted to do it, but when they got to the hospital entrance, she chickened out. She went white, had to sit down; then she said she had to go back to the hotel, that she couldn't go through with it. So they sat for ages, and Mistral talked to her, and it worked. As usual, when he looks at his sister, Linden is torn between amusement and emotion. She is such a bundle of nerves, that one, uncontrollable, unpredictable. Their father's face seems less distorted (or has Linden gotten used to it?), and Paul makes moaning noises that are both touching and embarrassing. Linden has the perfect excuse to use the Leica, to hide behind it, to protect himself.

Later, when he departs, leaving Tilia and Mistral with Paul, he bumps into Dominique in front of the elevator. He hesitates, only for a few seconds, and then asks her how can he talk to his father? He stammers, feeling ridiculous. He means to really talk, not just babble on about the river and the weather. She takes his question seriously. They ride down in the elevator together and walk to the exit on rue Saint-Jacques. She explains that sometimes families are put off by the strange expressions and noises that stroke survivors make. So if that bothers him, he can look out of the window, and try talking that way, in the beginning. And then he will get used to it. Linden doesn't dare tell her that his father's appearance does not inconvenience him; it is essentially confiding in his father that does. He thanks her and takes his leave.

Like an old friend, the rain greets him as he strides along boulevard de Port-Royal toward Montparnasse and the hotel. There are many people in cafés, he notices, having lunch, drinking, making merry, while half of the city is doused. He finds it perturbing how tragedy lurks in only some areas, not in others. Won't all of Paris be affected? Isn't that what they must learn to face? In the quiet of his room, he watches the live images of the president visiting the Javel neighborhood by boat, escorted by the mayor and the prime minister. Their expressions are solemn and lugubrious; behind them, another boat, this one full of journalists armed with cameras, follows. People shout out to the president from their windows: several insults, some pleas for help, many cries of thanks. The president answers everybody patiently, reaching up to shake hands, offering his sympathy, even responding to the few invectives. Yes, he should have come here before. Yes, he feels for them. Yes, he is here to help. As Linden looks on, a text message from Oriel shows up on his phone: *Hope your dad is OK? Tonight, meet me at 22 hours on corner of rue de Grenelle and rue de Bourgogne. We'll be in a patrol boat. Don't take your camera. No flash allowed. O xxxx.*

In the afternoon, Linden knocks on his mother's door. No answer. He catches the whine of a hair dryer and guesses she can't hear him. He waits for another five minutes and tries again when it gets quiet. This time, Lauren opens up, wearing a bathrobe, her hair still damp, dryer in her hand. She says she hasn't quite finished, and asks him to stay in the bedroom. The whirr starts again; she closes the bathroom door. Linden sits, thinking this may be the right time to talk to his mother about the next couple of weeks. If Paul's condition remains unchanged, they are all going to have to decide what to do. They can't stay in this hotel much longer. If Lauren must remain in Paris, then this must be organized. Do they have Parisian friends that could put her up? He can't think of many, and besides, the flood makes it more complicated. What about those friends Colin mentioned? Not a very good idea. Best to keep Colin out of it. His mother's phone buzzes, right next to him, on the bedside table. *JeffVDH.* It's that guy again. Her ex. Jeff van der Haagen. Linden shouts through to Lauren, "Phone ringing!," but again she can't hear him. After a few moments, a text message flashes on the screen. He shouldn't be looking, but he does.

> *My love, so glad to hear you're better. Call me when you can. Think of you night and day. Kiss you all over. J.*

Linden gets up, tempted to leave before his mother comes out of the bathroom. He doesn't know what is worse: his embarrassment at discovering his mother has a lover, or having to confront her, knowing he is fully aware of the situation. In a couple of minutes, she will emerge, and he will have to act normally, as if he saw nothing, as if nothing has happened. He doesn't feel up to it. He wonders what his sister will make of this; then he realizes Tilia probably already knows, or has guessed. He doesn't want to be part of this; he doesn't want to judge his mother, nor for her to think he is judging her. This is her private life, and it has nothing to do with him. He stands near the window, feeling uncomfortable. His parents' marriage? It's none of his business. He left home when he was fifteen. Their relationship is a mystery he refuses to look into. Why should he? Yet the text message has created ingress into that mystery, has forced him into their intimacy. He can't help thinking of his father. What does Paul know? How long has it been going on? Linden recalls the summer when Jeff and his family came to Vénozan, a hazy memory. Is this a recent affair? Or one of those long-lasting clandestine ones, like Candice and J.G.'s? More questions come. Are his parents happy? Have they always been happy? Had it been easy for Lauren to give up her country, her life, for a new one, for a new language she hardly knew, and still spoke badly? She was only nineteen when she met Paul. Had she felt forlorn when both her children left home? She was forty then. Perhaps that had been her hidden fragility: the prospect of being alone in that large house, with a husband who only listened to trees. The hair dryer stops at last. When Lauren appears, dressed in a dark sweater and trousers, Linden remains silent. He cannot bring himself to act naturally. His arms hang stiffly on each side of his body. He waits for his mother to discover the text message, to put two and two together. She slips her reading glasses over her nose, takes her phone in her palm. Linden looks away. The minutes drag by. Perhaps she'll say nothing. Perhaps she'll hide it all, like when she couldn't face the fact he was gay, like when she probably told her friends her son had girlfriends.

"You must be disappointed in me." His mother's voice is low, but he hears her perfectly. He shakes his head, raises a hand: He doesn't have to hear all this; he doesn't have to know. His voice comes out a little noisier than he expected. She sighs. There, she knew it; he's angry, and he has every right to be angry. How can Linden explain to his mother that he would rather she not unburden herself, that he doesn't need to be told all the details? His parents' personal life holds no appeal for him, and he marvels that she cannot fathom that. Lauren blunders on, laboriously, and for the hundredth time he thinks how different she is from her sister, who was intuitive, understated. Yet, he loves his mother, even if he knows she is self-absorbed, unsubtle, at times insensitive. She has a sharp sense of humor, which he finds endearing; she has often made him roar with laughter. Now, laughter is very far from his mind. He raises his hand again, interrupts her, tells her it's okay, that he understands. She doesn't have to go on. He's an adult. Why can't they stop talking about this, now? Lauren's face seems to sag. Gone is the resplendent mother who got all the attention. Lauren bangs her hand down on the table, hard, making him jump.

"Linden, just listen to me!"

Her tone is tense, filled with pain; tears glisten in her eyes. He steadies himself for what is to come. There are many, many things in her life she has done wrong. The good thing about reaching her age is that she can see these mistakes; she can pinpoint how they happened, why they happened. She's not out to make excuses, to wallow in self-pity. She knows exactly what she has done. Jeffrey, her old fiancé. Yes, Jeff is married as well. Yes, it sounds low and shameful. God, it isn't! It began years ago. She hardly sees Jeff. He lives in Boston with his family. They meet once a year, perhaps even less. Now that her parents are dead, she has no excuse to go to Boston. She writes to Jeff every day. They have been corresponding like this, on a daily basis, for fifteen years. He is her confidant, her best friend, her soul mate. He is always there for her, even if he is miles away, and she tells him everything. She is there for him in return. They have written pages and pages to each other, letter after letter, email after email, text after text. No, Paul doesn't know. At least she thinks he doesn't know. And would he care if he did? She's not sure. Linden asks her what she means. She gives a little dry laugh that he doesn't like. Linden just doesn't see, does he? Nobody does. Nobody sees. Nobody can tell. Paul is gentle, kind, and patient. He is not aggressive; he has never yelled at her, never hit her. It's just that Paul lives in another world. He doesn't see what they see; he doesn't hear what they hear. All he sees, all he looks out for are trees. Must she really explain this to him? Surely Linden must know. Surely, Linden suffered from this, as well. She knows Tilia did. Linden mutters he knows. His mother goes on, her voice still wobbly. Paul is content with her merely being there. Her presence is all he needs. The silence drives her mad. Over the years, she tried opening up to her husband. He always listened, but discussions never took place; Paul wrapped himself up in his customary reserve. She concedes she has more conversations with her housekeeper, Nadine, or even old Vandeleur, the gardener. She organized this very trip in the hopes that he would somehow interact with her, with his family at last. She thought it wasn't too late, that Paul would somehow learn to communicate, at seventy! Had she been so very wrong? And now, this tragic thing has happened: her husband is fighting for his life in a hospital. Is she going to be able to speak to him again? Will he hear her? Will he survive? She feels so guilty. Lauren begins to cry, gently. Linden wonders if Candy knew about Jeff, about her sister's difficulties. She probably did. Candy was close to Lauren; she knew how to keep secrets. He feels sorry for his mother for the first time, his nonchalant, exquisite mother who rarely seemed perturbed by the course of events. He has hardly ever seen her cry. He reaches out and pats her shoulder comfortingly; he says Paul is going to pull through, that she'll be able to see him soon, that she mustn't worry. He gets up, murmurs something about going back to his room, but she pulls on his hand.

"I want to talk to you about my other mistakes."

She sounds determined now, less tearful. Her wet face is turned to his. She says she'd been waiting for the right moment to tell him this, and that moment never came. So she's choosing now, even if they've had their fair share of emotions during the past week. She's been carrying this burden around for too long now; it's too painful. She wants to talk about his coming out. Linden was not expecting any of this. He sits down again, wordless, his heart beating a little faster. His mother clasps her hands together, flinching. What she is trying to say, and being utterly hopeless at it, is this: She's sorry. Sorry for reacting the way she did when he told her, thirteen years ago. Sorry for all those years when she never brought the subject up again, until she met Sacha. She let Linden down, badly. She has never forgiven herself. And that silly jealousy when he said Candy knew before she did: How could she have been so stupid, so uncaring? She had been overwhelmed by all the wrong feelings. To be honest (and she wants to be honest; she wants nothing but honesty between them right now), she had guessed he was gay when he decided to leave for Paris. She suspected he was being bullied at school. And yet she did nothing, said nothing, another terrible mistake. She knows why. She can say it now, but she couldn't back then. She said nothing because she was afraid. She was afraid of her son being a homosexual. It was the dread of being different, of standing out. The fear of having a child who was not like the others at school, especially in that narrow-minded provincial town, because of the name she bore, that name, Malegarde: a family of notables, a lineage of which Linden was the only heir. The last one to carry on the name. There was no one she could voice her fears to. There was no one she could talk to. She couldn't bring herself to say out loud "I think Linden is gay and I'm scared of that." So she let it go. She let him leave for Paris, and she can see him now, tall, thin, and unhappy, coming to say good-bye to her in the kitchen, his father waiting in the car to drive him to Montélimar to catch the train to Paris. Deep down, she knew her sister would offer Linden all the tenderness and comfort he needed, everything she wasn't capable of giving him there and then. She despised herself. She considered herself a hopeless mother. When Tilia left, and then got pregnant, she felt lonelier and more useless than ever. She didn't know how to talk to Linden; and there he was, becoming closer and closer to Candy every day. She let her envy get in the way. She could have talked to her sister, and she didn't. Another mistake. So many mistakes. She's the queen of mistakes, isn't she? When Linden had summoned up his courage that spring day in his flat on rue Broca, she had behaved disastrously. When she thought back to it, she wanted to scream. The worst part was when she had told him she didn't know how his father would react and that she left it up to him to talk to Paul. How could she have brought herself to say this to her son? Such cruelty! Such hard-heartedness! She sees now that it was once again her fear making her say these things, her terror of having a gay son. Her fear of saying to people: My son is gay. She loathed herself for this. She had wanted her son to be like all the other sons of people she knew. Yet she hadn't been raised by bigots! Her parents, however old-fashioned, were open-minded. They had taught their daughters to be tolerant, generous, impartial. So what had happened? It took her a while to figure it out. Years, in fact. She realized she had to banish the image of the son she thought she had, the so-called perfect son, the son who would fit in; the images of her son getting married to a woman, having that woman's child. She understood she had to stop lying to others about her son's sexuality, for the simple reason she couldn't face their reaction. It hurt now to think back on all those years when she didn't dare question Linden about his personal life, his boyfriends, even after his coming out. He must have found her callous. Time went by, and Linden's career took off. He became more famous than his father, in another field. She was proud, she really was, but there was this nagging feeling inside her, always. Linden was leading his own life, and she knew nothing about it, apart from his photographs. She just couldn't figure out how to talk to him, naturally. She brought it up with Tilia, who became impatient and told her off. And she could not discuss it with Paul. She never had. She did not dare. It was so stupid of her. Linden's personal life was a topic she never discussed with her husband. Did the reluctance come from Paul? No, she did not believe so. It came only from her, and with each year, the silence thrived. And then, in 2014, she met Sacha, with Linden, in New York. She had never met any of her son's boyfriends; she had never even heard their names. She had been nervous about this dinner; she was worried about this young man, this stranger. Linden had told her, candidly, by email, that he was in love, that he was moving to San Francisco soon, and that he wanted her to get to know Sacha. Lauren had been in Boston for a week in April 2014, for her mother's funeral, which Linden had attended. It had been a sad period for Lauren: her sister's suicide two years earlier, her father's death the year before, and now her mother's. She had agreed to stop by in New York, and Paul had flown back to France from Boston for an important dendrologists convention. The night that Sacha and Lauren met, she saw them walk into the restaurant, and her son's face was glowing with happiness. She saw only that, at first, the incredible light shining from Linden's eyes. And then she looked at the man standing beside him. The same light. The same radiance. She saw two people in love. She saw it, then and there. Why had she been afraid? She felt liberated! She would never lie again. She didn't need to. When she mentions Sacha, she always adds: my son's boyfriend. When she speaks to Paul, she simply says, Sacha. Paul has never asked anything about Sacha, but he knows exactly who Sacha is. What does he think of his son's living with a man? She has no idea. She has never mustered the courage to ask him. Linden says he hasn't, either, for the same reasons.

"Maybe you'll be able to talk to your father now. At last," says Lauren. A silence ensues, humming with all sorts of possibilities. Lauren is the first to break it. Does he remember that first dinner with Sacha? Of course he does! How could he forget it? Maialino, a restaurant overlooking Gramercy Park, fried artichokes as starters, prosecco sparkling in their glasses. Lauren goes on to describe how Sacha, whom she had barely met, made her laugh within the first ten minutes of their meal. She couldn't even recall what the joke was about; all she can see is herself choking with mirth into a napkin. Was it one of his imitations? Sacha was awfully good at impersonating famous people.

Lauren talks with more ease now. Her expression is less strained. There is one more thing she wants to say. Occasionally, people have strong reactions when they hear her son is gay. Well, last summer, for example. She was at a ladies lunch at Grignan, an elegant do at a pretty restaurant, down by the historic washhouse. She usually did not attend these events, because it meant dressing up and resorting to small talk, but a neighboring friend she was close to was also going. There was a table under the arbor, decorated with bouquets of roses, and a delicious meal. She was seated next to an emaciated woman from Montbrison who wore pearls: Madame Moline. Lauren was told Madame Moline had a splendid house up in the hills, with a magnificent garden, and she remembered Paul's having gone there to assess the trees when the Moline family moved in, a couple of years earlier. Madame Moline was thrilled to hear Lauren was Paul's wife. She had a warm remembrance of him; his knowledge of trees was immense. How lucky Lauren was to be married to such a remarkable person. And did Paul and she have any children? Lauren nodded yes, a daughter and a son. Madame Moline, while picking at her food jadedly, appeared to be most interested in the Malegarde family. She wished to know all about Tilia and Linden. What unusual names! Their father had chosen their names, Lauren said. And so Tilia was an artist in London and Linden a photographer based in San Francisco? Any grandchildren? Yes, Mistral, seventeen, a student. And what about Linden? Was he married? Lauren smiled. No, but he was planning to be. Madame Moline stretched her red lips into a smile. An American fiancée, like his mother? A young American man, Lauren told her. Madame Moline's lips seemed to shrivel. She frowned. A man, she repeated. Yes, said Lauren brightly, a young man. And because Madame Moline seemed completely lost, she added, "My son is engaged to a young man." Madame Moline blinked. She opened her mouth, dabbed it with her napkin, and still no sound came out of it. (In spite of himself, Linden chuckles. His mother's mimics are hilarious.) Lauren then said in a clear voice that her son was homosexual and that he was in love with a man. Madame Moline looked rattled; she kept staring at Lauren as if Lauren had grown a beard, or turned blue. Finally, she managed to articulate how very brave it was of Linden to have chosen to be a homosexual, very brave indeed. Lauren gazed back at the lady and said firmly that her son had not chosen to become homosexual; he was born that way. And she was proud of him, proud of who he was. Madame Moline took Lauren's hand. Her skin was parched and her fingers bony. Lauren was so incredibly courageous! Such unconditional love was admirable, like those mothers whose sons were in prison and who still loved them, even if they were murderers. Linden interrupts her, saying he cannot believe what he is hearing. Lauren smiles ironically. It is true; it is all true! Another close friend once admitted to her, when he found out about Linden, that he would have hated having a gay child. She had read such pity and distaste in his eyes that it had made her want to slap him. Another friend had crooned: Oh poor you, what bad luck! Perhaps the nastiest remarks were the flippant ones that were meant to be funny. Oh, so her son was gay? Well, wasn't that something to do with the mother? Did Lauren mollycoddle him, or what? In the end, wasn't it all Lauren's fault? She had learned to distance herself from this, even if at times those remarks still stung her.

As he takes Lauren into his arms, hugging her close, Linden realizes it never occurred to him that his mother could be criticized because of her son's homosexuality. It seems unexpected and unfair that she, too, would have to go down that dark road of intolerance, of rejection. Her words ephemerally resuscitate the suffering of his own journey toward self-acceptance, the rebellion against the shame others had persisted in sustaining around him.

Lauren steps away from her son and strokes his face. Her eyes are wet again.

"I'm so proud of you, Linden. I'm sorry it's taken me all this time to tell you."

⁓✤⁓

There is no more public lighting in this part of the capital. Ahead, the motorboat waits in the darkness. The glow of flashlights guides Linden and Oriel along the narrow metal walkways of desolate rue de Bourgogne. Three policemen greet them; the divisionary commandant, Bruno Bouissy, and his two adjutants. Linden cannot distinguish their faces, but he makes out weapons carried against their bodies. For the second night running, the commandant says, gangs of pillagers have been reported in the district. The seventh arrondissement is a traditionally wealthy one; that's why the looters are active here. They have also been targeting the eighth, specifically rue du Faubourg-Saint-Honoré, with its numerous luxury boutiques. They're looking for jewelry, for leather goods, for cash. They're very organized, apparently; they come in silently on paddleboards and canoes, sometimes improvised ones, created with planks and crates fastened together, making the most of the unlit streets. They carry stepladders and mallets. How do they operate? Very simple: A couple of them guard the boat while another climbs up the ladder, smashes a window that hasn't been shuttered, and breaks in. Then valuables are hauled down with bags. It takes only a few minutes. Most of the apartments here have been evacuated, but a few stalwart dwellers remain. No one hears the gangs, and even if someone does, most residents are terrified. Landlines are out of order, and mobiles no longer function in the area, so the police cannot be summoned. The only way to fight the thieves and arrest them is to patrol the streets by boat, incessantly, but there aren't enough dinghies, and there aren't enough men. Crime is on the rise, in rhythm with the water, points out Commandant Bouissy. People are freaking out, worrying about how they will make ends meet, how they will eventually be reimbursed. Several shops have been plundered, and it's getting worse near Nanterre and Gennevilliers, northwest of Paris. There is little solidarity, one of the captains adds grimly. Oriel says she hates this egocentric world where selfies rule, where no one bothers to find out if their neighbor is all right. As they climb into the fluvial brigade motorboat, Linden notices it has stopped raining. This is the first time it has relented since he arrived on Friday. Oh, but the rain will be back, says the adjutant driving the boat. That is the problem; it will be back.

The night air is icy, burdened with the stink of putrefaction and drains. The moon peers out from behind clouds, casting a supernatural nacreous light on the flooded streets. Paris looks like an obscure and sinister Venice, a drowned metropolis gradually sinking into oblivion, incapable of putting up a fight, yielding to the unhurried and lethal violence of its demented river. The commandant tells them he has never seen anything like this in his life. The past four days have been crazy. The Seine's power of destruction is unimaginable. This morning, he flew over the hub of the Parisian agglomeration, Île de France, by helicopter and what he saw was unreal. The river has altered the landscape, gobbled up quaysides, park, and streets, transforming places into different ones, redrawing maps, doing as it pleases. The ravages in the suburbs, all along the river's course upstream and downstream, from Melun to Mantes-la-Jolie, and beyond, are dreadful. Even within Paris, despite all efforts, some neighborhoods are not getting the same consideration. Priority is going to the eighth, where water now threatens the presidential palace, and the big department stores on boulevard Haussmann, Printemps and Galeries Lafayette, have been closed in haste. They can't keep up with the general panic and the delinquency, the burgled shops, the suffering, the commandant admits sadly. They are not prepared for this. They have learned to deal with terrorism, but faced with the unleashed frenzy of nature, they are powerless. The truth is, he adds, the government is overwhelmed, trapped in a skirmish between the prefecture, the city hall, and the mayors of suburban towns, while experts blame climate change, excessive deforestation, environmental degradation, but at the end of the day, no one comes up with solutions.

Motor quietly chugging, the boat turns left at the bottom of rue de Bourgogne into rue de l'Université, passing through marooned place du Palais-Bourbon, its crowned statue now encircled by a pond. Farther on, in the distance, to their left, Linden can glimpse the bulk of the Invalides, its golden dome glistening in the moonlight. The Seine has swallowed up the esplanade and all intersecting streets, creating a boundless lake. The wind blows violently; the water slaps against the boat. When they get to the other side, nosing into the continuation of rue de l'Université, the wind can no longer reach them. The silence is even more profound here, the darkness, too. The tall buildings around them seem abandoned, sepulchral, as if no one had ever lived there. The boat glides left into rue Surcouf. Why here? Linden wonders. Why back here? Why this street? He almost smiles at the irony of it. Why do these trips bring Linden back to untold stories of pain and regret? First Candy, now Hadrien; first rue Saint-Charles, and now rue Surcouf. Because of the gloom, he can't read the numbers above the doors, but he knows it is number 20. Commandant Bouissy explains that the river level, compared to that in other streets, is very high here. The sector comprised between boulevard de la Tour-Maubourg and avenue Rapp is much lower than elsewhere, situated in a hollow basin. This is where the flood is the deepest, he says, in all of Paris, worsened by the gush coming underground through the RER train rails right beside the river. Parisians with ground-floor lodgings here have water up to their ceilings. There are no lights visible through the windows, just the flicker of candles here and there. Slowly, the policemen shine their search lights over the façades, and although Linden's eyes follow the yellow circles of light roaming over stone, he sees none of it. He is nineteen years old again. Third floor, door on the right. The silkiness of Hadrien's skin, the heat of his mouth. Eighteen years ago, but it still feels like now. He has not forgotten anything. One spring morning, a young man had walked into the photo lab near Bastille where Linden worked. The young man, who was about his age, had the loveliest smile he had ever seen. He seemed shy, incapable of looking Linden in the eye, at first. He was there to have a couple of black-and-white prints duplicated and framed. Linden hardly noticed the photographs; he saw only the young man's hands, slim and tanned. Since Philippe, there had been no serious boyfriends; just affairs, none of them important. Linden often felt lonely in the small room he rented on rue Saint-Antoine; his daily existence seemed dreary. The blue-eyed stranger and his shy, sweet smile somehow gave him hope. Later on that day, as Linden left the lab to go home, the young man was waiting a little farther on, on rue de la Roquette. That was how it began. Linden took him back to the tiny room beneath the roof. Hadrien had caressed Linden's face, kissed him slowly and ardently. In Hadrien's arms, Linden felt as if he had found a secret place where he felt safe. They met again, and again, always at Linden's place. They had to be careful; Hadrien lived with his parents, and he had not told them he was gay: He had even invented a girlfriend so that they would stop asking questions. Hadrien studied history at the Sorbonne. He was an only son. He was a gentle young man, serious and earnest. Linden remembers his voice, soft-spoken and melodious. Their affair lasted a year, and it gave Linden hope and confidence; he felt less lonesome. Hadrien's love filled up the emptiness. Sometimes, they talked about the future. Hadrien was afraid of his parents' reaction; he wasn't ready to tell them. His father, especially, often made homophobic remarks, saying gays should be locked up, or hanged. He felt his mother might understand better, but he was too scared to tell her. There was no one he could talk to, or turn to. Not even his friends. How lucky Linden was to have been able to tell his aunt so easily, and how wonderful her reaction had been.

Linden's reminiscences are interrupted by the loud sputter of the walkie-talkie. Apparently, the police caught a gang red-handed on nearby rue Malar—three robbers and their entire booty. The men have been handcuffed and are being taken to the police station on avenue du Maine. Linden nods, pretends to be pleased, but his thoughts are not with the arrest. He sees the door of number 20 now, on the right, next to the restaurant. It is an unpretentious, pale edifice, more modest than the imposing buildings next to it.

There is no candlelight at any window. Do Hadrien's parents still live here? He remembers the apartment well, even if he came here only twice. It was a little dark; the sun never filtered in. The morning it happened, Hadrien's parents had been away on a trip to Spain. His father was a teacher; he and his wife left at each school holiday. They thought they were safe. They could never have imagined the parents would come back earlier than planned. Hadrien had begged Linden to spend the night with him in the family home. Only one night! They could sleep in the big bed for once. He'd change the sheets before his parents got home. He would cook a fine meal! Linden had not been able to say no to Hadrien's enthusiasm. Neither of them heard the key in the lock. They were fast asleep, naked, in each other's arms. The first thing Linden had heard was a strangled yell. He had opened his eyes and seen a middle-aged man and woman standing there. They seemed outraged. It had happened so quickly. The strident shriek of the voices; the father, beside himself, his face scarlet, telling them how repulsive they were, how vile, how nauseating; they were dirty, disgusting faggots. The hands, pointing, like claws. Linden and Hadrien had crawled out of bed, vulnerable, recoiling under a torrent of insults; they had gotten dressed, hurriedly, awkwardly. Tears were streaming down Hadrien's face. Impossible to forget what the father had said, his words spewing out: Hadrien was not wanted here anymore. He and his poof of a boyfriend were going to get the hell out of here and never come back. Did Hadrien hear that? Was it clear? The venom in that voice, the hatred. Hadrien was no longer their son. It was over! A homosexual son? Never! He was nothing but a failure. He was an embarrassment to the entire family. What would his grandparents think? His aunts and uncles, his cousins? Had he thought about that? And had he thought about him, his own father? His own mother? Hadrien's father said he wished his wife had had a miscarriage when she was pregnant. There would be no more money for Hadrien, either, ever, nothing, not a centime. Hadrien should be ashamed of himself. People like him were perverts. They were not normal. They belonged in prison. There were medical treatments for people like them. In other countries, homosexuals were executed, and perhaps the fear of that could knock sense into them! Didn't they see there was no place for them in this world? Didn't they see nobody wanted them, that nobody pitied them? Linden had dragged Hadrien down the stairs. They had gone straight to Linden's place on the Métro. They didn't dare hold hands, but during that long ride home on line 8, Linden longed to comfort Hadrien. Nearly twenty years later, Linden still feels the weight of that moment. He is glad the lack of light is preventing Oriel from seeing his face. Hadrien had never complained; he never mentioned the episode. It was as if something had been broken within him. He lived with Linden for a while, continued his studies, diligently. Then he found a job in a bookstore, moved out, and they no longer remained in touch. It was Hadrien's choice. A few years later, Linden saw on Facebook that Hadrien had gotten married, that his wife and he had had a baby. There was a family photograph, with Hadrien's parents in the background, proud smiles on their faces. Linden couldn't get over the photograph. He showed it to his friends, some of whom had known Hadrien when they were together. One of his friends, Martin, had said Hadrien looked like a lamb being led to slaughter. When Linden moved to New York in 2009, full of exciting projects for his future, the pain he felt when he thought about Hadrien had lessened a bit. He met other men, he traveled, he worked hard, but he knew he would never forget. A year and a half ago, just after his Parisian trip with Sacha, he had received a message from Martin. Hadrien was dead. Martin had no details; he had read it in *Le Figaro*'s "Carnet du jour." Hadrien was thirty-five years old. What had happened? There was no way Linden could find out. He searched online, but nothing came up. Over and over, he had asked himself why and how Hadrien had died. There were no answers, only questions and doubt. He felt the same suffocating torment that came with Candy's death, the same waves of inconsolable sadness that left their mark.

The motorboat slinks down rue Saint-Dominique, past numerous shops bolted in vain against the flood. All stocks and basements

must be underwater. Like rue Saint-Charles, this used to be a busy
street, teeming with traffic and passersby. It is now a dreary, watery wasteland without a soul in sight. Up ahead, the silhouette of
the Eiffel Tower emerges like a gaunt gray phantom. The black
water ripples around them; on its surface, a pallid moon floats like
a drowned face staring up in tomblike silence. The team is now
going to check on passage Landrieu, a peaceful, narrow lane with
no shops between rue Saint-Dominique and rue de l'Université, a
place where many tourists rent lodgings for a couple of days or a
week. As far as they know, the apartments here are empty and in
need of surveillance. Last night, there was a break-in at number 4, on
the upper floor of a lavish loft leased out for parties and events.
The burglars got away with computers, sound systems, and hard
drives. Linden looks up at the moon, unsuccessfully trying to
banish thoughts of Hadrien. Oriel's shout startles them all.

"Listen! There is someone crying!"

The motor is turned off, and they all strain their ears. At first,
they hear nothing, and even Oriel wonders if it wasn't her imagination. One of the adjutants says many house pets have been
abandoned, another sad truth of the flood. The other night, a desperate, starving cat had sounded quite human. Now they all hear it:
a muffled, faraway wail. It is a child. It takes them a while to locate
it, past the modern blocks that rise at each opening of the passage.
The men angle their search lights up to the dark windows. The
child continues to cry, a thin, piercing whine, leading them to it.
Perhaps the child is too small to come to the window. They paddle
on, halting in front of number 10; the sobs are coming from here.
On the third floor, a window is slightly ajar. They shout up, shine
their lights along the glass. No response. Commandant Bouissy
scrambles up a rescue ladder held in place by the two others. The
rocking motion of the boat makes Linden queasy. Oriel whispers
to him she has a bad feeling about this; this is exactly the kind of
situation she has been dreading. The commandant has now pushed
the window open, and he climbs inside. When he appears again,
moments later, there is a toddler in his arms. He shouts down to

them, his voice altered. There is a dead woman in there. They need to call for extra help.

Later, Linden and Oriel learn this is the first official casualty linked directly to the flood. The victim was a twenty-eight-year-old woman from Poland, whose working papers were not in order. She worked illegally as a cleaning lady for low-cost rentals. The studio on passage Landrieu where she had been found belonged to a friend, who had agreed to put her and her child up for a few weeks. The concierge of number 10, who had been displaced a few days ago, and who was now in a shelter near the place de la République, told the police she had never noticed the woman's presence, nor that of a child, or if she had, she didn't remember. There were so many comings and goings in that flat, which was sublet on the Internet to different clients. Nobody had checked on the woman. The police said she probably died of seasonal flu. She had been dead since Sunday, since the water rose. Oriel felt it was more the lack of caring that killed the Polish woman. What was going to happen to this poor kid? Another boat came, taking away the body of the woman, wrapped in a sheet, and the weeping child, curled up in a police officer's arms. For a long moment, Linden and Oriel don't speak.

It is midnight. The captain leads the boat toward pont de l'Alma. Their team has more night watches to do in the seventh arrondissement, until dawn. The moon radiates in a freezing blue-black sky, illuminating the swollen watercourse. There is a higher spot at the end of rue Cognacq-Jay, just before the bridge, and they head there. As they step out of the boat, icy water shoots up to their shins. They wade through it, teeth clenched. The place is completely deserted. The Seine is now drenching the Zouave's shoulders. The bridge has been entirely closed off by metal barriers and it seems to be poised on top of the river. The commandant explains the pont de l'Alma was rebuilt in 1974, because the lower ancient structure was in danger of collapsing. The new steel arch is higher and wider, but as a result, the statue of the Zouave was reinstalled eighty centimeters higher. So, in reality, the river should be up to the

Zouave's neck. It is a tragic, silvery spectacle; Linden wishes
he had his camera with him. Discreetly, he takes a photo with
his phone.

They board the boat once more, and it turns back down rue
de l'Université, crossing the Esplanade over to rue de Lille, by the
submerged and barricaded Musée d'Orsay. Paris seems deathly,
plunged in silence and obscurity. The City of Light has been snuffed
out, stripped of its liveliness. The only sound they hear is the put-
ter of the motor echoing off the stone edifices. Rue de Verneuil is
pitch-black; the commandant holds up a powerful floodlight so the
captain can see where he is going. The tall buildings are built close
together in this small street, creating a stifling impression. Linden
thinks of all the empty apartments, of all those who had to flee in
haste, wondering what to leave behind them, what to take. There
are many art galleries on rue Jacob, where they now slide through
in the same thick silence. How many have been affected? The commandant says that even in the northern Parisian quarters, which
have not been flooded, the atmosphere is the same as here: unin-
habited, dead quiet. No more nightlife. Restaurants are becoming
emptier and emptier; theaters and cinemas have dwindling au-
diences. Parisians are either leaving the city or staying at home,
waiting for the Seine to recede. The capital is at a complete stand-
still. Not to mention the anxiety of expecting mothers, the sick,
the elderly. Electricity is only barely working in half of the city. No
wonder it's driving them all mad! How many out there are cold,
wet, hungry, and furious? Hundreds! Thousands! He certainly hopes
the peak comes soon. The situation is unbearable. God knows what
will happen if this goes on. The experts say it could be tomorrow;
they're saying the Seine could go over the level of 1910, which was
8.62 meters. It could reach the highest level ever recorded, that of
1658, up to 8.96 meters, which would mean more damage in the
fifteenth and seventh arrondissements, with water sneaking to
unprecedented places, all the way up to the seventeenth, to Wa-
gram, to Batignolles; in the third, to boulevard de Sébastopol and
rue de Turbigo; and in the fifth, to rue Buffon and avenue des

Gobelins. The cost of all this will be colossal, adds the commandant bitterly. It will take months, even years, for everything to get back to normal. The Seine's ire has only added to the general feeling of dissatisfaction toward the authorities for not coping and not foreseeing the crises, and is not abetting a vulnerable nation still nursing its wounds since the first terrorist attacks targeting it. The flood will divide France all the more.

❧

When Linden returns to the hotel, late, there is a note under his door from Lauren.

> *I want to see your father tomorrow. I must. I spoke to*
> *the doctor. He says I can go. Please take me.*
> *Love Mom xxx*

The images of a sinking Paris had, momentarily, taken Linden's mind off his parents. He lies on the bed, weary, checks the time. Two o'clock in the morning. That's 5:00 P.M. in San Francisco. For Sacha, it's still Wednesday. He reminds himself that Sacha has meetings at that time with his staff, every day. He'll have to call him later, or tomorrow. He sends him the photograph of the submerged Zouave in the moonlight. He sleeps fitfully and awakens to the sound of a knock at his door. It is still dark outside, just after eight, and the rain is back, pattering against the window, just like the policeman said it would be. It is Mistral, telling him they are ready and asking if he can come down. Agathe has managed to order them a taxi, as Lauren feels too weak to walk to the hospital. They meet for breakfast. The hotel is more or less empty now, save for them. To Linden's surprise, Colin is there, debonair, impeccably dressed and shaved, smelling of Floris aftershave. He greets Linden heartily, clapping him on the back, acting as if nothing had happened. Linden has often observed his brother-in-law in this Jekyll and Hyde mode, switching from intoxicated barbarian to polished gentleman overnight. Tilia looks on, imperturbable, sipping her coffee. Their marriage is a mystery. How does she put up with it? Colin lying, again and again, convincing his entourage he is heroically controlling his drinking, not even realizing how pitiful he is. Linden wonders how long the couple will last. Colin is laying it on too thick, pouring out Lauren's tea, bouncing up to get a fresh croissant for Mistral, all smiles.

Leaving them to their breakfast, Linden concentrates on the news, reaching out for the morning newspapers. The Seine will reach its peak today, Thursday, rolling in at a frightening 8.99 meters at pont d'Austerlitz. Can the city take it? He reads the river has turned a violent, stinking yellow, flowing ten times faster than normal. Experts are worried about hazardous waste being swept along by floodwater, about the alarming mass of refuse, of decomposing plants, of putrescent organic matter. Sullied by toxic chemicals, by metal contamination, the fetid water dominates the city with its tenacious and noxious miasma. All the newspapers scream out the same headline: NATIONAL DISASTER; all use the same words: *ruin, devastation, unemployment, paralysis.* Dismayed, Linden reads on, discovers the Apple Store on rue Halévy was ransacked during the night. The capital's two opera houses, Garnier and Bastille, have both been inundated. (Sacha will be very upset to hear this.) The famous English-speaking bookstore, Shakespeare and Company, situated near quai de Montebello, has been, as well. Several photographs make Linden wish he had taken them: Notre-Dame, shrunken and altered, literally squatting on the river like a wounded creature; the Jardin des Tuileries entirely smothered by a lake, doused trees thrusting out like desperate arms. Saint-Michel fountain is spewing sludge; the École des Beaux-Arts, on rue Bonaparte, is no longer dry. Major power cuts are slowing down the city, as many electrical processors are underwater. The brand-new Ministry of Justice, an imposing block of glass and steel, situated on higher ground at Aubervilliers, is safe. Linden discovers bitter criticism of the recent relocation of the gigantic Hexagone Balard, dubbed the "French Pentagon," housing the new Ministry of Defense in the fifteenth arrondissement. It had apparently been built on stilts to prevent being flooded, but it has been damaged, even if no one knows to what extent. Uproar had commenced: Why had it been constructed on that floodable spot in the first place, just like the nearby, and out-of-order, Pompidou hospital?

At Cochin Hospital, Linden waits in the corridor until his family has spent the time they need with Paul. His room is too small for all of them to be with him at the same moment. Tilia comes out looking preoccupied. She thinks their father looks less well this morning. Paler skin, more sunken eyes. Using her bossy-sister voice, she asks a nurse if they can see Professor Magerant and is told the ward is short-staffed this morning; there have been difficulties with all new patients arriving from flooded hospitals. Tilia sits down next to her brother. How she hates being here; how she hates talking to nurses, waiting for doctors, all that bullshit. When Linden doesn't answer, she glances at him, tells him she's never seen him look so tired. He wonders if she has any idea of how maddening she is? He responds with a tight-lipped smile. Then she says something that frightens him: She says fiercely that their father is not going to make it. She can tell; she knows. Linden explodes. What the hell is she talking about? Adamantly, she shakes her head. Their father is dying, and deep down they all know it, and they can't even say it out loud. They can't face it, and they're bloody well going to have to. Linden wants to slap her. How dare she? How dare she destroy their hope? He feels like throttling her. When their mother steps out, in tears, Tilia pulls herself together, and he wipes the fury off his face. They both get up to comfort Lauren, and when Linden's eyes meet Tilia's over their mother's head, there is steely determination in his. The message to his sister is clear: Tell our mother he is going to be all right. Tell her we all have to believe. Lauren murmurs she is in shock; she can't get over how thin and old their father looks. She can't bear it. It takes them a long moment to calm her down.

Linden will spend all morning here with his father. They can go; he'll be in touch. He says this reassuringly. He watches them leave, Lauren suddenly frail next to Mistral, whose arm is around her shoulders. Back in the room, the first thing that strikes him is how ill his father looks today. Was Tilia right? He must remember not to reveal his anxiety to his father. He stands by the window, glancing out at the gray wetness; he can feel his father's eyes on him, watching him. The small, unventilated room is silent. Linden picks up the low murmur of voices, the click of footsteps outside in the corridor. The moment stretches out, and it seems interminable. The rain continues to drip. He listens to his father's breathing for a while. He could continue to stand here, watching the drizzle. It would be easy. He could also turn around and speak honestly to his father for the first time in his life. The choice is there in front of him, like a crossroad. He doesn't hesitate very long.

"Papa, I want to talk to you about Sacha."

As soon as Linden pronounces Sacha's name, it feels like doors opening with a smooth whoosh, like a path snaking out in front of him, a path full of promise and possibility, and he flings himself down that path. Sacha is standing next to them, filling the room with his presence, the way the sun ignites a wall. Sacha, he says, is the man he loves. Sacha is short for Alexander. His dad is from San Francisco and his mother is from L.A. Sacha is his age. He is left-handed. He likes to cook, and he does it beautifully. Doesn't this sound trite? Linden wonders as he speaks. Is this the right way to do it? He rushes on, tautly. They met at the Metropolitan Opera House, on Manhattan's Upper West Side. Sacha's love for opera is like Paul's love for Bowie. It's visceral. As a child, Sacha took violin lessons, which he never continued when he grew up, but his teacher once took him to see *The Magic Flute* when he was seven. Papageno, the comical bird catcher garbed in a feathery costume, charmed him with his fetching tune. Sacha came home singing the aria at the top of his lungs. That's how it started. Then he was smitten with *Don Giovanni*, especially Leporello, the peevish manservant. By the time he was a teenager, he wanted only opera in his earphones. Other kids listened to Brandy, Madonna, or Dr. Dre; Sacha stuck to opera. That night in 2013, Linden was taken to the

Met by his agent, Rachel Yellan. She had tickets to see *La Travi-ata,* and she had insisted, in that rather imperious tone of voice, that Linden join her at Lincoln Center. He had been living in New York for nearly four years now, and he knew how much he owed his agent. She had put all the energy she had into getting him those first jobs that launched his career. He didn't have the heart to de-cline. It was an opening night, and Rachel had said he must look smart. No jeans and sneakers, please! He was expecting to fight off ennui, but to his surprise, he found the performance diverting. He savored the melodious, sensitive nuances despite his untrained ear. He had read in the program that *traviata* meant "fallen woman." The young German soprano who played Violetta, the ill-fated cour-tesan dazzled by love, astonished him with her vitality. Dressed in scarlet, she strutted up and down the stage, climbed sofas, flung herself on the floor, pouring all her emotions into her voice. Lin-den used to think opera singers were static middle-aged dames with double chins. Paul chuckles at this. Linden takes it as an encour-agement. During the interval, Linden went to the bar to get cham-pagne for Rachel, who was chatting with friends. He saw Sacha from the back first. He spotted him because he was tall, as tall as he was. Black hair, parted in the middle, reaching to his shoulders. When he turned around, Linden saw long black eyebrows, a curved nose, hazel eyes. Not good-looking in a classical sense, but quite mesmeric. He heard his laugh. He remembers thinking what a de-lightful laugh it was. He couldn't help observing the striking stranger as he was waiting for the champagne. He watched him listen to his friends, nod, laugh again. The man was wearing a suit, a white shirt, no tie. He wore a necklace of some sort around his neck, but Lin-den couldn't tell what the ornament nestling on his collarbone rep-resented. The man took off with his friends and Linden watched him leave. He wondered who he was, what his name was. He felt sure he would never see him again, and somehow that made him sad.

Linden pauses. Why is he telling his father this? Because he wants Paul to know; he wants Paul to know who Sacha is, and who

he is, as well. He says it all out loud. There will be no more holding back. Linden plucks up his courage, clears his throat. The second part of the opera was as spellbinding as the first. The young
soprano sang with passion as she drew near her inevitable demise.
Lying on her deathbed, in a heartbreaking aria, she bade farewell
to her dreams, "Addio del passato," begging God to have mercy on
her. Sacha's favorite part. The subtle, haunting fusion of her voice
and the orchestra affected Linden unexpectedly. All of a sudden, it
was no longer the young soprano he saw onstage, but Candice, who
had killed herself a year before, unable to face life. It was excruciating for Linden to behold; the music dug into his heart with such
potency, he had to wipe his eyes. It was then that he noticed him,
the tall, dark man, a few rows away, sitting and looking quietly at
him. It took his breath away. It was impossible to drag his eyes from
the stranger's. It was Rachel who introduced them to each other
moments later, in the crowd on the way out. It appeared she knew
him well. Sacha was a keen opera lover. The ornament around his
neck was a small silver drop. It would look silly on any other guy,
but not on this one. "Linden Malegarde, meet Sacha Lord. I think
you two might get along." Another pause. This is harder than he
thought. He starts stuttering again, which unnerves him. You can
do it, says Sacha's voice inside his head. *Come on, Linden, do it. Do
it for me. Do it for us. Talk to your father. Tell him. Tell him everything.
Don't be afraid.* Linden tries to keep his voice light and breezy, but
at times the emotion takes over and seeps through. Maybe Paul
is wondering, What is so special about Sacha? Why Sacha? Why
him and not some other guy? It's simple, and it goes something
like this: Sacha is the kind of person who makes others happy. It
could be seen as a natural gift, he supposes. Sacha gives off special energy; it contaminates, in a good way. Perhaps it's his enthusiasm, the fact Sacha likes to listen to people, that he's interested
in them. That's how he began his start-up, because he wanted to give
those with great ideas a chance. He likes getting people together;
he likes creating, communicating, mapping out, imagining. Linden tries to explain what Sacha's start-up is about, how it works.

He's worried a technical exposé might bore or tire his father. What would Mr. Treeman have to say about Silicon Valley? Linden tries not to think about his father's responses. If he does that, he might as well stop. Sacha's start-up analyzes the influence of digital technology on everyday life, hunts out new apps, experiments with them, funds them. Linden wonders if Paul knows what an app is. Paul doesn't even have a smartphone, let alone a computer. He might as well try to explain. Apps cover a huge range of various sorts of actions. What Sacha does is hunt out any promising digital inventiveness; for example, a smart dude created an app that worked with recycled mobile phones to protect rain forests. How? The phones were rigged to branches, and if they ever picked up the sound of chain saws, the phones would automatically call the guards. There are many concepts out there, and some of them sound downright ludicrous, but Sacha listens to every single one of them. Each person who contacts Sparkden.com with a project has Sacha's attention. Sacha always looks ahead. The past doesn't interest him much; he's fascinated by what the future holds, however dystopian that future may seem. The list of app possibilities in every domain is endless: tracking moods, sleep, dreams, improving posture, controlling budget, weight, monitoring health, projecting favorite videos and photos on walls from a phone, transforming surfaces into keyboards or musical instruments. Is his father following all this? He hopes so. Another point: Sacha is a great boss. He never patronizes or bullies. The twenty people working for him worship him. Oh, but he does have failings, like everyone else. Paul mustn't think he's perfect; he isn't! He spends his life glued to his phone, which drives Linden crazy. He is at times impossibly impatient and stubborn. He flies off the handle, and then blames his conduct on his histrionic mother, Svetlana, who is a quarter Russian. He's a hopeless driver; he becomes incensed in traffic jams and then daydreams at green lights, heedless of the hooting behind him. He's a bit of a prankster, too, which can occasionally be annoying; he loves playing tricks, disguising his voice over the phone (which he is very good at). Sometimes Linden thinks Sacha should have been an actor.

Linden feels the path is not taking him the right way, where he wants it to go. He must leave this sunny, frivolous area, heading in a darker direction. That's better, but it's less easy. He's afraid he'll start faltering again. Linden says he guesses that maybe he isn't the son Paul wanted to have. Perhaps Paul is disappointed. His father often said, when Linden was small, that he was the last of the Malegardes. The last male heir. The last one to bear that name. His father seemed to think it was important. Perhaps Paul is saddened that his son will never have a child with a woman. Perhaps Paul doesn't want to hear all this chat about a man. About the man Linden loves. Silence. Linden still doesn't dare look at his father. What might he read there? Repulsion? Resentment? Instead, he stares at the rain dribbling down the pane like teardrops, and it is again Sacha he sees: Sacha rooting for him, urging him on. He plants more power into his voice; it's getting all thin and teary again. Linden felt different before he was ten years old. He hadn't known how to express it. It was such a confusing sensation. At first, when the kids at school called him those names, he had felt shame; he had even wanted to die, to run away, but not anymore. No, not anymore. Isn't he talking too fast? The words rush out, almost jumbled. Shouldn't he slow down? He takes a deep breath, resumes. He knows Sacha is the person he wants to spend the rest of his life with, the person he wants to grow old with. He had never thought of getting married until Sacha. He had never even envisaged a family until Sacha. Now, a wedding and a family are part of their future, part of their plans. In 2013, the year he met Sacha, people took to the streets in France to demonstrate against gay marriage. Paul probably remembers that small children were dragged to these rallies, wearing pink and blue T-shirts that read ONE DAD, ONE MOM. While there were many walking the streets, the majority of citizens approved the law, which was passed, as Paul no doubt knows. Linden is not ashamed of what he is; he wants Paul to know this.

He has many friends who still cannot admit to their families that they are gay. They lie, and they pretend, because they are afraid. They invent other lives, other loves. That is their choice, and he respects it, but he does not want to be trapped in duplicity. Perhaps, in the beginning, Linden should have talked to Paul. It wasn't easy to open up to his father. Did Paul ever sense this? Linden had tried. At times, Paul seemed so wrapped up in his trees that he wondered if his father had ever wanted to see the real world. Or simply, are trees the real world to Paul? If that is the case, he can understand, because taking photos is like putting on armor, sliding a protective shield between reality and his own vision of it. Linden had chosen to come out to Candice because he sensed she would understand. She did. Years later, he spoke to Lauren, who did not react as well as her sister. It had wounded him. Today, Linden is not sure his father understands, or accepts what he is. All he knows is that he is at peace with himself. If his father cannot bear who he is, what he is, then Linden will learn to live with it. He will face it. With Sacha's love, he can do this. The most important thing for him is not to lie to his father. He cannot pretend to be someone else. So now Paul knows. Paul knows everything there is to know about his son.

Linden is still facing the windowpane, his breath drawing bubbles of vapor on it. He turns around. From where he is standing, he can't see his father's eyes. Linden comes closer, bracing himself for what he will discern there. What if it is rejection or disgust? What will he do? Turn around and leave? The dread within him looms; he can't help thinking back to the abhorrence in Hadrien's father's face, to the words he spat out: *dirty, disgusting faggot.* Shuddering, he reaches for his father's hand. He sits down, looks straight at Paul. What he discovers takes his breath away. The blue eyes shine out to him, and he reads such love there that tears come; powerful and tranquil love, as if the weight of his father's hand, encompassing and tremendous, were resting on his shoulder, as if his father's arms were wrapped around him in one of those brief bear hugs he used to give him when he was a kid. Paul is trying to speak, but only garbled words come out, and Linden doesn't care; he lets the tears run unchecked. His father loves him. The force of that love. That's all he knows. That's all he sees.

⚜

Linden lingers in front of Professor Magerant's office, hoping to see him. His assistant tells him the professor is still in the operating room and won't be back for a while. Nurses are looking after Paul again. While Linden waits outside, Dominique emerges from another room, her knitting in her hands. He tells her he's alarmed by his father's condition, and she nods. She noticed the degradation, as well. She'll see Paul now. Does Linden mind? Linden says of course not; he's going to spend most of the day here anyway. He settles into a chair and sends a message to Sacha. Dominique reappears after a few minutes. Her face seems flushed.

"Your father needs you to go get something for him."

Flummoxed, Linden asks her what she means. She explains that there is something Paul wants Linden to fetch from the house in the Drôme. Linden stares at her. What is it? She says she doesn't know. She wrote his words down on a piece of paper, which she hands him. Nonplussed, Linden reads: *Tallest lime. Blocked-up hole where dead branch used to be, halfway up, left as you face the valley. Get Vandeleur to help.* Again, he asks her what the object is. Dominique shakes her head. Paul wouldn't say; he just said his son must reach down the hole and bring it back. Linden looks at her with wariness. Paul can't talk, so how can she know all this? She replies calmly, saying he can talk; it's difficult to understand him, but she knows how. That's her job, interpreting people who have had strokes. She asks Linden who Vandeleur is. The gardener, he tells her. He's been working there for years; he descends from a British army officer. He's someone his father trusts. They wait till the nurses leave before entering the room. When they are alone with Paul, Dominique inquires about the object in the tree. Paul's pale face seems to scrunch up even more, but a sound does come out of his mouth, and Linden has no idea what it is. Paul repeats it several times, but Linden still can't make it out. Dominique nods. She says it is a box. A metal box in the tree. His father wants him to go get a box hidden in a tree, he asks, trying to keep the incredulity out of his voice; his father wants him to do this now? More unintelligible gurgles emanate from Paul. Dominique listens vigilantly. She translates: Yes, he wants Linden to bring it to him. As soon as he can. He says it's very important. Linden says he doubts he'll get a train; most of them have stopped running because of the flood. How will he get to Vénozan? It's over six hundred kilometers away. Dominique suggests quietly that perhaps he could drive. Linden glances over at his father. In the ashen, misaligned face, the blue eyes glow with intensity. There is no way he can back down before them, even if he's apprehensive about leaving his father in this state. He nods, tells Paul he'll get the house keys from Lauren, rent a car, and be on his way. The parched lips bend into the semblance of a smile. Linden bends down to kiss his father's cheek, wondering what this means, wondering what he will find.

To his surprise, Linden rents a car easily at the Montparnasse station. He is told that's because the tourists are all gone—a disaster for business, for everything. Luckily, the tank is full, and that's good news, because he is warned he will have a hard time finding gas in the city. It will also take him a while to leave Paris. He even gets an upgrade, a sleek black Mercedes for the same rate as a humble Peugeot. At the hotel, Lauren hands over the house keys to her son. She has no idea about the box in the tree; neither does Tilia. Mistral wants to go with him, and Linden rather likes the idea, as the trip will take him over six hours, but Tilia says firmly she needs her daughter by her side. It is almost noon. If there is no traffic, he can be at Vénozan by six. It will be dark then, and complicated to locate the tree, Tilia points out. Lauren says he should get a good night's sleep once he's there, then leave early tomorrow morning. That sounds good, he agrees. Lauren gives him Vandeleur's number and the one for Nadine, the lady who looks after the house, in case of a problem. She'll call Nadine while he's on his way and ask her to put the heat on in his room, fresh sheets on his bed, and to leave dinner for him in the fridge. Linden grabs his phone, his Leica, some rolls of film, and a change of clothes. He waves good-bye to them as they watch him draw away. It feels odd to be at the wheel of a manual car again; it takes him a little while to master the sensation. The robust Mercedes is a pleasure to drive. He heads to porte d'Orléans as wispy rain draws feathery streaks on the windshield. The A6 highway traffic is dense, as predicted. Linden turns on the radio; a provocative female voice is saying how the flooding is having positive effects; Parisians are fascinated by the event, and many love affairs are beginning on the bridges. The voice goes on to mention that the Latin motto of the city of Paris is *fluctuat nec mergitur,* which means "tossed about by the waves but does not sink." Isn't that what they all need to remember? she quips. The facetiousness annoys Linden; he changes channels. A news flash announces the archbishop of Paris is praying in Sacré-Coeur Basilica for the flood victims during a special Mass: the arch-bishop's morose tone exhorts listeners to care for one another, to leave their selfishness behind, in the name of the Lord. Linden cuts him off, as well. And then . . . Is it a coincidence? Hardly! An acoustic guitar twanging in an ethereal fashion fills the Mercedes: the unmistakable beginning of "Starman." Linden turns the vol-ume up and finds himself singing along, accompanying Bowie's impish "low-oh-oh" and "radio-oh-oh" with gusto, belting out at the top of his voice that there's a starman waiting in the sky, only to discover the driver in the next car staring at him unabashedly. He can't help laughing, only a trifle self-conscious, and the car picks up speed now, at last, putting malodorous, damp Paris behind him. In the masses of articles published after Bowie's death in 2016, he read that everyone had their own special Bowie. He wonders what the singer really represents for his father. A man who loves trees could have been soothed by the mellifluous accents of Charles Trenet or Charles Aznavour, or by Georges Brassens's gruff southern accent, not far from his own, and yet it was an eccentric Englishman who fascinated him—a skinny, gawky guy with orange hair and chalk white skin who shaved off his eyebrows and wore makeup. It is precisely that, which Linden finds astonishing: his father's veneration for an artist so dissimilar from himself.

Guilt comes over him unexpectedly. Was he right to drive off like this, without even speaking to Professor Magerant? And what the hell is in that box? Why is the box in the tree? How long has it been there? The usually busy highway grows more and more empty; he wonders why. Near Beaune, three hours away from Paris, he stops for a sandwich and a coffee in a deserted cafeteria. Afterward, he connects his phone to the car audio system so that he can play his own music and make and receive calls. Another 180 minutes before he reaches Vénozan. He daren't try his home number. It's too early in the morning in San Francisco; Sacha won't be getting up for another hour. He'll give it a go later. He calls Tilia, tells her to warn Magerant that he's gone to get something for their father. She says she will, and that Mistral will be spending the day with her grandfather, which reassures him. As he draws nearer to Lyon, the traffic gets denser, and the rain vanishes, offering him his first glimpse of a blue sky in seven days, since he landed last Friday. It fills him with a sort of hope, spurs him on. After a sluggish passage through Lyon, the road becomes fluid again. Just two hours to go. The light is dwindling gradually, the sky glowing pink with the setting sun. Linden feels tired now; there's an ache in his neck and back, but he wants to keep at it. When he leaves the highway at Montélimar, night has fallen. It is cold, though not as cold as in Paris. Mistral calls to say Paul is asleep and that Tilia spoke to the professor: Paul is going to be put on new medicine. There is no need to operate for now, the doctor said. The road twists through the hills toward Grignan, Sévral, Nyons, and in spite of himself, Linden can't help feeling joy in returning to the land of his childhood. He hasn't been back for four long years. When he parks the car near the house, the cool night air enveloping him as he steps outside smells of moss, wood, and rich, moist soil. He breathes it in avidly, stretching his weary limbs. The full moon glows down upon him magnanimously. He unlocks the front door; it lets out a famil-

iar groan and click when it is pushed open, and the heavy iron door-
knob still draws the same cold imprint in his palm.

Nothing has changed. He is greeted by the scent of lavender and
roses, with a touch of beeswax. He could be stepping back in time,
in a flash. The entrance is warm, thanks to Nadine, who also left
a couple of lights on for him. In the kitchen, the table is set for
one. He checks the fridge: fresh soup, ratatouille, rice and chicken,
a slice of *tarte aux pommes*. There is a note for him on the kitchen
table from Nadine, in her small, neat handwriting: She hopes his
father will soon be back home. Linden suddenly remembers (how
could he have forgotten?) that cell phone reception is hopeless here.
The only way to get a decent connection is to walk up the hill, beyond
the swimming pool, higher and higher, holding your phone up like the
Statue of Liberty—nothing he feels like doing right now. He finds
it chilly in the big living room, so he moves to his father's office
while his dinner is gently heating up. No more lavender and rose
scent here, but more the acrid flavor of tobacco. This is Paul's
room, where he can't be disturbed, where he comes every morning, sitting behind that old-fashioned writing desk, to answer his
letters, to make his calls, to write his conferences papers. Paul sits
facing the valley, which can't be seen now because the curtains are
drawn and the shutters closed. On the walls hang framed leaves
pressed under glass from all kinds of different trees: ginkgo, yew,
beech, cedar, sycamore. The only visible photograph is the one
Linden took in December 1999 of the storm at Versailles. Paul's
Bowie vinyl records are preciously stacked here, next to the old record
player. Paul has always refused to succumb to digital recordings,
asserting that analog formats have a richer, truer sound. Linden
glances through the records, chooses *Blackstar*, Bowie's last album,
the one he knows less well. He clicks the old stereo on, sliding the
record out of its case, a gesture he hasn't done in a while but one
that he has watched his father accomplish so often. Static crackles
on his skin as he manipulates the record, making sure he doesn't
get his fingers on the surface. He gently lowers it onto the turn-
table, positioning the tone arm to the outer edge. Then he sits at

his father's desk, his hands spread on the old scratched surface. The music rises, opulent and intense, wrought from audacious, sometimes disconcerting harmonies, interleaved with abrupt outbursts of weird sound effects, the fizz of a synthesizer, and an almost religious chant. After a full four minutes, as Linden tries to fight off his perplexity, a sheer high note picks its way through the confusion and Bowie's voice rings out, true and clear, sending a shiver down Linden's spine, something about an angel falling. As he listens, entranced, his hands stroking the worn wood, memories resurface randomly, and he doesn't push them away. Paul teaching his son to drive; once, he got furious because Linden drove straight into a fence, making a dent in the car. Months later, when Linden obtained his license, motoring his father all the way to Lyon, Paul was proud. Linden remembers that pride, how Paul would nod to all the unknown people they passed, chanting, "It's my son driving. Hey, look, it's my son at the wheel!" Paul, kneeling in front of the mantelpiece, showing him how to start a good log fire. His deft hands, crumpling newspaper up into small balls, stacking tinder into a sort of grid, then balancing two split logs on the very top. Paul letting Linden light the fire with a long match, saying, "You need to let the fire breathe. Don't overfeed it. Give it time to grow." Paul teaching him to swim, his father's thumbs firm under his armpits. Paul never wanted to use those little floater wings other kids had. He said his children had to learn without them, like he did. The first thing he taught them was how to hold their breath underwater, and then how to float on their backs, without being afraid. Linden would put his head on Paul's shoulder: Look up there at the sky. See what you can see. Birds, clouds, or a plane maybe, or a butterfly? Put your head way back; hold out your arms. There! You're floating, all by yourself! When Linden was nearly ten years old, his father took him on an excursion up the Lance mountain, which rose behind Vénozan in a long curved arc. His father said it would take six or seven hours, that it wasn't always easy, but that he could do it. Tilia wanted to go, too, but Paul had insisted this was between father and son. How well Linden remembers that phrase:

"between father and son." They left early in the morning, on a
crisp April day, carrying food and water in their backpacks. They
climbed up through lavender fields, cherry orchards with blossoms
sending sweet perfume their way, then cut though thick woods.
The first pass was easy to get to. It became a little tougher from
there. Linden felt breathless, but he forced himself to keep up
with his father, putting his feet where his father had tread. Paul
climbed steadily and swiftly, knowing exactly where he was going.
Sometimes he'd point out the stump of an old oak, or the ruins of
an abandoned farm. After a while, once they left the forest and
reached the plateau lining the highest part of the mountain, moving through the second pass, they stopped for lunch. They were
alone, just the two of them, sitting on a flat boulder. Paul split the
bread, ham, and cheese with his knife, handing slices to his son.
His father didn't speak, but Linden felt intensely happy. The sun
scorched the tip of his nose. He listened to the wind, blowing stronger
as they edged closer to the pinnacle. They set off again, rising up
through steep pastures peppered with rocks and bushes. The grass
was short and yellowed, parched in places. Linden felt tired all of
a sudden; his legs ached, and he nearly sprained his ankle on an
unsteady stone. Just as he was about to fall back, to murmur he
couldn't do it, that his father had been wrong, he was too small, he
would never make it up to the top, Paul's hand shot out to grab his,
just like when he was younger, and he held on to it, feeling his father
yank him upward, as if a new energy was streaming from his father's
arm to his. At the top of the mountain, the view was magnificent,
like a reward, and it made Linden laugh out loud with awe. An ancient stone cross was implanted there, and he reached out to touch
it. His father said they could see all the way to the Italian border,
over the Alps, and Linden believed him. He felt as if he were standing on top of the world: Endless layers of hazy blue and green
spreading out in front of him like a vast carpet dotted with crests
and peaks, and if he stretched out a finger, he imagined he could
caress them. The splendor of the image remained imprinted in his
mind. His father finally spoke. He said it all seemed calm, so peaceful,

didn't it? Linden nodded. His father then said something he never forgot. When nature got angry, Paul said, there was nothing man could do about it. Nothing at all.

In the grain of the wood, Linden's fingers follow grooves and incisions, feeling his father's presence beat there like a pulse. How old is this desk? It has probably been in this room since his great-grandfather Maurice's day, although it was less shabby then, its corners less rounded. On the left, fountain pens and blotting paper, a jar full of pencils and ballpoints, a magnifying glass with a curved handle, an ashtray, a lighter, and the snow globe that Linden remembers so well and which he now picks up to shake. Flurries spin around miniature white birch trees studded with tiny red-and-brown robins. Linden pulls on the brass handle of the top drawer, which opens with a squeak. He finds writing paper, its pages curling with damp, stamps, an old black wallet, which smells of tobacco, in which he discovers a forgotten fifty-franc banknote and a school picture of a plump-faced Tilia, age nine or ten, which makes him grin. At the back of the drawer is a cemetery of old copper coins, rusty scissors, and a jumble of obsolete keys. On the right of the desk, next to the telephone, there are stacks of paper, unopened mail, with stamps from all over the world. It's extraordinary how all these tree lovers get in touch with Paul. Linden knows his father answers every letter he gets. Paul doesn't own a computer, or a typewriter; he does it all by hand. Linden reads a long paragraph on a single sheet of notepaper. Several sentences and words have been crossed out and rewritten. He guesses it is the unfinished draft of a speech his father was working on before he left for Paris last Friday. His father's large, sprawling handwriting has never been difficult to decipher. Trees. Always trees. And now the box in the tree, in the oldest lime. What is the significance of that box? Why did his father want him to come here and fetch it? Linden goes into the kitchen to get a tray, on which he places his food. This room has few happy memories for him. This is where they had breakfast, lunch, and dinner every day. Lauren never used the formal dining room, which she considered not cozy enough. Linden sees himself in that chair, there, by the window, thirteen or fourteen years old, told off by his mother because he wasn't sitting up straight; burdened with the daily teasing and taunting at school, which he didn't have the courage to bring up. How lonely he was; how sad he felt. Is this why he seldom comes here? Because it brings back that pain, that rejection? Doesn't Vénozan deserve a second chance? Must it always bear the scars of his adolescence?

Installed in his father's office, Linden eats his meal hungrily. The ring of the phone startles him. It's his mother, making sure he got there safely. She says she called Vandeleur, that he'll turn up first thing tomorrow morning. Paul had a peaceful day, but he still seems very tired. She's worried. She says she thinks Professor Magerant looks worried, too, but she can't get anything out of him. Tilia had a go at him, and Linden can imagine what that means. The professor had remained surprisingly calm. He told them only that they were changing the medical treatment. Nothing more. It was frustrating. Linden comforts her the best he can, but he can feel the disquiet grow within him, as well. When he finishes talking to his mother, he uses the landline to dial Sacha's cell phone. The call goes straight to voice mail, which is rare, as Sacha's mobile is usually always on. He tries Sacha's direct line, and gets his assistant, Rebecca. No, she hasn't seen Sacha yet this morning, but she'll let him know Linden called. She checks the agenda. No, there are no outside meetings scheduled for Sacha today. Linden hangs up, marginally bothered. In the nearly five years they've been together, he has never been unfaithful to Sacha. He has never even wanted to. He hopes and believes Sacha feels the same way. He trusts Sacha; he always has. At present, with a new tenuousness rocking the base of his world, he wonders. He is aware of the magnetic effect Sacha has on other men. He's seen it. It is instantaneous, potent. Sacha seems blind to it, but surely he must be conscious of it. He calls the cell phone again, asking Sacha to ring him at Vénozan, leaving the number for him. There's so much he wants to share with him. He'll start by recounting how he described Sacha to his father, so that after a while, it felt like Sacha was there, in the room with them. How is he going to put words to what he felt when he understood his father loved him? It was the warmest, most beautiful and precious sensation, and just thinking about it brings tears to his eyes, brings him back to the boy he was, following Paul around in the garden, listening to him talk about plants and nature. Another memory surfaces: Paul pointing out the big black carpenter bees to his small son, explaining the males never sting, they can't, and he can even catch them in his hand, which he promptly does, while Linden looks on, quaking. Look how beautiful they are, with their shiny black bodies and metallic dark purple wings; Linden mustn't be afraid, even if they make such a loud noise and look menacing. The females will sting only if they feel they are under attack. Linden just needs to let them alone. One summer day, his father gently deposited a male carpenter bee into his palm. It felt tickly and quite terrifying, because the insect seemed huge in his tiny hand, but he felt his father's pride, and it made him glow inside.

Linden puts his dinner things away, clears up, and makes his way upstairs. He has never felt frightened in this house, but it does seem particularly silent tonight. For once, the mistral is not blowing at all. He enters his old room. He left here twenty-one years ago, and his mother had it redecorated, but as soon as he finds himself within these walls, he suspects he might harvest the angst of the sad, harassed teenager again, shedding the know-how of the sophisticated, worldly photographer. He decides he won't be enduring any of that despondency tonight. It is a small inner tussle leaving the painful memories behind, but he does it quite effortlessly. He has a quick shower and slips into bed. He thinks of his father again. There is so much catching up to do, so many conversations to have. How will this be possible? Paul won't be able to board a plane for quite a while, he imagines, because of his stroke. Well then, in that case, Linden will have to return to Vénozan, this time with Sacha. They must both make time for this. He sees it clearly: the white wrought-iron table, candles flickering in the soft evening breeze, the sun setting on the right of the house, sending its final golden rays over the valley, all the way up to the gigantic cypress trees standing in a row, the ones Paul calls "the Mohicans." He sees Lauren and Sacha laughing, with Paul looking on, his father's eyes always roving back to his army of trees clustering around the house: the old oak with its splintered trunk, the two towering planes, the maple and the elm, familiar landmarks of Linden's childhood. What will happen to this house when Paul and Lauren are gone? Who will look after the land, the arboretum? It is the first time this cheerless thought comes to him. Not Tilia, surely; she seems attached to her life in London, her daughter, her art, her hopeless husband. He thinks now about all the decisions that will have to be made once his parents are no longer here. The idea of the estate being sold or razed makes him wince. No matter how unhappy he was here as a teenager, this house, this land, is part of who he is. The child that Linden and Sacha will adopt one day will carry both their names. That child, the one they so often talk about, the one who is woven into their future, will come to know this land; of that, he is certain.

Linden had left the door open so that he could hear the phone ring from his parents' room if Sacha called back, but what wakes him is the cavernous clang of the doorbell penetrating his sleep. He is astonished to see it is nearly nine o'clock and that sunlight is peeping through the curtains. The doorbell jangles again, mightily. Linden dresses in a hurry, pads down in his bare feet, wrestles with the lock. Vandeleur is standing there, a wide grin on his freckled face, and it is Linden's childhood beaming at him. The bright red hair has tapered to a sandy gray, the shoulders seem less broad, but Vandeleur's green eyes still twinkle above his bulbous nose. He calls Linden "little chief," like he always has, slapping him on the back with a powerful square hand. What's all this business with the boss? The boss, in the hospital? Can't be possible. Got to get him out of there fast. Is the boss on the mend? He must be, because Vénozan will never be Vénozan without the boss. His hoarse, rough voice is perhaps a little less brash. Linden takes him into the kitchen for a cup of coffee, then runs upstairs to get his shoes. He explains what he is here for. Vandeleur stares at him, incredulous. What? The boss wants to dig a hole in the old lime? *That* lime? The oldest one? Linden nods. They must get to work now. God knows how long it will take. There is a box in the tree that his father needs. Vandeleur nearly drops his coffee. Does Linden mean a treasure, or something like that? Linden can't help smiling. The seventy-year-old gardener has the expression of a five-year-old being taken to the circus. When Linden steps outside, he is dazzled by the golden sunlight. It is so strong, he has to close his eyes, and yet how delicious it feels on his skin. The past week in Paris has been similar to living in a cave. He mentions this to the old man as he follows him to the shed, where they pick up tools. Vandeleur says he has never seen anything like the Paris flood, which he's been watching on TV. He wants to know what it was like, those watery streets, the desolation. Hell, answers Linden. As they walk up to the arboretum, carrying the ladder between them, as well as a sledgehammer, Linden realizes there is nothing watery around them, only grass, trees, and blue sky. The pure wintry air courses through his lungs, invigorating and refreshingly fragrant. How far away sodden, stinking Paris seems! When they get to the top of the hill, he turns to look at the valley behind him: the house nestling in the hollow where the winding path ends, the sky immense, unencumbered by bulky clouds. The wind lies low today; only the tips of the trees at the top of the vale sway with a gentle whisper. Yes, Linden has missed this land, this place that saw him grow up. He has missed it much more than he thought.

All the trees of the arboretum sport their winter garb: naked black branches, not a leaf in sight. Spring is still far off. They know exactly when to blossom—Linden recalls Paul telling him this as a boy—launching the formation of their lush pale green bower with absolute precision. Vandeleur's voice is a little ragged from the climb. The boss used to love playing here as a kid. He'd come here every day. He had a tree house in one of these. Does Linden know that? Linden nods. Vandeleur continues. The boss still comes up here all the time, sometimes alone, sometimes with him. Not much talking going on. Just looking out on the land and checking how the trees are doing. The tallest lime is easy to pick out, looming high over the others, its huge gnarled branches stretching out like gargantuan arms, its thick, twisting roots reaching deep into the gravelly hill. How can Linden not think of his father when he is standing here, right under his favorite tree? He can almost hear Paul's voice, explaining to him how rain was greedily sucked up by the tree, branches and leaves opening up like cupped hands to catch each raindrop, sending them streaming down the trunk in rivulets, feeding the thirsty roots. Vandeleur sets the ladder against the lime. He scratches his head. Is Linden sure they're supposed to slash into this one? Linden says he's sure. Vandeleur doesn't seem convinced. It sounds crazy to him. This is the boss's favorite tree. Linden says he knows, that he was named after it, *Linden* means "lime" in English. Vandeleur guffaws. He never guessed that at all! He thought it was just a fancy American name! But he knows *Tilia* is the Latin term for it. So, the boss has a thing for lindens, doesn't he? He and the boss fight about this old tree's age all the time. Vandeleur thinks it's over four hundred years old, and the boss says three hundred. Cut into it? It just doesn't make sense. This tree is like royalty. This tree is the master of the forest. Vandeleur puts his hand on the old bark with reverence. Is this really what the boss ordered? Linden reads aloud from Dominique's note. "Tallest lime. Blocked-up hole where dead branch used to be, halfway up, left as you face the valley. Get Vandeleur to help." The old man starts at the sound of his name, then nods. He'll do what the boss wants. Linden says he'll go up to find the hole while Vandeleur steadies the ladder. He climbs up gradually, surprised at the girth and height of the tree. He had never imagined it was so enormous. He can now glimpse the small lopsided hole clogged up with cement, on the left, where a dead branch used to be. The ladder doesn't quite reach high enough; he wonders how he is going to manage. As he twists around, figuring it out, the ladder wobbles.

"Don't take a tumble, now, little chief," warns Vandeleur from below. "Wouldn't want two Malegardes in the hospital, would we?"

From the top of the ladder, the gardener seems very far away. Linden asks for the sledgehammer, which Vandeleur hauls up to him, but try as he might, the tip of the mallet is still far from the blocked-up hole. He has to haul himself up higher to reach it. He can make out a sturdy, thick branch where he can place one foot, slowly pushing himself off the ladder with his right hand, the other holding the sledgehammer. It's an easier maneuver than he thought, although he can't look down anymore; it's giving him vertigo. The sensation of being high up in the vast naked tree is elating. Linden wishes he had his camera with him. How is it he had never thought of taking pictures from up here? Above his head, the branches coil toward the sky, and he can feel the wind blowing through his hair. The air up here is crisp, pure; he could stand on this branch and breathe it in for ages. An astonished woodpecker peeks at him from a higher bough. Vandeleur yells. What the hell is little chief doing? He's worse than his dad when it comes to admiring trees! Linden chuckles. Time to get on with it. The hole is accessible now, and he starts swinging the tool into it, doing his best to keep his balance. The old cement disintegrates quite easily, crumbling into a fine gray residue that coats his head and gets into his eyes. Vandeleur shouts that they don't block gaps in trees like that anymore; they don't use cement. The thing is, they need to stop bugs or birds from getting into the nooks, which could be dangerous for the tree. Linden coughs, wiping the powder off his lids. Vandeleur says he'll get one of the other gardeners to close it up again the way they do it now, with a thin metal flap or screening. Linden scrapes away the last of the cement with his hand. The hole gapes open, about the size of a watermelon. He has to edge closer, inching along the branch, sledgehammer still in hand. Gingerly, he eases his fingers into the orifice, until Vandeleur bawls at him to use the gloves he put in his jacket pocket. No way should Linden put his bare hand in there! There could be a nasty surprise! Insects or birds or Lord knows what! Linden pauses, slips the gardening gloves on, balancing the sledgehammer on his thigh. Then he tries again, forcing his fist through the cavity. He feels a humid sponginess, like moss or weeds, and pushes his wrist right in, turning his hand around clock-wise. Nothing resembling a box meets his fingers. Could his father be wrong? Is the box still here? Perhaps it has moved, with time, into the center of the tree? In that case, he will never get hold of it. Disappointment floods him; what is he going to tell Paul? Did he come all this way for nothing? He slides his arm in farther, mar-veling at the deep cranny within the tree, like a secret passage, and then he touches it, the sharp corner of a metallic object. He hollers out to Vandeleur that he's got it; he can feel it. He just has to pry it out; it seems stuck. A fierce struggle ensues; his cheek is squashed against the coarse bark, his fingertips sliding powerlessly over the slippery edges of the box. It's almost as if the tree won't relinquish the box. Linden finds himself muttering to his namesake, talking to the tree as if it could hear him. "Come on, linden, don't do this to me. Let go of it. Let me have it." He has an idea. He slides the end of the sledgehammer right into the hole, straining the handle up against the corner of the box with all his might. He hears a faint squelch, and when he darts his hand in again, the box moves more easily now, like a loosened tooth. It takes further effort to pull it gently out toward him, bringing it to the light and the air, like a strange, outlandish birth, but all of a sudden, the box is in his hand, and he stares down at it in awe while Vandeleur crows with tri-umph. It is a small biscuit tin, covered with moss and crawling with ants, which he blows away. Gingerly, he makes his way down the tree, his head spinning. Vandeleur asks him for the sledgeham-mer, which he hands down, then for the box, so Linden can use both his hands, but he won't let go of it. The ladder seems awfully far away. His legs feel weak. He lets Vandeleur's voice direct him. Little chief needs to take it easy now; there's no hurry. One step after another, that's right. Once his trembling feet are on the ladder, Linden regains his strength and climbs down adroitly. Vandeleur peers at the box, asks Linden if he's going to open it. His father didn't say to open it, Linden points out: He just said to bring it to him, that it was very important. Vandeleur wants to know if it's heavy; Linden places it into the worn-out old palms. The gardener lets out a whelp of surprise. It's as light as a feather! He shakes the box, holds it to his ear, like a kid trying to hear the ocean in a seashell. Is it money? Linden says he has no idea. He is tempted to find out, but he doesn't feel comfortable in front of Vandeleur. He'll do it later, in the car, when he's alone, on his way back to Paris. He promised to come back fast; he should be on his way.

When Vandeleur has gone, and when Linden has locked the front door, it is approaching eleven o'clock. He takes a few quick photographs of the house and the valley with his Leica. Just before he left, he called Mistral, Lauren, and Tilia from the landline to say he had the box and was on his way. He couldn't get through to any of them. He wondered if it was to do with the flood and the mobile coverage not functioning. He tried Sacha's cell phone and the home number as well, and got voice mail each time. Linden takes to the road with somber thoughts, stopping at Montbrison for gas. The sun is rising higher into the sky. The box sits on the seat next to him; he looks at it from time to time. Heading north to Montélimar, to the highway, he passes Grignan, the town where his parents met, with the castle high on its stony promontory. The roads are clear; he can drive fast and smoothly. He turns on the radio and discovers, to his dismay, there has been a night of terror in Paris. Marauding gangs attacked shops after nightfall, starting with the Champs-Élysées and neighboring avenue Victor-Hugo, causing thousands of euros of damage to a capital enfeebled by the flood. Hundreds of hooded looters then stormed through the dark streets of Montparnasse, poorly lit because of electricity outages, smashing windows and stealing everything they could get their hands on, from electrical items to clothing. The mobs came from outlying districts, determined to engage in lawless mayhem and to clash with the police. Horror-struck, Linden listens. Boutiques on rue de Rennes were ransacked in a matter of minutes, one after the other. The supermarket near the corner of boulevard Saint-Germain was emptied and set on fire. Police, bombarded all night long with bottles and bricks, admitted being overwhelmed by the scale of the attacks, because many officers were already busy guarding flooded areas. Firefighters struggled with blazes for hours. Hundreds of people were arrested; fifty or more were injured. A tearful old lady says she has never seen anything like this since the student insurrection of May 1968. Linden reaches for his phone, meaning to call his family to check if they are all safe, but he is unable to locate it. He pulls over at the next rest area to hunt for it, looks under the seat, in the back, in his bag, and realizes with dread he forgot it, left it plugged into the socket in the bedroom. He feels lost and helpless without it. He knows none of his family's numbers by heart, let alone Sacha's. He bemoans the fact he has no address book, not even a slip of paper with important numbers jotted down. How could he have been so reckless? He does have backup in his iPad, but he left that at the hotel. Cursing, he takes off again, going faster than he should be, a dull foreboding in the pit of his stomach.

The news on the radio does little to alleviate Linden's disposition. The level of the Seine has started to recede ever so gradually, but the water still annexes half of the city, and it can't really be called water anymore, declares the journalist deprecatingly, more like vast stagnant pools of oily slush reeking of cesspools. Chaos. There is no other word for what is going on in Paris. Pumps are unable to suck up the muck, as it is too thick and gritty. Stinking rubbish both piling up and floating about is another major sanitary problem. Exasperated inhabitants have decided to burn trash wherever they can, fashioning wild bonfires on every available street corner, another hazard. Linden can hardly believe his ears. Can it get any worse? Will Paris ever pull through? The voices on the radio continue their unsettling litany. Should he turn it off or find music to listen to? On the other hand, he tells himself he needs to know what's going on, what he's returning to. He learns the Red Cross is launching a larger disaster response, and that more donations are needed to allow their workers to assist thousands of freezing, homeless Parisians with food, shelter, and emotional support. Clearly in the grip of an unparalleled crisis, Paris seems beset by ancient class, racial, and political divisions; the recent upheavals are not encouraging acts of solidarity and altruism. The lack of coordination between governmental officials, relief organizations, and the military are making headlines worldwide. The person being blamed in the press appears to be the president, who is being accused of not being able to rally his troops to deal with the disaster. The president's major opponents have not stopped condemning him, judging his administration lethargic and incapable of meeting the needs of all those affected by the flooding. But on social media, the young president is revered by the majority of Parisians, who are convinced he is doing everything he can in a dramatic and unprecedented situation.

When Linden reaches Lyon, two hours later, he stops in a self-service cafeteria for gas and a snack. He makes calls using his credit card from a run-down pay phone that looks like it hasn't been used for years. It is practically impossible to get any information without the Internet, he realizes. He finally obtains directory assistance and asks for the number of Cochin Hospital and has a panic-stricken moment finding a pen and a piece of paper. A woman standing nearby drinking coffee proffers both. The hospital takes ages to answer, and when he does get through, the jaded person on the other end of the line does not react well to his impatience. Professor Magerant's direct line rings and rings into thin air. Why is no one responding? Where is his secretary? The woman who lent him pen and notepaper takes pity on him. Doesn't he have a cell phone? Linden ruefully admits he forgot it. She hands him hers with a smile. How kind! How unexpected! Using it, he goes online to find the hotel number, dials it, and is told his family is out. He assumes they are at the hospital. He uses the lady's phone again to scavenge for another number online for the hospital, manages to find the nurses' office on his father's ward. Again, the endless ringing tone. Finally, a female voice responds; the woman sounds as if she's in a hurry. She says she can't hear him. Can he please speak louder? He says he is the son of Paul Malegarde, who's in room 17. He just wants to tell his family he's on his way. He'll be there as fast as he can, in under four hours if the traffic is good. She says she still can't hear him correctly. Can he repeat the message? A sort of rage comes over Linden. He wants to shout, to insult her, to use the nastiest possible words. Instead, he hangs up, riled, giving the mobile back to its owner. He has no more time to waste. The lady asks him if everything is okay; she has a pleasant, honest face. He nods briefly, thanks her, and sprints back to the car. He knows he's driving too fast, that he should be careful, but he can't help speeding ahead, hands gripped on the wheel, the ominous sensation churning within him. The highway becomes more and more congested as he nears Paris, and when he reaches Nemours, only an hour away, he finds he has to halt in the bumper-to-bumper traffic. As he sits immobilized in an interminable queue of stationary cars, fury sweeps over him again, red-hot, like a scorching blaze. Minutes tick by and still the line is not moving forward. He feels like bashing his head against the steering wheel, imagines blood trickling from his battered forehead. He tries calming down, breathing gently, emptying his mind.

The box glimmers in the fading daylight, as if it were calling out to him. He stares at it. His father didn't tell Dominique *not* to open it, did he? Linden reaches out for it, cradling the cold metal in his hand. A solitary ant crawls over his palm; he flicks it away. He could open it now. Perhaps this traffic jam is fate's way of telling him to do so. Stranded, stuck, without his phone, what else is there for him to do? He clasps it between his fingers, trying to pry the top up. He fiddles with it for a while, maddened; the lid feels like it has been glued on. He remembers the ballpoint pen the lady lent him and that he forgot to give back. It's still in his jacket pocket. He fishes it out hastily; bends the clip on its side all the way back. With the point of the clip, he presses hard on the corner of the box. It clicks open. Linden lifts the lid off carefully. The inside is surprisingly intact. No bugs, little humidity. He discovers an unsealed envelope, peers inside. There are several pages of paper, neatly folded, and two short yellowed articles from a newspaper. The date on the first one is August 5, 1952. "The body of a young girl found at a private property at Vénozan, near Sévral, on August 3 has been identified as that of Suzanne Vallette, sixteen, from Solérieux. The police suspect foul play." The second article dates back to August 10, 1952. "A man connected to the rape and murder of Suzanne Vallette is in custody at Nyons. He is a 35-year-old shepherd from Orelle with a criminal record." Who is Suzanne Vallette? What had she got to do with Paul? Mystified, Linden unfolds the sheets of paper. A loud honk from behind makes his heart race; the column of cars is moving again. Nervously, he drives onward, the papers spread out on his knees. The traffic is slow-moving, but not slow enough for him to read safely, and it drags on all the way to Paris, where the rain has stopped at last. A dark blue sky glows above the highway. When he reaches porte d'Orléans, Linden is hastily able to decipher the opening paragraph of the first page at a red light. He recognizes his father's familiar handwriting. There is no date.

> *I will start with the tree. Because everything begins, and ends, with the tree. The tree is the tallest one. It was planted way before the others. I'm not sure how old it is, exactly. Perhaps three or four hundred years old. It is ancient and powerful. It has weathered terrible storms, braced against unbridled winds. It is not afraid.*

Linden wonders what the rest of the papers contain. What will he discover? Why are they so important to Paul? Will he have time to read them before he gets to the hospital? Probably not. He must drop off the car at the Montparnasse station. Shouldn't he drive straight to Cochin Hospital? But where would he park around there? Should he return the car and then dash to the hospital? While he dithers, horns blare behind him again. He decides to drive to the hospital; he'll return the car later. A sort of desperation mounts within him. He turns right into rue du Père-Corentin, not expecting the blockage awaiting him there. For twenty minutes, he sits in the car, fuming. He sees, as he draws slowly nearer, that a unit of policemen is stopping all cars heading into rue de la Tombe-Issoire. As Linden rolls the window down, the icy night air rushes in, nauseating with pungent smoke. No more rain, but a putrid rotten-egg stench that makes him to want to retch. Where is he going? a policeman asks. To the nearby hospital to see his father, Linden says. He is asked to show his identity card and the vehicle registration documents. Is he a tourist? Is he aware that driving through the city is not recommended, due to the flood and the recent rampaging? He says he's not a tourist; he's French and he is here with his family. Can they please let him through? His father is waiting for him at Cochin Hospital. His father is very ill. These men look drawn; they have dark circles under their eyes. They must have had a tough night. He feels sorry for them. The policeman takes his time, glancing from the card to his face. Finally, he lets Linden pass. He warns him that he'll find it hard to park. He is right. Linden spends another interminable moment or two looking for a free space around the hospital, tension rising within him. He loses his temper, swearing at the top of his voice, sounding like Tilia, hitting the wheel with furious hands. At his wits' end, he leaves the car on the pavement on rue Méchain, knowing he'll get a fine. There's no other solution. The freezing, foul-smelling city around him seems inimical and alien. He runs as fast as he can to the principal entrance on rue Saint-Jacques, the box tucked in his pocket. It takes him another minute to reach the building where his father is.

The inside lights glare at him, hurting his eyes. Linden feels out of breath as he waits for the elevator, mouth dry, heart pounding. Why this anguish? Paul will be upstairs in room 17; Mistral, Tilia, and Lauren are there, expecting him; perhaps Dominique is with them as well. He'll hand over the box to his father jubilantly. He'll make Paul chuckle by telling him about how he and Vandeleur carried the ladder, how it didn't reach high enough, how the box was stuck deep in the tree, and what a struggle it had been to pull it out, and that a surprised woodpecker had gawked at him all the while. He'll tell Paul about the loveliness of the land, the light, the air, how he had wanted to stay up in the tree and feast his eyes on everything the valley had to offer. He had seen the beauty of Paul's world. He belonged to that world, too. All this, he will tell his father.

Out of the tail of his eye, Linden notices a person approaching swiftly from his left. The elevator door slides open with a beep; he steps forward, meaning to get in, but the blurred contour of the individual drawing near him comes into focus and he turns his head. A tall, dark-haired man stands next to him, so close, he can breathe his familiar odor. He needs a couple of seconds to understand who is stretching his arms out to him. Light-headed with happiness, Linden pulls Sacha close, his disbelieving fingers reaching up to caress strands of the long black hair. Sacha's arms intertwine behind his back, clasping him tight. The past week has been a jumble of raw emotions fueled by the rising, wild river, seven strange days that have tampered with Linden's acuity. He tries to find the right words. All he can murmur is "My love. My sweet love." Sacha quivers, as if he is cold. Surprised, Linden detects long shudders coursing through his body. Why is Sacha so silent? He hasn't uttered a word. Glancing over his shoulder, Linden sees the dingy wall of the hospital entrance, posters tacked onto boards, lusterless linoleum. A woman sitting in a plastic chair seems fast asleep; a nurse pushing a patient in a wheelchair lumbers by. Is Sacha crying? Bewildered, Linden tries to take one step back so that he can look at him, but Sacha won't let him, cradling him desperately, hanging on to him with all his might, as if the thing he wants the most in the world right now is to protect Linden from whatever lies ahead, buying him a little more time, building him an infinitesimal dam of ignorance, because he knows Linden will remember this moment, this Friday, for the rest of his life.

Linden gently pulls away, bracing himself for what he will read in the beloved eyes. He doesn't want Sacha to say the words; he doesn't want him to pronounce them. He puts his palm on Sacha's cheek and notices with wonder how unsteady his hand is. Sacha speaks at last. They called and called. They understood there was a problem with Linden's phone, or that he had forgotten it. There was no way they could reach him. It had happened in the middle of the afternoon. It had been peaceful. Paul was holding Lauren's fingers. It took place just like that, with her in the room, and no one else. Lauren came stumbling out, all the color drained from her face, incapable of talking.

Linden thinks of his mother, witnessing that last breath, that last heave of the chest. How painful that must have been for her. How heartbroken she must be. The tears come now, spurting from Linden's tired eyes. His father is gone. He remembers the last time he saw him, just yesterday, when he bent down to kiss him good-bye. Linden feels numb, unable to move, to react. He wants to sit down; he wants to be able to wait here, to rest, to say nothing, to gather up his strength, just for a while. He knows he can't. Upstairs, they are waiting for him. How are they? How are they taking it? Sacha says Tilia is impressive. She is the one holding them together. Tilia? Linden is surprised. He thought she would have collapsed. No, she hasn't. She certainly hasn't. She is up there comforting Lauren, who is desperate, as well as Mistral, who has broken down. She is dealing with all the procedures. She has spoken to the doctor, to the nurses. She is calm and compassionate.

Linden rides up in the elevator, Sacha's hand tight in his. The door to room number 17 is closed. He knows his father's body is behind that door. He knows he will have to lay eyes on it at some point. He will have to see his father in death, just like he will have to watch his father's coffin lowered into the ground in the small green cemetery at Léon des Vignes. It is an ordeal that awaits him and that he will not shy away from. He follows Sacha to the waiting room a little farther down. There is his sister, her arms wrapped around his mother and his niece. Colin sits in front of them, his head in his palms. They see him; they cry out his name and the tears come again. There is an intense, confusing moment of sorrow where sentences seem chaotic, interrupted by sobs.

It is later, when they have been able to speak more straightforwardly, when they have comforted one another somewhat, that Linden pulls the box out of his pocket. He tells them that this is what Paul wanted him to bring back from Vénozan. There are papers inside, but he hasn't had time to read them all yet. He is going to do that right now, right here. He takes the first page and starts to read.

He reads slowly, taking his time, pausing to draw breath. Sometimes he glances up at Lauren, at Tilia, for courage, for support.

When Linden comes to the last page, he hands it over to his sister. Tilia's voice fills the small room, at first unsteady and hesitant, then taking on power, and it is almost—almost—as if Paul were there, standing at the threshold, his hands in his pockets, his blue eyes shining out to them.

≈

I heard its footsteps come closer to where I stood. Every time it took one step, the leaves and the grass rustled to warn me. It thought it was making no noise, but I heard it perfectly. I heard it almost too loud. Every single part of me was straining to listen. Now I sniffed its stink, sweaty and boozy, like those drunken field hands I sometimes saw hanging around the farm before my father ousted them.

I leaned against the tree, my eyes closed. I was so still, I was like a branch. The monster came awfully close, but it passed on by, lurching, mumbling under its breath.

The rain began to fall, thick and steady and strong. No storm, no thunder, just the rain gushing down. I heard the monster run away, swearing. I thought of Suzanne getting wet and I began to cry again. The tree sheltered me like a huge umbrella.

I fed all my terror into the tree. It took my fear and made me part of it. The tree held me. It locked me into itself. Never had I felt such protection. Never had anyone or anything safeguarded me this way. It was as if I had become the bark, as if I had slipped into the cracks and fissures, past the moss, past the lichen, past the insects crawling up and down the trunk.

And there, in the heart of the linden, I knew no monster, no horror, would ever find me.

❦ Acknowledgments ❧

Thank you, Nicolas Jolly, Laure du Pavillon, Catherine Rambaud, and my precious first readers.

Thank you to photographers Charlotte Jolly de Rosnay, David Atlan, Alexi Lubomirski, and Mélanie Rey.

Thank you to Laurence Le Falher, for her New York knowledge.

Thank you, Laetitia Lachmann.

Here are the five books that helped me write this one:
Paris Under Water, Jeffrey H. Jackson (Palgrave Macmillan)
Paris coule-t-il?, Magali Reghezza-Zitt (Fayard)
The Secret Life of Trees, Colin Tudge (Penguin)
The Hidden Life of Trees, Peter Wohlleben (Greystone Books)
On Photography, Susan Sontag (Penguin)

Contact:
www.tatianaderosnay.com